THE LIVING

Also by Matt de la Peña

Ball Don't Lie

Mexican WhiteBoy

We Were Here

I Will Save You

THE LIVING

Matt de la Peña

DELACORTE PRESS

Text copyright © 2013 by Matt de la Peña
Jacket art copyright © 2013 by Philip Straub

Visit us on the Web! randomhouse.com/teens

Educators and librarians, for a variety of teaching tools, visit us at RHTeachersLibrarians.com

Library of Congress Cataloging-in-Publication Data
Peña, Matt de la.
The living / Matt de la Peña. — First edition.
pages cm
Summary: After an earthquake destroys California and a tsunami wrecks the luxury cruise ship where he is a summer employee, high schooler Shy confronts another deadly surprise.
ISBN 978-0-385-74120-0 (hc) — ISBN 978-0-375-98991-9 (glb) — ISBN 978-0-375-98435-8 (ebook) [1. Survival—Fiction. 2. Natural disasters—Fiction. 3. Diseases—Fiction. 4. Cruise ships—Fiction. 5. Mexican Americans—Fiction.] I. Title.
PZ7.P3725Li 2013
[Fic]—dc23
2012050778

The text of this book is set in 12-point Goudy.

Printed in the United States of America

10 9 8 7 6 5 4 3

First Edition

For my beautiful wife, Caroline

Shy stands alone on the Honeymoon Deck. Cooler full of ice-cold water bottles strapped across his chest.

Waiting.

It's day six of his first voyage as a summer employee of Paradise Cruise Lines. Towel Boy at the Lido Deck pool by day. Water Boy at night. But the money's good. Like, game-changing good. He calculates again how much he'll have pulled by the time school starts back up. Three eight-day voyages, plus tips, minus taxes. Be enough to help his mom out and still score some new gear and a pair of kicks, maybe take a female out to dinner.

Shy moves to the railing, picturing that last part.

Him with a girl on an actual date.

He'd get a reservation at a nice spot, too. Cloth napkins. Some fine girl sitting across from him in the classy-ass booth. Maybe Jessica from the volleyball squad. Or Maria from down the street. All eyelashy smiles as whatever girl glances at him over her menu.

"Get whatever you want," he'd tell her. "You ever had surf 'n' turf? For real, I got you."

Yeah, he'd play it smooth like that.

When it's overcast at night, the moon above the cruise ship is a blurry dot. The ocean is black felt. Can hardly tell where the air ends and the water starts up.

You can hear it, though.

That's another thing Shy never would have thought before he landed this luxury cruise gig. The ocean talks to you. Especially at night. Whispering voices that never let up, not even when you sleep.

It can start to mess with your head.

Shy spots a passenger stepping out of the Luxury Lounge. The thick glass doors motor open long enough to let out a few notes from the live orchestra. Inside there's a formal event going on called the Beacon Ball. Harps and violins and all that. Hundreds of dressed-up rich folks drinking champagne and socializing. Shy's job tonight is to offer water to anyone who steps outside for air.

Like this dude. Middle-aged and balding, dressed in a suit two sizes too small.

Shy moves in quick with his cooler, asking: "Ice-cold bottle of water, sir?"

The man looks at the sweating bottle for a few seconds, like it confuses him. Then a grin comes over his face and he digs into his wallet. Holds a folded bill toward Shy between two veiny white fingers.

"Sorry, sir," Shy tells him. "We're not supposed to—"

"Says who?" the man interrupts. "Take it, kid."

After a short pause, for show, Shy snatches the bill and buries it deep inside his uniform pocket. Like he always does.

The man uncaps the water bottle, takes a long swig, wipes his mouth with the arm of his suit jacket. "Spent my entire life trying to get to this place," he says without eye contact. "Top scientist in my field. Cofounder of my own business." He looks at Shy. "Enough money to buy vacation homes in three different countries."

"Congratulations, sir—"

"Don't!" the man snaps.

Shy stares at him for a few seconds. "Don't what?"

"Don't tell me what you think I want to hear." He shakes his head in disgust. "Say something real instead. Tell me I'm fat."

Shy glances at the ocean, confused.

The guy's definitely fat, but if Shy's learned anything during his first six days on the job, it's that luxury cruise passengers don't want anything to do with real. They want a pat on the back. "Tell a dude how great he is and get paid." That's his roommate Rodney's motto. But this guy isn't fitting the formula.

The man sighs, asks Shy: "Where you from, anyway, kid?"

"San Diego."

"Yeah? What part?"

Shy shifts the cooler from his left side to his right. "You probably never heard of it, sir. Little place called Otay Mesa."

The man laughs awkwardly, like it pains him. "And you're trying to *congratulate* me?" He shakes his head. "How's that for irony?"

"Excuse me?"

He waves Shy off and re-caps his bottle. "Trust me, I know Otay Mesa. Right down there by the border."

Shy nods. He has no idea what the guy's getting at, but Rodney warned him about this, too. How eccentric luxury cruise passengers can be. Especially the ones whose front teeth have already turned pink from too much red wine.

It's quiet for a few seconds, Shy readying himself for his exit, but the man turns suddenly and points a finger in Shy's face. "Do me a favor, kid."

"Of course, sir."

"Remember this cowardly face." The man taps his own temple. "It's what corruption looks like."

Shy frowns, trying to find the logic.

3

"This is the face of your betrayer. Me, David Williamson. Don't you ever forget that! It's all in the letter I left in the cave."

"Not sure I'm following, sir."

"Of course you're not following." The man uncaps his water bottle again and turns to the ocean. He doesn't drink. "I've made a career out of hiding from people like you. But tell me this, kid: how am I supposed to go on living with all this blood on my hands?"

Shy abandons his search for meaning and focuses on the guy's comb-over. It's one of the more aggressive efforts he's ever seen. The part starts less than an inch above the left ear and dude's expecting a few wiry strands to cover a serious amount of real estate.

Maybe that's what he means by "hiding." Down to three defiant hairs and still believing he has that shiny-ass dome fully camouflaged. It reminds Shy of little-kid logic in a game of hide-and-seek. How his nephew Miguel used to bury his face in a couch cushion, thinking if he couldn't see you, you couldn't see him either.

Shy hears flutes and harps again and turns his attention to two older women who've just come out of the lounge in sparkling party dresses. They're both laughing and holding their high heels in their hands.

"Hello, ladies," he says, moving toward them. "Care for an ice-cold bottle of water?"

"Oh yes!"

"Honey, that sounds marvelous!"

He hands over two bottles, amazed that wealthy women can get so worked up over free water.

"Thank you," the taller one says, leaning in to read his name tag. "Shy?"

"Yes, ma'am."

"Now, that's a curious name," the other woman says.

"Well, my old man's a curious guy."

They all laugh a little and the women open their waters and take well-mannered sips.

After the Paradise-recommended amount of small talk, Shy steps away from the women and goes back to looking at the dark sea that surrounds them. Thousands of miles of mysterious salt water. Home to who knows what. Big-cheeked bottom dwellers and slithering electric eels, whales the size of apartment buildings that swim around all pissed off they don't have real teeth.

And here's Shy, on the top deck of this sparkling white megaship. Two hundred thousand tons and the length of a sports arena, yet somehow still floating.

He remembers his grandma's reaction when she first learned he was applying for a summer job on a cruise ship—two weeks before she got sick. She ducked into her room, came out seconds later with one of her scrapbooks. Turned to several articles about the rise in shark attacks over the past decade.

Shy had to take her to the local library and pull up an image of a Paradise cruise liner on the Internet.

"Oh, *mijo*," she breathed, all excited. "It's the biggest boat I've ever seen."

"See, Grandma? There's no way a shark could mess with one of these things, right?"

"I don't see how." She looked at the screen and then looked back at Shy. "I have pictures of their teeth, though, *mijo*. They have rows and rows. You don't think they could chew right through the bottom?"

"Not when the bottom's like eighteen feet thick and made of pure steel."

Shy is staring blankly at the ocean like this, remembering his grandma, when out of the corner of his eye he sees a blur climbing the railing.

He spins around.

The comb-over man.

"Sir!" he shouts, but the guy doesn't even look up.

Shy cups his hands around his mouth and shouts it louder this time: "Sir!"

Nothing.

The two older women now see what's going on, too. Neither moves or says a word.

Shy rips off the cooler and sprints across the width of the deck. Gets there just as the man lowers himself over the other side of the railing and goes to jump.

Shy reaches out quick, snatches an arm. Grabs for the man's collar with his other hand and balls the material into his fist. Holds him there, suspended against the ship.

Everything happening so fast.

No time to think.

This man dangling over the edge, twenty-something stories up from the darkness and too heavy for one person, slipping through Shy's fingers.

He hooks his right leg through the railing for leverage so he won't get pulled over, too, and shouts over his shoulder: "Get help!"

One of the women hurries toward the lounge, through the glass doors. The other is shouting in Shy's ear: "Oh my God! Oh my God! Oh my God!"

The comb-over man locks eyes with Shy. Shifty and bugged. Up to this point his hand has been gripping Shy's forearm. But now he lets go.

"What are you doing!" Shy shouts at him. "Grab on!"

The man only looks below him.

Shy tightens his grip. Grits his teeth and tries pulling the man up. But it's impossible. He's not strong enough. Their positioning is too awkward.

He looks over his shoulder again, yells: "Somebody help!"

The second woman shuffles backward, toward the lounge. Hand over her mouth. The water bottles from Shy's cooler rolling around the deck behind her.

Shy can feel the man's elbow starting to slip through his fingers. He has to do something. Now. But what?

Several seconds pass.

He lets go of the collar long enough to clamp on to the man's arm with his left hand, too. Just below the elbow. Both of his hands in a circle now. Fingers linked. Shy's whole body shaking as he holds on. Sweat running down his forehead, into his eyes.

His leg in the railing beginning to cramp.

A few more seconds and then he hears a ripping sound. The man's suit coming undone at the arm. He watches helplessly as the seams pull apart right in front of his eyes. Slow-motion-style. Black threads breaking, dangling there like tiny worms.

Then a loud tear of material and the man drops, screaming. Eyes wild as he falls backward. Arms and legs flailing.

He disappears into the darkness below with hardly a splash.

Shy! someone calls out.

But Shy's still staring over the railing, into the darkness. Trying to catch his breath. Trying to think.

Shy, I know you can hear me.

Other passengers moving out onto the deck now. The hum of hushed conversations. A spotlight snapping on above him, its bright beam of light creeping along the surface of the water. Revealing nothing.

Stop playing, bro. We need to hurry and get to Southside.

The ocean still whispering, same as before. Like nothing whatsoever has happened, and nothing will.

Shy glances down at his hands.

He's still gripping the man's empty sleeve.

THE LIVING

Day 1

1
Rodney

"Seriously, Shy. Get up."

Shy rolled over on his cot.

"Don't make me smack you upside the head."

Shy cracked open his eyes.

Big Rodney was standing over him, hands on hips.

Shy looked around their small cabin as reality came flooding back: no sleeve in his hands. This, a completely different voyage—bound for Hawaii, not Mexico. The man jumped six days ago, meaning it'd been almost a full week now.

"I know you didn't forget, right?" Rodney said.

"Forget what?" Shy sat up and rubbed his eyes. He knew this answer would stress Rodney out, though—because everything stressed

Rodney out—so he smiled and told the guy: "I'm playing, man. Of course I didn't forget. You see I'm already dressed, right?"

"I was gonna say." Rodney ducked into the bathroom, came back out with an electric toothbrush buzzing over his teeth, mumbling something impossible to make out.

Shy got out of bed and went to his dresser, pulled a brown paper bag from behind the safe he never bothered using.

Tonight was Rodney's nineteenth birthday. A bunch of people were supposed to celebrate on the crew deck outside of Southside Lounge. When Shy's shift at the pool ended at nine he'd come down to his and Rodney's cabin to shower and change, but he wound up crashing hard. This was a minor miracle considering he'd hardly slept the night before. Or the night before that. Or the night before . . .

He peeped the clock: already after eleven.

Rodney ducked back into the bathroom to spit, came out wiping his mouth with a hand towel. Guy was surprisingly nimble for an offensive lineman. "I said, you were thrashing around in your sleep, bro. You dreaming about the jumper again?"

"I was dreaming about your mom," Shy told him.

"Oh, I see how it is. We got a second comedian on the ship."

The suicide might have happened six days ago, on a completely different voyage, but every time Shy had closed his eyes since . . . there was the comb-over man. Sipping from his water bottle or talking about corruption or climbing his ass over the railing—guy's meaty arm slowly slipping through Shy's sissy grip.

Even worse, halfway through the dream the man's face would sometimes morph into Shy's *grandma's* face. Her eyes slowly filling with blood from her freakish disease.

Shy tossed the paper bag to Rodney.

"Bro, you got me a present?" Rodney said. "What is it?"

"What do you want it to be?"

Rodney studied the ceiling and tapped his temple, like he was thinking. Then he pointed at Shy, told him: "How about a beautiful woman in lingerie?"

Shy gave an exaggerated laugh. "What, you think I'm some kind of miracle worker?"

"I'm playing, bro," Rodney said. "She doesn't have to be beautiful. You know I'm not picky."

Shy pointed at the bag. "Just open it."

Rodney unfolded the top and pulled out the book Shy got him: *Daisy Cooks! Latin Flavors That Will Rock Your World.*.

"They had it in the gift shop," Shy told him.

Rodney flipped it over to look at the back.

"If you're gonna be a famous chef," Shy added, "you need to know how to do tamales and empanadas. Me and Carmen could be like your test audience."

Rodney looked up at Shy with glassy eyes.

The gift proved Shy remembered their first conversation on their first voyage together. When Rodney mentioned his dream of becoming a New York City chef.

But tears?

Really?

"Come on over here, bro," Rodney said, holding out his arms.

"Nah, I'm good," Shy told him, moving toward the door. Rodney was an enthusiastic hugger who didn't understand his own strength. And Shy wasn't the touchy-feely type.

"I mean it, Shy. Come give your boy some love."

Shy went for the door handle instead, saying: "We need to hurry and get you to your party—"

Too late.

Rodney grabbed him by the arm and reeled him in for a bear hug. Shy imagined this was what it might feel like to be squeezed to death by a Burmese python.

"You're a good friend," Rodney said, his voice cracking with emotion. "I mean it, Shy. When I become a world-famous chef and they put me on one of those morning TV shows to do a demonstration . . . Watch, I'm gonna name a dish after my Mexican compadre. How about the Shy Soufflé?"

Shy would've come up with some crack about Rodney having more of a face for radio, but he couldn't think straight. Rodney was cutting off all the oxygen to his brain.

2
Crew Within a Crew

Shy and Rodney sat down at a table on the crowded balcony where Carmen, Kevin and Marcus were guarding a stack of steaming pizza boxes.

"Took you long enough," Marcus said.

Rodney pointed at Shy. "Talk to him. He was having another nightmare about that guy he saw jump."

Shy stared at Rodney. Guy was crying over a cookbook not fifteen minutes ago. Now he wanted to call people out for nightmares?

Carmen opened the top box, said: "They just dropped these off for you, Rod. Happy birthday, big boy."

"Happy birthday," they all echoed.

Rodney thanked everyone with an over-the-table hug and slid the first slice onto his paper plate. Then he took a second and third.

The smell of pepperoni and cheese hit Shy so hard he barely had time to drool over Carmen. His stomach growled as he reached into the box with everyone else. He dotted off the extra grease with a napkin, folded the thick slice as best he could and took a sideways bite.

There were two crew lounges on board, one on each end of the ship, but this was their favorite. The Southside Lounge.

Paying passengers had every amenity imaginable. Luxury spas and pools. Multiple full-service casinos. Five-star restaurants. Dance clubs. Theaters. Gourmet food stations that stayed open all night. But the real action was down here on the crew level. At around midnight, once most of the work shifts had ended, there were parties up and down the halls, in the bars, spilling out of the lounges. A mix of good-looking young folks from all over the globe.

It was especially crowded tonight because it was the beginning of a brand-new voyage. No one was burned out yet, and there were plenty of fresh female faces to scope out—Shy's favorite pastime. The tables were all overflowing. Everyone drinking and talking and laughing. Playing poker. A group of Japanese girls were at the bar doing shots. A few Brazilians moved their sweet hips to the reggae beat against the far wall.

An older black man Shy remembered from his first voyage sat by himself near the railing, writing in a leather notebook. Hair gray and wild. Braided chin beard. He looked like some kind of black Einstein, or a terrorist—but all he did on the ship was shine shoes.

It was kind of weird having some old dude on the crew, but Shy doubted kids his own age had the shoe-shining skill set.

Two Thousand Dollars Richer

As everyone else discussed their few days away from the ship, Shy thought about one of his own recent birthdays. Couple years back his mom and sis and grandma had taken him to a college hoop game. At halftime they called out three seat numbers, asked the people sitting in those seats to proceed down to the court level for a chance to win prizes. Shy couldn't believe it when his sis pointed out he was sitting in one of the lucky spots.

He made his way down to the hardwood with the two other contestants, stood in front of the packed arena as the emcee explained the rules. Each of them would shoot a layup, a free throw, a three-pointer and a half-court shot. If you made one shot you got a gift certificate for Pizza Hut. Two shots got you free tickets to the next home game. Three, a suite for you and five guests. If you made all four shots, including the one from half-court, you got a two-thousand-dollar savings bond from the bank that sponsored the arena.

The first shooter was an old dude with tufts of gray hair popping out of his ears. He missed every shot.

The second shooter was a short-haired mannish-looking chick in Timberlands. She made the layup and the free throw.

Then it was Shy's turn.

He laid the ball in off the glass and then buried the free throw with quickness. He sank the three, all net, and listened to the crowd begin to stir. As Shy dribbled out to half-court, the emcee announced: "If this young man can make one last shot from half-court, ladies and gentlemen, he'll go home tonight two thousand dollars richer!"

Shy stood a few steps behind the half-court line, looking up into the crowd. A bunch of folks were on their feet, cheering. A rush like no other. He spotted his mom and sis clapping, his grams leaning over the railing, snapping photos he knew would end up in one of her famous scrapbooks. He pulled in a deep breath, then turned to the distant hoop, took a dribble and a couple quick strides and heaved the ball from down near his waist.

He watched the rock sail through the air in super slo-mo. Watched it smack off the backboard and go straight through.

The crowd erupted.

The bank sponsor came out to half-court and presented Shy with an oversized check. Two Gs. Shy held it up, almost laughing. Because nothing like this was supposed to happen to some anonymous kid like him. He was just a dude from down by the border. Didn't they know?

Shy reached for a second slice, still buzzing off the memory. He wondered how long before his laughter might make a comeback. He'd never admit it to anyone, but seeing a guy fall from the ship had sort of messed something up in his head. Shit was hard to process.

He took a bite and decided he should scan the balcony again, see if there were any new females as fine as Carmen. It was a little game he sometimes played. He was only half finished when he realized Kevin was staring at him from across the table.

"What's up?" Shy asked.

"We need to talk," Kevin said in his subtle Australian accent. "Soon as you're done eating."

"I still gotta close down Lido," Shy told him. The pool area was his final responsibility for the night.

"I'll close it with you, then."

Shy shrugged and took another bite of pizza. It was strange to see Kevin so eager to talk. They didn't work together, though, so Shy didn't see how he could be in trouble.

He watched Rodney hold up a fresh slice and say: "You know who made this for us, right?" He pointed a thumb back at himself. "Head chef comes to me right as I'm clocking out, says, 'Oh, I'm sorry, Rodney. We just got an order for four pies. It'd really help out if you could get them in the oven before you leave.' Bro, I had my apron off and everything."

"And you actually did it?" Marcus said.

Rodney shrugged. "No choice."

"Damn," Carmen said, looking to Shy. "They had your boy prepare his own birthday dinner."

"Wish they had him deliver it, too," Shy said. "Then we could've stiffed his ass on the tip."

They all cracked up some, even Rodney, who said: "Speaking of tips, tell everyone what the jumper slipped you before he hopped in the soup."

Shy reached into his uniform pocket, held up a hundred-dollar bill. "Forgot all about it till we boarded today."

Rodney shook his head and pulled another slice. "I was like, what'd you do, bro? Give the guy a happy ending?"

"Just a bottle of water," Shy said, staring at the comb-over man's money. Technically, the crew wasn't supposed to accept tips. But that never stopped anyone. This tip seemed different, though. Like it'd be messed up to spend it on some dumb shit.

Carmen held out an open palm, told him: "Might as well hand it over, *vato*. That's exactly how much you owe me for being your friend."

Shy made like he was placing the money in her hand, but the second her manicured fingers started curling around the bill, he snatched it back and shoved it in his pocket. "Gotta be quick," he told her.

Carmen made a face and pinched the back of his arm.

Shy felt better when he noticed Kevin laughing with everyone else. Whatever he wanted to talk about couldn't be *that* big a deal.

"Lemme get this straight," Marcus said, wiping his hands on a paper towel. "If you would've just peeped the tip right away, you could've saved this cat's life?"

"How you figure that?" Shy asked.

"I'm saying, someone slips *me* a Franklin, my ass goes on high alert."

"Maybe I'm just good at what I do." Shy shot him a sarcastic grin.

"Not," Carmen said.

"Yeah, okay." Marcus laughed and bit into his pizza slice.

"Some passengers just like to tip like that," Kevin said. "They wanna impress everybody."

"I got tipped fifty for adjusting a karaoke mike," Carmen said. "Two voyages ago."

"Man or woman?" Rodney said.

"Man. Why?"

"You know all these rich white dudes got a warm spot for you, Carm. You're like their jalapeño *chalupa* fantasy."

Carmen reached across Shy and slugged Rodney in the shoulder. It was impossible for Shy not to stare at her shirt riding up her beautiful brown back.

"Shoot," Marcus said, "fifty seems kind of high for the Mexican platter."

Carmen grabbed a piece of crust out of the half-empty pizza box and heaved it at his head. Marcus ducked in time, though, and the crust went sailing over the railing, into the Pacific. "I guess chicken and waffles are supposed to be fine dining," she said.

"Compared to a bowl of wack taco salad?"

Everybody was cracking up now, including, Shy noticed, the group of Swedish crew members at the next table over.

"For the record," Rodney said, "everyone here is the fine-dining version. Look around you, bro. Paradise only hires attractive people."

Shy watched them all sort of glance around the table at each other. They didn't need to, though. Rodney had it right. Pretty much everyone on the crew was attractive, especially the group Shy kicked it with.

Kevin was a rugged, outdoorsy Australian. Messy blond hair and three-day stubble. At twenty-two he was the oldest and most worldly at the table. When he wasn't mixing martinis on a Paradise cruise ship, he was posing for pictures all over Europe as an underwear model.

Marcus was the ship's resident hip-hop dancer. A pretty-boy black kid from Crenshaw who was a secret tech head. He was all cut up from popping and locking, contorting his body in ways that didn't seem possible. Whenever Marcus dropped his uniform top on the pool's main stage, during a scheduled dance demonstration, Shy would watch everyone stare at his abs without blinking. Even skeletal old white ladies from Confederate states.

Carmen was the only female in their group. She was eighteen and half Mexican like Shy, from a town not far from Otay Mesa called National City. She hosted karaoke every night and sang in some of the shows. First time Shy met her, he could barely speak. She had to wave a hand all in front of his face, laughing, and ask Rodney if he was mute.

Only problem with Carmen was she had a fiancé back home. Some wealthy white kid in law school. She left the diamond in her cabin, she claimed, because wedding rings work like kryptonite on tips.

Eventually their eyes all settled on Rodney.

He lowered a half-eaten sausage slice, said: "What?"

A table full of grins.

"Bro, I don't count," he said. "There's a reason they keep my big ass locked up in a kitchen."

Everyone laughed.

Rodney was a six-four farm boy with a bad flat top. Crooked teeth. A few months ago he'd moved from Iowa to Irvine to try and play college football for the Anteaters. His strength coach hooked him up with a job on the ship assisting the head chef in the Destiny Dining Room. In his free time, Rodney read romance novels and ate Costco-sized bags of gummy bears and listened to Christina Aguilera on oversized headphones.

As everyone finished eating, Shy thought about how he fit into the equation. He wasn't an underwear model like Kevin, he knew that. But he was tall for being half Mexican. And he played ball. The girls back home called him "pretty boy" and said he was a catch—though a catch in Otay Mesa was probably different from a catch on a Paradise cruise ship.

Shy was still kicking this around as he weaved through the balcony crowd to toss his greasy paper plate into the trash by the bar. When he turned back around, he found Kevin standing there. "Ready?"

"Sure," Shy told him. "But what's going on?"

"Overheard something earlier." Kevin threw away his plate, too. "Figured you should be properly warned."

Warned? A wave of nerves passed through Shy's middle.

"Lido Deck, right?" Kevin said.

Shy nodded. As he followed Kevin through the crowded balcony tables, toward the exit, he looked over his shoulder at Carmen.

You okay? she mouthed.

Shy shrugged and went through the door.

3
Man in a Black Suit

Shy followed Kevin up several flights of stairs, through the ship's atrium, which was straight out of an art magazine. Oversized paintings hanging from every wall, fresh flowers arranged in large colored vases, cascading chandeliers, classical music playing softly on well-hidden speakers.

They gave smiles and subtle head bows whenever they passed a passenger couple out for a late-night stroll.

"Ma'am."

"Sir."

They trekked all the way to the other end of the ship and out onto the Lido Deck, where Shy was to spend the majority of his working hours this voyage. The ship psychiatrist had decided it was best to keep Shy off the Honeymoon Deck—at least until he'd had the proper amount of time to "deal with the suicide." Then he'd handed Shy a bottle of pills that were supposed to ease his mind. But all the first one did was make him feel hollow and numb. Like a fake person. He tossed the rest of the bottle in the trash.

They crossed to the far end, where the infinity pool sat sparkling in the moonlight. There were some people still hanging out in the Jacuzzi, even though it had been closed for over an hour. A guy and three girls. When they saw Kevin and Shy approaching, the guy stood up and said: "Time to wrap it up, right?"

"Sorry, sir," Shy told him. "I have to close down for the night."

The guy hopped out of the Jacuzzi dripping wet and looked down at the girls. "You heard the man. Time to move it indoors."

Shy watched the three bikini girls climb out of the Jacuzzi. They were younger than most of the passengers, mid-twenties maybe, and they looked good as hell. Only a few fractions of a notch below Carmen when she was in a two-piece—and that was saying something.

The guy had already put on a shirt and cargo pants, and he walked over to Shy and Kevin, saying: "Must be a hassle shooing people out of the tub every night. Sorry 'bout that, guys. I'm Christian, by the way."

Shy shook the guy's hand and introduced himself.

Kevin did the same.

Christian was straight out of a GQ ad. Light-blue eyes and chiseled chin. Tiny bit of scruff around his face. Longish sandy-blond hair to his shoulders, still wet and dripping down his shirt.

"Come on, Dr. Christian," one of the girls called.

The guy winked at Kevin and Shy. "Just made it through med school. We're doing a bit of celebrating. See you guys around." He turned and started toward the atrium, the girls falling in line behind him. Shy watched them go, wondering what it would be like to live another kind of life. To be on the path to becoming a doctor. To be the one waited on instead of the waiter. It was something he'd never even considered before stepping foot on a luxury cruise.

Soon as they were gone, he turned to Kevin and said: "So, what'd you wanna warn me about?"

"Had his hands full, didn't he?" Kevin said, staring at the wet footprints the girls had left behind. "I was certainly willing to help a bloke out. All he had to do was ask."

"I'm with you," Shy said, and he began dragging white lounge chairs back where they belonged, pulling off discarded towels, readjusting seat backs. There were over two hundred chairs, and every morning, before the sun came up, they had to be perfectly aligned.

He rounded the second row and veered toward the housekeeping room, saying: "The warning, Kev."

"Right," Kevin said, picking up a towel Shy had dropped. "So, after I board the ship this morning, I go directly into the bar to do my prep. But the cellar door's locked, which is a pain in my ass. I have to hike it all the way up to Paolo's office to get the key and—You've met Paolo, right?"

"Head of security." Shy pushed open the door to housekeeping and heaved the stack of towels off his shoulder and into the wash bin. Kevin tossed in his towel, too. Claudia, a German woman Shy had met on his first voyage, waved and wheeled the cart toward laundry.

"I forgot," Kevin said. "You spent a few hours with him after the suicide, no? Anyway, I can't go in his office right away because someone's in there. A man in a black suit. And guess who he's asking Paolo about?"

"Me?"

"You."

Shy stopped. "Why?"

But he had a feeling he already knew why.

The comb-over man.

"Like a good mate," Kevin said as Shy resumed straightening lounge chairs, "I wait behind the door, out of sight, and listen. Black suit wants to know about this Shy bloke. Who is he? Where's he from? What did he and the jumper discuss before things went bad? And he's using tough talk with Paolo, which I've never seen on board a Paradise ship. Paolo outranks almost everyone, you know? So this guy's probably not crew."

Shy shook his head in frustration. "How many times do I have to explain shit?" he said, facing Kevin. "I gave the guy a water. When he tried to jump I grabbed his arm, but he was too heavy. I couldn't hold on. What else do they wanna hear?"

He was leaving out his strange conversation with the comb-over man, of course. Had yet to mention that part to anyone. But it didn't make any sense. And he figured the less interaction he said they had, the quicker they'd let him get on with his life.

So much for that theory.

"Easy," Kevin said. "Don't go shooting the messenger now. Anyway, sounds to me like Paolo relayed the right information. But the man in the black suit wasn't satisfied. He wanted your file. And your work schedule."

Shy yanked a damp towel off a chair. "This is crazy, Kev. Did Paolo *give* it to him?"

"Don't know," Kevin said. "Sounded like they were wrapping up at that point, so I stepped away from the door."

Shy shook his head some more and walked a last handful of towels to housekeeping, dropped them into an empty bin. How was he supposed to put shit behind him when everyone kept bringing it back up?

He turned toward the fancy Jacuzzi, flipped off the jets and the waterfall and the heat, started covering it with the special lid. All Shy wanted was a summer job before his senior year. And when his counselor brought up the connections she had with Paradise Cruise Lines, it sounded different, exotic. If he had it to do over again, though, he'd apply for something more normal instead. Like Subway or Big O Tires. No one tries to kill themselves while buying a set of damn Goodyears.

"Don't you get it yet?" Kevin said, shadowing Shy. "These aren't regular cruise ship passengers we're dealing with. They're the richest of the rich. We've had ex-presidents. Actors. Donald Trump was on my first voyage."

"What if I went and found this dude first?" Shy said. "Maybe I could talk to him. Get it out of the way."

"Could try that," Kevin said, glancing over Shy's shoulder. "I'm thinking he must be FBI, something important like that. And if the jumper didn't say anything to you before he went, you have nothing to worry about, right?"

Shy moved over to the infinity pool, pulled the fancy skimmer out of its holster. He didn't know what to think as he fished out a tiny scrap of paper, a hair band, a couple small bugs. The FBI? Nothing like this had ever happened to him before. He wished he could fast-forward through the rest of this voyage, get back to his simple life in Otay Mesa—though even that was messed up now that his grandma had passed.

Shy noticed Kevin glancing over his shoulder again, shoving his hands in his pockets.

"Well, that's a bit odd," Kevin mumbled.

"What?" Shy said.

Kevin stared at the ground, shaking his head. Then he spoke to Shy in a quiet voice. "Don't go turning around or anything, but I think someone's been watching us this whole time."

"Who?" Shy said. "The guy in the black suit?"

Kevin shrugged.

"The one you saw?"

"I'm pretty sure."

Shy froze, pool skimmer in hand. He could feel his heart start beating faster inside his chest. Things seemed more serious all of a sudden. Like maybe he was actually in trouble for something.

"Look," Kevin said. "Handle your business out here and go to your cabin. First thing tomorrow morning I'd have a chat with Paolo."

Shy put away the skimmer.

He could feel the guy's eyes burning a hole in his back. Or was his mind making it into a bigger deal than it really was? Either way, he didn't feel like being out here alone. "Hey, Kev," he said in a quiet voice. "You think you could hang for a few more minutes?"

Kevin shot him a look that said he had his back. "I'm not going anywhere."

4

Insomnia

Shy couldn't sleep.

Again.

He tossed and turned on his cot, listening to the rise and fall of Rodney's snoring, watching the digital numbers switch places on his clock radio. He stared up at the ceiling, unable to stop his mind from spinning. . . .

He imagined the man in the black suit sneaking into his room, wearing a ski mask. Inching a machete closer and closer to Shy's exposed neck until it pierced his skin and blood ran all over his sheets and his blankets and his flat-as-shit pillow.

He imagined the comb-over man slipping through his grasp, only this time they were handcuffed together and Shy was pulled overboard, too. Both of them falling falling falling toward a swirling ocean that sucked them in and held them in its clutches like the Bermuda Triangle.

Shy pictured the last few hours of his grandma's life. How she started clawing at her own skin in the hospital bed. His mom crying from outside the quarantine room. Pounding her fists against the thick glass and screaming at the nurses. Shy unable to move or speak or even breathe.

It was almost three in the morning when Shy finally gave up on sleep. He threw off his blankets and went to Rodney's computer to check his email.

Only one message in his in-box.

From his mom.

Could they please Skype tomorrow? Between his shifts? She had some possibly worrisome news she'd rather not share over email. "Please, Shy," the email read. "I know you're busy on your ship, but find a few minutes for your mom. I'm a bundle of nerves right now and I really want to talk to you."

Shy read it two more times without blinking.

Last time she wanted to talk was after his grandma was diagnosed with Romero Disease. And when Kevin wanted to talk it was about some guy in a black suit who'd been asking about him. The same guy who was watching them at the pool.

All these "talks" eventually turned to bad news.

He typed a message to his mom saying he'd log on to Skype at some point between two and two-thirty. Tomorrow afternoon. Then he closed the computer and left the cabin to wander the halls and think.

The entire ship was like a ghost town. Tumbleweed rolling past in Shy's imagination. He kept expecting to find a pack of black-suit-wearing FBI agents lurking around every corner, but every corner was empty.

The ship's great weight pitched subtly under Shy's shell tops. Tiny movements in the floorboards that made him feel uncoordinated as he climbed a few flights of stairs. His whole body tired and achy from lack of sleep.

He moved through one of the premier-class levels. Rustic light fixtures made to look like old-style lanterns, spotless framed mirrors, doors made of real wood with brass handles and brass locks and brass knockers.

So much money went into these premier decks.

The hallways alone.

How would it feel, he wondered, if he'd been born someone else? Not a housekeeping crew member who couldn't sleep, but a first-class passenger coming back from a night of killing it at the casino. He'd key open one of these fancy doors, toss his winnings on the oak table. Strip out of his clothes while watching the ocean through his cabin window. Climb into bed next to his smoking-hot wife and pull the silk covers up under his chin.

People in premier class probably fell asleep within seconds.

Shy climbed back up to the Honeymoon Deck and stood at the railing in the exact spot where he'd dropped the comb-over man. His first time back to the scene of the crime. Even hooked his right leg into the railing to remember what it felt like. But the only thing it made him feel was stupid, so he pulled his leg back out and just stood there, staring down at the dark water.

Listening to its constant whispering.

Still unable to make out any meaning.

Seemed like forever ago that the bus dropped him off for that first voyage—though it had only been eleven days. He remembered looking out the window as his bus squeaked to a stop. There was the massive, sparkling ship at anchor. It towered over everything around it, even what was on land, and he couldn't wrap his head around the immensity of it. The giant hull perfectly white, lined with orange-bottomed lifeboats and row after row of single square windows. The glass-covered atrium reaching up from the highest deck, into the sky. Thick synthetic cords jetting out of the bow, tied to solid steel hitches built into the pier. The name "Paradise" written across the side in huge calligraphy letters.

It stood there in the water, motionless.

Waiting for him.

Now Shy was aboard that ship for a second time, staring out from the empty Honeymoon Deck. The ocean stretching out endlessly in front of him. Far as the eye could see. Nothing but water and more water.

It made Shy feel incredibly alone.

A tiny, insignificant human.

This sudden awareness crushed down on him and stole his breath, and for a split second he understood how someone could be moved to jump.

5

Carmen

After wandering a while longer, Shy found himself outside Carmen's cabin, knuckles raised in front of her door, ready to knock.

But he couldn't knock.

It was three-thirty in the morning.

He lowered his fist and just stood there a few minutes, trying to think.

On his first voyage, he and Carmen had hit it off right away. They realized they were from the same area, went to rival high schools—though Carmen had just graduated. Then they discovered something else they had in common. Romero Disease.

Shy had lost his grandma.

Carmen, her old man.

They talked and talked that night. Carmen crying in front of him. Leaning her head against Shy's shoulder at one point, and him telling her, "It's okay, Carm, it's okay," even though they both knew it wasn't okay.

Shy turned and started back to his own cabin.

He only made it a few steps down the hall, though, before he heard a door creak open.

Then a tired voice: "Shy?"

He turned, saw Carmen peeking out from behind her door. Eyes puffy from sleep. Hair reckless. An oversized guy's T-shirt barely covering her long brown legs.

"What are you doing up?" she said.

"Couldn't sleep."

She rubbed her eyes and yawned. "Again?"

Shy shrugged.

The girl looked so good it made his heart hurt. A few strands of thick brown hair in her face. Full lips and dark eyes. Chest stretching out the vowels of her vintage-looking Padres shirt. He did his best to keep his eyes on *her* eyes so she wouldn't think he was being sketchy.

He cleared his throat. "How'd you know someone was out here, anyway?"

Carmen frowned as she considered this. "I woke up and . . . I don't even know, I just went to the door. I had a feeling you'd be here. Is that weird?"

So she wouldn't see his smile, Shy leaned over to retie his shoelace. He double-knotted and gathered himself and then stood back up, saying: "Anyways, I was out walking and I passed—"

"Hang on," Carmen interrupted, and she ducked back into her cabin.

Shy stared at her closed door, butterflies now going in his stomach. Back home he'd been with a respectable number of females. He was the starting point guard on his hoop squad. Found occasional notes stashed in his locker. Girls sometimes stepped to him at a house party or on a basketball road trip. And he always played it mellow. But with Carmen—even just as friends—it was a different story. He never really had a handle on his vibe. Felt awkward, even. Maybe because she was a year older. Or because she had a fiancé. Or maybe because he actually cared what she thought.

The door reopened and Carmen came all the way into the hall this time. She was wearing baggy sweatpants now and holding her laptop and a nearly full bottle of wine with a plastic cup over the top.

"Sit," she said.

Shy sat.

Carmen sat on the floor next to him and opened up her iTunes. "My roommate's sleeping," she said, putting on some Brazilian music, lowering the volume. She unscrewed the wine cap, poured some into the lone cup. "We'll have to share."

"For real, though," Shy said, making like he was about to get up. "I wasn't trying to pull you out of bed."

"What, you can't share a cup with me? You think I got cooties?"

He smiled. "You shouldn't have to suffer 'cause I can't sleep."

Carmen rolled her eyes and took a sip of the wine. "That first night we met. You remember the long conversation we had at Southside?"

"Yeah."

"At the end of it, what'd I tell you?"

Shy remembered her exact words, remembered the tears he saw going down her cheeks. "You said I could stop by whenever I wanted to talk. Didn't matter what time."

"So?" Carmen said, swirling the wine in her cup. "What are we gonna talk about, then?"

Shy settled back in and took the cup from her, pulled a sip of his own. Cool red wine running down his tired throat, settling in his tired stomach.

It was nice sitting here with Carmen.

In the hall.

Listening to music.

Everyone else on the ship miles away in their sleep.

"Kev says some suit guy's been asking about me," he told her. "Maybe FBI or something."

"That's why Kev followed you out to the pool?"

Shy nodded. "The guy might've been watching us, too. Kev thinks the whole time we were talking."

"Ay, creepy."

Shy shook his head. "I can't believe people are still asking me questions."

"They're being thorough, I guess," Carmen said. "You know these passengers are all, like, super important, right? Costs a grip to go on a Paradise cruise."

"That's what Kev said."

"Now if it was me or you who went overboard . . . trust me, there wouldn't be no FBI involved."

"Doubt they'd even slow down," Shy said.

Carmen shook her head. "Probably speed up."

They both smiled a little and Shy took another sip of wine, passed the empty cup back to Carmen, watched her pour it full again.

"I also got an email from my mom," he said. "She wants to Skype tomorrow. Says she's got some bad news."

Carmen cringed. "Any idea what it is?"

Shy shook his head. "Ever since my grams, though, first thing I always think about is that stupid disease. I swear to God, Carm, if my mom's sick . . . I don't even know."

"Tell me about it," Carmen said. "Anytime one of my little brothers even rubs his eyes I freak out." She reached over to her keyboard and skipped to a different song. Then she looked up at Shy, shaking her head. "We both know how awful it is, that's why."

"I heard they might have meds soon."

"I heard that, too," Carmen said. "Not that it does jack shit for my papi now. Or your grandma."

Shy looked at the ground.

As they made their way through another cup of wine, Carmen caught Shy up about her mom's quilting. Ever since her old man passed, her mom had been on a quilting binge. Quilts hung from every wall in their apartment, she said. They covered every couch and bed and end table. If the woman wasn't working or sleeping, she was needling her way through another quilt.

Shy told Carmen about the job his older sis had just landed at the elementary school across the street from their building. She was gonna be a teacher's aide. She'd make a little money and the hours were the same as his nephew Miguel's preschool, so she wouldn't have to pay for day care.

"What about your fiancé?" Shy asked, figuring he should ask about that part of her life, too.

"What about him?"

"I don't know," Shy said. "What's his story?"

"He's good," she said. "Busy like usual."

Shy nodded. "He got one of those quilts on his bed?"

Carmen laughed. "You know it. One with a bunch of little musical notes sewn into it. Not that Brett knows shit about music."

Shy grinned and took the wine handoff. Pulled another long sip. He was already feeling it and he decided it might help him sleep.

"Know what's weird, though?" Carmen said. "We *still* haven't talked about my papi. Me and Brett."

"Seriously?"

Carmen nodded. "Don't get me wrong, he's always been there for me. And he handled all the stuff for the funeral. But I don't know. He's never once stopped and asked me how I feel."

Carmen's eyes were fixed on the wine inside the cup for a few long seconds, like she was thinking. Then she looked up and said: "He's buried under them law school books, though. The first year is supposedly the hardest so they can weed out all the fakers."

Shy nodded. He always felt sort of jealous hearing about Carmen and her man. But if they were gonna be friends, he figured he had to occasionally ask about shit like that.

And that was what he wanted, right?

For him and Carmen to be friends?

Or was it impossible to be friends with a girl you thought was mellow and smart and beautiful?

Shy snatched the wine out of her hand and downed the last of it in one go. Handed back an empty cup.

Carmen went to refill it again, but there was only a tiny bit left. As she held the bottle upside down, letting the last few drops fall into the cup, she changed the subject to their current voyage. Neither of them had ever been to Hawaii, and since they'd both have half a day off, she made him promise he'd take a surfing lesson with her. And go with her to get real shave ice on the north shore. Then she looked at him all concerned-like and said: "Could I ask you a personal question, Shy?"

"Go 'head." He was feeling so buzzed now he was willing to answer pretty much anything. Even if she asked something crazy like how long it took him to stop wetting the bed as a kid.

"Do you think about it all the time?" she said. "How that guy fell with you right there?"

Shy shrugged. "I guess so."

"What was it like?"

Shy could picture the comb-over man now. His eyes darting all over the place. His arms and legs going as he fell toward the blackness. "He let go of my arm," Shy told her. "He wanted his life to be over. It's what he chose. With that disease, though, you don't get no choice."

Carmen looked down at the cup, nodding.

It went quiet between them for a few long seconds. A shared feeling of loss hanging in the air like a gas. Then Carmen cleared her throat and switched the subject back to Hawaii.

6

Space Sancho

They talked a while longer before Shy said: "Anyways, I should probably let you get back to bed."

"I don't work till later on," Carmen said. "So it's on you, dude."

"I'm supposed to be at the pool by seven. Guess I should at least try for a couple hours." He poked the top of her bare foot, said: "Thanks for talking."

"No worries." She picked up the empty bottle and spun it so the label was facing her. "Before you go, though. You know the rules. Tell me one new thing about you."

Shy stared at the wine bottle, thinking.

Carmen ended all their one-on-one conversation this way. It was her thing. He usually told her something basic. Like he didn't have a middle name. Or he'd lived in LA for a year with his old man. Or his Spanish was the worst of anyone in his family and sometimes he laughed at a joke even when he didn't understand. But tonight he was feeling confident from the wine, and he wanted to say something important.

"Well?" she said.

Shy looked up at her, trying to think. But he didn't know what to say. It all seemed too dumb for the moment.

"Come on, Shy," Carmen said. "We only met each other like two weeks ago. There's a million things you could probably tell me."

He shrugged. If he couldn't think of anything cool, he'd just say what was in his head. "I was on the Honeymoon Deck a while ago, looking at the water, and I thought of something."

"What?" she said.

"I don't know. In the grand scheme of things, we're like little specks of dust."

Carmen smiled. "Check out Shy getting all deep."

"For real," he said, wanting to explain himself. "At one point I was staring up at the sky, and you know what I realized? There's no way we're the only living humans in the universe. It's impossible."

Carmen put a hand on one of Shy's shell tops, said: "Don't tell me you're one of those UFO people."

He shrugged. Now that he was talking, he wanted to keep going. Maybe that was the only way he'd understand what he felt. "I'm talking about planets we can't even see with the highest-powered telescopes. Ones in completely different solar systems."

Carmen was grinning now. "I'm gonna go 'head and put this on the wine."

She was right, Shy was seriously buzzing now. He felt like he could say anything that popped into his brain. "And you know what my theory is?"

"Please, enlighten me."

"I think on one of those faraway planets there's a space version of me and there's a space version of you. And I bet our space versions met earlier in life. In junior high. On the swings at the park or something. And they probably hit it off in about two point five. Like love at first sight or whatever. And since that day they've been all about each other."

"Oh, is that right?" Carmen looked like she was about to bust out laughing, but Shy didn't even care. Now that he was flowing, he didn't want to stop.

"I bet they're on a ship right now," he continued. "Just like us. Only billions of miles away. And they're drinking wine and talking about life."

Carmen shook her head and tried to pour more wine into the empty cup. Nothing came out, though, so she set the bottle back down. "So technically," she said, "you're like my space Sancho, right? My other man in another world."

"On that distant planet," Shy heard himself say, "I'm your *only* man."

Carmen leaned back against the hall wall and crossed her arms, looking all skeptical. "How do you even know if the space us gets along? We probably fight all the time."

"Nah, we never fight," Shy said.

"You sure?"

He nodded. "'Cause we talk about everything. Even sad stuff. And the space me always asks how you feel."

Carmen grinned at Shy and shook her head.

He didn't even know what he was saying anymore. Shit was just popping into his brain. "There's actually a test people can do," he told her. "Right here on earth. To find out if their space versions are compatible."

"I'm sure there is."

"See, most people get caught up in the kissing and the feeling on each other. But really it's more simple than that. It's about how two people fit when they hold hands."

"You're like a fifth grader," Carmen said, rolling her eyes. "You know that, right?"

But Shy also saw her glance down at his hands. And now that he thought about it, he honestly believed you could decide if you were right with a girl by how it felt holding her hand. "Maybe we should check our fit," he suggested. "Just to see."

Carmen laughed him off and changed the song playing on her computer. When she looked up again, and saw that Shy was still staring at her, she said: "You're being serious?"

Shy shrugged.

He couldn't believe it. She was actually considering his test. Butterflies started flapping all around in his stomach. He never thought she'd really do it.

"Fine," Carmen said, acting like it was no big deal. She held her right hand out to him, palm up.

Shy took it gently into his, pulled a nervous breath and said: "It's a three-part test, all right? First we gotta check things out the regular way, like two people watching a movie in the theater."

They held hands on Shy's knee.

It felt more alive than anything he'd ever known.

"Okay," he said, nodding. "That's pretty soft right there. I'm not gonna lie." His heart was now trying to leap right out of his body. "What do you think?"

"I don't see no fireworks, if that's what you mean."

Shy smiled a little, but quickly forced his face back to being regular. "Next we gotta check it with our fingers linked." He slipped his fingers into hers and held her hand softly, looking in her eyes. The warmth of her skin spreading through his hand and into his arm, into his entire body.

"Yeah," he said. "That's a pretty solid match. You feel it, right?"

Carmen didn't answer this time.

Her face seemed serious all of a sudden.

Shy swallowed down hard on his nerves. He was sort of in over his head now.

"Okay, one last test," he told her. "But it's maybe the most important. You slip your index finger into my pinkie. Like this."

He hooked Carmen's index with his pinkie, their fingers now dangling there together. Shy's breaths short and quick and uncertain. Both of them staring down at their hands.

They looked up at each other at the exact same time.

"Hmmm," Shy said, rubbing on his chin, wondering if she could tell his whole body was actually shaking. "Maybe I was wrong. Maybe our space versions are messing up—"

Carmen cut him off cold when she leaned forward suddenly and kissed him on the lips, kissed his words right back into his mouth.

Gently, though.

And quick.

Her lips slightly parted and her eyes closed and then it was over—Shy sitting there stunned, holding his breath, staring at her perfect brown face. Perfect soft lips. Her big brown eyes reaching deep into his chest, uncovering his lonely heart.

He let go of her finger and placed his hands on the sides of her face. And he looked at her for a few seconds. The way he'd always wanted to look at her.

Carmen.

His blood marching through his veins like a New Year's parade and his breaths now quick and desperate.

He leaned forward and kissed her again. Longer this time. And more powerfully. Carmen's fingers going through his hair and then her lips brushing against his ear as she breathed out his name.

"Shy."

It came out quietly, sending sharp tingles all across his skin.

She pulled back to look at him again.

Shy's chest going in and out and in and out as he tried to think about what was happening. But it was impossible to think.

He was here. With Carmen.

But at the same time it felt like he was far, far away, out on the ocean somewhere, bobbing on the surface, listening to its ceaseless chatter. Or farther still, all the way on that distant planet he'd just told her about.

She shoved him against the wall and kissed him again. Desperately this time. With an urgency he'd never experienced. Like they were wrestling. Gripping each other's wrists and pushing and clawing, and Shy was lost in this fight, kissing her back with everything he felt and feeling her body against his body and breathing her into his lungs.

They toppled over, onto the floor.

Carmen above him now.

He accidentally kicked over the wine bottle, heard it slowly rolling down the hall. Her hair covering his face like a secret hiding place. Her hands gripping at his skin.

And then she stopped.

Just like that.

She pushed away and looked at him, out of breath.

Face of confusion.

Shy sat up, too. He started to say her name, to try and bring her back, but she covered her mouth and quickly turned away from him.

And that was when Shy knew.

He'd messed up everything with the only girl who understood.

Day 2

7
Towel Boy

Shy felt like he'd been asleep for about three seconds when his alarm started blaring in his ear.

He sat up quick and shut it off.

Six-thirty in the morning.

His first thought as he held his throbbing head: no way he'd make it through work today. He was too exhausted. Too hungover.

Then a second thought: Carmen.

His stomach dropped.

Last night when he said he was sorry, she had ducked back into her room without a word. He had to talk to her as soon as possible. Clear the air. Go back to being just friends or whatever they were supposed to be.

Rodney turned over on his cot, eyes still crusted closed, drool pooling on his pillow. Massive sock-covered feet hanging off the end of his cot. Seemed like the guy didn't have a care in the world. Why couldn't it be like that for everyone?

Shy forced himself out of bed to pop some aspirin. Then he dragged his Paradise polo and shorts into the tiny bathroom for a cold shower.

The sun was just starting to rise into the cloudy sky when Shy re-opened his towel stand on the empty Lido Deck. Early mornings at sea were breathtaking, and they usually made him feel brand-new. But today all Shy felt was used up and stressed out.

As he placed a folded towel at the foot of all two hundred deck chairs he replayed his night with Carmen. He felt sick about it. Damn liquid courage. All that space shit he'd talked. The hand holding. Hooking up with Carmen was both everything he wanted and the worst thing that could've happened.

He mopped the deck and removed the Jacuzzi cover and turned on the heat and the jets, and then he fished a few more bugs out of the pool with the skimmer and treated the water. The whole time he kept his eyes peeled for Carmen. Usually she'd cut through the pool area at some point with her morning coffee. On her way to the Normandie Theater. And they'd kick it for a few minutes.

But he was over an hour into his shift now.

And still no sign of Carmen.

Shy forced himself to think of other things instead. Like the suit guy Kevin warned him about. He'd go talk to Paolo between his shift here and his afternoon shift at the gym. Then there was the Skype he was supposed to do with his mom. If something bad had really happened back home, he didn't know what he'd do. He was stuck way out here on a ship. Middle of the ocean. No help to anyone.

Soon scattered passengers began trickling out onto the deck. A few shivering kids lining up for the water slide, their moms and dads standing around sipping coffee, introducing themselves to one another. An old couple under a Paradise umbrella rocking old-people sunglasses and reading electronic books.

Across the deck, the Island Café had opened and the smell of bacon and sausage and waffles filled the air. The clinking sound of silverware on plates and early-morning chatter. The aspirin was finally working on Shy's headache. He scored a coffee from the café and took it back to his stand, where he sipped at it and studied the dark clouds in the distance and watched people.

By ten the pool area was half full.

Shy handed out fresh towels, miniature golf equipment, Ping-Pong paddles, swimmies, scuba masks. Cocktail waitresses moved through the rows of lounge chairs, taking orders for espressos, Bloody Marys, mimosas. The ship emcee announced the day's activities and reminded passengers that the duty-free shops had just opened in the main promenade.

Still no sign of Carmen.

And nobody in a black suit—though Shy doubted anyone would wear a suit out by the pool when it was like ninety degrees. The guy would probably have changed into shorts or something. Which meant Shy didn't even know what he was looking for.

By noon the deck was humming and the sun beat down in front of clustered rain clouds. Almost every lounge chair had been claimed. Elegant women in wide-brimmed hats and bikinis, reading magazines, eating the fruit out of their tropical drinks. Men sleeping in sunglasses or watching the pool, bulging stomachs already bright red from the sun.

Just like on Shy's first voyage, the women were all better-looking than the men. And younger. But this group was a little quicker to tip. He already had a small wad of cash in his pocket as he made another pass through the crowd, replacing used towels with freshly laundered ones.

Whenever the used bin filled up he'd cart it across the deck to housekeeping and hurry back with fresh warm stacks.

He was so busy now he hardly had time to think.

And not thinking was clutch—like somebody should bottle the shit and sell it ten bucks a pop.

On his third trip back from housekeeping, though, he stopped cold.

Carmen.

8

The Glare Off a Diamond

She was on the other side of the pool, maybe twenty yards away, wheeling an amp and a microphone stand toward the far staircase, which would lead her down to the theater.

Shy parked his towel cart by his stand and started toward her, brainstorming how to best present his apology. But just as he rounded the Jacuzzi a passenger in a cowboy hat flagged him down.

"Hey there, bud," the man said. "Wanna check out the ring I'm about to give my soon-to-be-better-half?"

Shy tried to muster a Paradise-worthy smile even though the question had caught him totally off guard, and he was in a hurry. "Uh, okay, sir." He glanced in Carmen's direction, saw that she had stopped at the outdoor bar to talk to one of the cocktail waitresses. Katrina.

The man unzipped the leather fanny pack resting underneath his stiff-looking beer gut and reached inside. He had a little gray mixed into his mustache and sideburns. Legs so spindly and white Shy wondered if it was the first time he'd ever stepped into a pair of shorts.

He pulled out a small blue box. "Springing this on her tonight at dinner," he said, looking all proud of himself. "She doesn't have a clue." He flipped open the box, and the knuckle-sized diamond caught the sun, nearly blinding Shy.

"Wow, sir. It's really big."

"Impressive, right?"

"Very." Shy glanced at Carmen again—still talking to Katrina. He needed to wrap up the big show-and-tell session and go catch her before she left.

"Over seven carats," the man said. "I'm guessing you've never seen a seven-carat diamond before."

"Not even on TV," Shy told him, leaving out the part about him not giving a shit.

"Well, I'm in oil, boy. Big oil, just like my daddy. We're oilmen. And you know what all the top oilmen have in common?"

"What's that, sir?"

"When we decide to do something, we do it big."

Shy snuck another glance at Carmen and Katrina, then looked back at the ring. He tried to think up something else to add as the man kept talking, something flattering—'cause maybe that was where he'd gone wrong with the passenger who'd jumped—but he was drawing a blank.

The oilman stopped himself, mid-sentence, and followed Shy's eyes to Carmen. "Young lady," he called to her suddenly.

Carmen pointed at herself, mouthed: *Me?*

He nodded. "Come on over here a second, will you?"

Shy kept his smile going, but inside he was in a bit of a panic.

Last thing he needed was for his and Carmen's first interaction since the hookup to be chaperoned by Roy Rogers.

Carmen said something to Katrina, then wheeled her amp toward them wearing a Paradise smile of her own.

"You gotta check out this ring," Shy told her, trying to play like everything was normal between them. But the fact that she didn't even look at him seemed problematic.

"Oh, this isn't just any ol' ring," the man said, tapping the Tiffany's box closed. "But first things first, sugar. What's your name?"

"Carmen."

"Gorgeous name for a gorgeous gal. And where you from, Ms. Carmen?"

She glanced at Shy for a fraction of a second, then told the man: "I'm from San Diego, sir."

"Originally, I mean," the man said. "What race are you?"

Carmen was as good as anyone at laying down the fake cheerful vibe. But Shy could tell by her eyes, she wanted to boot dude in the *huevos*.

"Guess," Carmen said.

"All right." He got a big grin and looked her up and down, spending a few extra beats on her cleavage. "I gotta warn you, though. I've been all over the map on business. And I know my women."

When the guy took Carmen by the arm, and actually spun her around so he could peep her backside, Shy started getting pissed, too. If they were anywhere besides a cruise ship he'd have already swiped the ring and Carmen's hand and been halfway to Ensenada.

"Brazilian?" the man guessed.

"Close," Carmen said, rolling her eyes at Shy.

"Portuguese?"

"I'm Mexican American."

"Mexican? Really? What kind of Mexican?"

Carmen actually laughed out loud. "Just plain old Mexican, sir. Same as this guy." She pointed at Shy. "We're both half."

Shy was staring the oilman down now, waiting for the next bit of racist shit to come flying out of his mouth.

"Wow," the man said. "You all look different from the Mexicans we got in Texas."

"Believe it or not," Shy told him through a fake-ass grin, "not all Mexicans look the same, sir."

Carmen stepped on Shy's foot and shot him a dirty look. But it wasn't like the guy heard a word anyway. He was too busy pulling another woman into the mix, a slender twenty-something brunette in a black one-piece.

Shy took Carmen's elbow, asked her in a quiet voice: "Could I talk to you for a minute?"

She brushed away his hand without even looking at him. "Nah, I wanna see this *culo*'s ring."

Shy stared at the side of her face.

So he was definitely the one taking the rap for last night. Like he'd executed some premeditated master plan, and Carmen was just an innocent bystander.

Okay.

"Where are you dining tonight?" Shy heard the oilman ask the woman in the one-piece.

She looked at him, confused. "Destiny?"

"And what time's your seating?"

"Eight-thirty."

"Well, how about that?" the oilman said, turning back to Carmen and Shy. "She'll be there for the big show."

"What show?" the woman said, curious now.

"I'm asking my lady friend to marry me tonight at dinner. In front of everyone. They're even giving me a microphone." He held out the Tiffany's box again, popped it open.

"Jesus!" Carmen said, staring at the massive ring.

The other woman held a hand against her chest.

Shy studied the two of them. Eyes all bugged. Mouths hanging open. He wondered if pretty girls looked at expensive rings the way guys looked at pretty girls. And where'd that leave a no-money-having high school kid like him?

There were now a few other female passengers huddled around the oilman's ring. A cocktail waitress Shy had never met. An older gray-haired man and two pretty girls around Shy's own age. The older man turned to look at Shy, and Shy turned away from the girls. One of them was probably his daughter.

He leaned toward Carmen and tried again. "Seriously, though, I really need to talk to you."

She glanced at her watch. "No can do, Mr. Space Sancho. I'm already running late." She patted him on the shoulder and added: "I did write out some new rules for us, though. If you're lucky I'll even tell you what they are. You're on break during the late dinner, right?"

Shy nodded. Things were even worse than he thought.

"Meet me at the Destiny hostess stand and we'll watch Romeo propose. Then, if I'm feeling charitable, we can talk."

She spun around her amp and microphone without a goodbye, started wheeling her way toward the staircase.

Shy didn't have a good feeling about these new rules.

He watched Carmen's ponytail sway back and forth across her back like a lazy pendulum, telling himself: *Don't look at her legs, don't look at her legs, don't look at her legs.*

He looked at her legs.

9

A Dinner Invitation

When Shy returned to his towel stand, he apologized to the small group of people that had gathered there. He ducked under the counter, handed out a few fresh towels, a dart set, a pack of cards, a Game Boy. He had everyone sign the checkout sheet on his clipboard with their cabin number.

He looked up as the last person in line stepped forward—one of the girls he'd just seen checking out the oilman's ring. "We need stuff for Ping-Pong," she said, pointing over her shoulder. Standing a few yards behind her was the other high-school-aged girl and the man with gray hair.

"Let's get you guys set up," Shy said, reaching into one of the drawers in front of him. He grabbed three paddles and a pack of

Ping-Pong balls, handed them to her over his stand. "Best paddles we got right here. Just took them out of the package yesterday."

She didn't even look at them, just gave a bored expression and said: "Do I have to, like, sign my name or something?"

Shy pointed at the sign-in sheet, watched her pick up the pen and write her name. Addison Miller.

She was even prettier up close. Straight blond hair down past her shoulders. Light-green eyes. A few scattered sun freckles on the bridge of her nose and along her cheeks. Strange how a pretty girl's face could instantly put Shy in a better mood.

"So, you any good?" he asked, motioning toward the paddles.

She frowned like his question was the lamest thing she'd ever heard. "We're only playing because my dad's making us."

Before Shy had a chance to respond, a floppy-haired kid stormed up to the stand, saying: "Hey, asshole!"

Shy looked down at him. "Excuse me?"

"What, are you deaf?" he said in his squeaky little voice. "I called you an asshole. I just came over to get stuff and you weren't here."

The kid was maybe ten years old and rail thin. Hair hanging over his eyes. He looked like a damn Muppet.

Shy forced a smile even though he wanted to toss the kid into the pool. "Sorry 'bout that, little man. But I'm here now. So, what can I do for—?"

"Don't call me 'little man' either," the kid snapped. "Just because I'm young doesn't mean you can disrespect me."

Shy was speechless.

The gray-haired man suddenly appeared, saying: "Whoa, whoa, whoa. What seems to be the trouble over here?"

The kid pointed a finger at Shy and barked: "This asshole's not doing his job."

Shy no longer wanted to toss the kid in the pool, he wanted to pin his little Muppet head against the towel stand.

The gray-haired man smiled at Shy. "This one's got a mouth on him, doesn't he? What do you think"—he glanced at Shy's name tag—"Shy. Do we push him overboard?"

The blond girl rolled her eyes at her dad.

"Maybe we do, sir," Shy said, trying to play along.

The kid cursed under his breath again, then said: "Just give me a stupid golf club and a ball."

The other girl was there now, too, looking entertained as she ran her fingers through her long black hair.

Shy turned to open the closet behind him, saying: "Let's see what we can do for you, money. Ah, here we go." He handed over a slightly bent club and the most nicked-up golf ball he could find. "This should be perfect for you."

The kid inspected the ball with a disgusted look on his face, but he didn't say anything. Just turned and started up the stairs behind him, toward the Recreation Deck, where the miniature golf course was.

Soon as the kid was out of sight, the gray-haired man held out his hand to Shy, said: "Jim Miller."

Shy shook hands with him. "Shy Espinoza. Thanks for stepping in with that kid."

"Somebody had to," he said. "You've already met my daughter Addison. And this is her friend Cassandra."

"Nice to meet you guys," Shy said, giving them a proper Paradise smile.

Cassandra flipped her hair from one shoulder to the other and popped her gum. Addison rolled her eyes again. Shy could tell neither of them wanted any part of this conversation.

"So?" Addison said, tilting her head at her dad. "Are we going?"

But her dad was still grinning and staring at Shy.

Addison grabbed her dad's arm and started pulling him away, saying: "You're the one who wanted to play this stupid game in the first place."

"Wait, I have an idea," the man said, turning to the girls. "You guys keep complaining that there's no one your age on the ship, right? Well, Shy is."

The girls looked at each other with exaggerated frowns. "Uh, he *works* here," Cassandra said, like the thought of hanging out with anyone on the crew was absurd.

"What does that matter?" the man said. "Tell you what, I think we should invite the young man to dinner with us."

"Ew, Dad," Addison said. "You're being really creepy."

"It's okay, sir," Shy interjected—because he didn't want any part of this either. "I actually don't think we're allowed to—"

"I insist," the man said. "You'll join the three of us for dinner. A couple nights from tonight, soon as I get back from the island. If you're scheduled to work I'll speak to the captain myself, get everything squared away."

Shy just stood there, grinning. What island? he wondered. Hawaii? Weren't they all going there together?

The girls were now shooting dirty looks at the man. They didn't want to eat with Shy, and Shy didn't want to eat with them. The math seemed simple enough. But this guy was strangely persistent.

"I'll have someone notify you where to be," the man said.

"God, Dad," the blonde said, "you're totally embarrassing yourself." She finally managed to pull him away from Shy's towel stand, and the three of them started toward the Ping-Pong room on the other side of the pool.

Shy watched them go, trying to figure out what had just happened. There was no way he was going to dinner with passengers. Didn't matter how good-looking the girls were, it would be torture. Plus, it wasn't even allowed. And where was this guy going in the middle of a cruise? Then again, Shy reminded himself, passengers could pretty much do anything they wanted if they had enough money. And the gray-haired guy made it sound like he was all buddy-buddy with the captain.

Shy glanced down at his sign-in sheet, studied the girl's information. Addison Miller. Even her name sounded stuck-up. That's one of the things he liked best about Carmen. Hottest female on the ship, crew or otherwise, and she acted like she didn't have a clue.

Shy looked up at the sky where dark gray clouds were rolling in. If they eventually blocked out the sun, it would mean more people working out during his gym shift, which would mean more work for him. He scanned the pool crowd again, readying himself to do one final towel pass before he went on break. He was surprised to find Rodney lumbering down the length of the Lido Deck.

"Shy!" he called out as he rounded the Jacuzzi.

A few passengers turned to look at him.

When the guy finally made it to Shy's towel stand he stuck a meaty forearm up on the counter and leaned over to catch his breath.

"What the hell, Rod?" Shy said.

Rodney pulled in a couple deep breaths, then stood up straight and looked Shy right in the eyes. "You need to come with me. Right now, bro."

"Why? What happened?"

"We've been robbed!"

10
News from Back Home

Rodney unlocked their cabin door, held it open for Shy to go in first. Their stuff was scattered all over the floor. Empty drawers hanging open and clothes strewn everywhere. Both their cots stripped and flipped. Pillows pulled from their cases. All the family photos Shy had stashed in his backpack now scattered across the desk next to Rodney's open laptop.

"I didn't touch anything," Rodney said, moving across their small cabin. "Wanted you to see exactly how they left it."

Shy scooted his pics together first, staring at the one on top—his grandma manning the griddle, patting down one of her famous tortillas. Why would anyone go through his personal shit? It didn't make sense.

"Came back from the kitchen," Rodney said, "and I saw our

door wasn't all the way closed. Figured you were in here sleeping or something. But then I walked inside . . ." Rodney waved a hand toward the mess. "Who would do this to us? Nobody's allowed down here except crew."

Shy spotted his passport lying under his cot. Spotted his wallet on a pair of wadded-up jeans. He reached down for them, found his C-note still tucked safely inside the billfold of his wallet. Same with his bank card and ID. He turned to Rodney. "None of my stuff's missing."

"Mine either," Rodney said.

If it wasn't a robbery, maybe it was the guy in the black suit. But why break into the cabin and go through their stuff? Why not just ask about the suicide directly, like ship security already had? Like the cops who were waiting for Shy on land when they disembarked from his first voyage?

Rodney straightened out his mattress and sat down, leaned his elbows on his knees. "I feel violated, bro."

"Tell me about it," Shy said, shoving his wallet and passport into his safe and locking up. Maybe he was in more trouble than he realized. What if they were looking for someone to blame for the guy jumping? What if they tried to frame him?

"It's not like a regular job," Rodney said. "We don't get to go home at the end of our shift. We *live* here."

Shy felt bad Rodney had to suffer, too. Just because they were roommates. *He* wasn't the one who let a passenger fall, who wasn't strong enough to hold on just a few minutes longer. Shy felt like he should back up, explain everything he knew about the suit guy to Rodney. But there wasn't time. And he wasn't even sure the suit guy was really to blame.

"Look," Shy said. "After my shift at the gym, I'll go talk to Paolo. See what I can find out."

Rodney nodded. "I'd go myself, but I have to head back to the kitchen in twenty minutes."

Shy glanced at his alarm clock.

Two-thirty.

Damn.

"Hey, Rod?" he said. "I know this isn't the best timing, but is it cool if I use your computer real quick? I promised I'd Skype with my mom."

"No problem," Rodney said, standing up. "Need me to vacate?"

"Nah, it's okay," Shy told him. "I appreciate it."

He sat at the desk and turned on Rodney's computer and waited for it to boot up—Rodney already straightening up behind him. Shy was starting to feel like a prisoner on the ship. People were spying on him. Breaking into his cabin. And there was nowhere to hide. He wiped a few beads of perspiration off his forehead and swallowed. His throat felt like it was closing up.

The screen lit up and Shy logged on to Skype and dialed his mom. As it rang, he glanced around their trashed cabin again, shaking his head. Soon as his gym shift was over he was definitely tracking down Paolo. He needed some answers.

In a few seconds his mom's face popped onto the screen. He could tell she'd been crying.

Shy sat up and leaned toward the computer. "What is it, Ma? What happened?"

She wiped a hand down her face and took a deep breath. His mom was tough. He'd only seen her cry a couple other times in his life. It had to be bad.

"You okay?" Shy asked.

She shook her head.

"What is it? What happened?"

"It's Miguel, honey."

The name alone knocked the wind out of Shy. He'd never even thought of that. "What, he's sick?"

She didn't say anything.

"Don't tell me it's Romero, Ma. I can't even hear that right now."

His mom started crying again.

Shy pounded a fist on the desk. First his grandma. Now his little nephew? "You already took him in? You talked to a doctor?"

His mom wiped her face with a wad of tissues and breathed for a few long seconds. "We went first thing this morning," she said in a shaky voice. "They have medicine now. The doctor told us as long as the patient starts on the meds within twenty-four hours, his chances are good."

"They keeping him overnight?" Shy asked, thinking about expenses.

His mom nodded.

"And the medicine probably costs a lot, too, right?"

"Money's the last thing on our minds, Shy."

"I know." But Shy also knew his sister didn't have insurance. No way she could afford this on her own. Neither could his mom. "I want you to do something for me, Ma. I want you to cash that bond I won at the game. Give the money to Teresa."

His mom was shaking her head. "We *have* money. Teresa's friends have been very generous—"

"Cash the bond, Ma. I'm serious."

"I didn't message you for money, Shy. I wanted you to know what's going on back home."

"I understand that," Shy said. "But you gotta do this for me. I love that little kid." He felt a lump going in his throat. He'd shared a room with Miguel since the day Teresa brought him home from the hospital. They were more like brothers than anything else. "It's the only thing I can do from way out here."

"You do *so much* for this family," his mom said. "You have since the day your dad left."

Shy wiped more perspiration off his forehead. "Working on this ship was a mistake."

"Shy, you listen to me. You remember Teresa's bunnies?"

He didn't say anything.

"You remember, don't you?"

He did.

His sister had two bunnies when they were little. She got them for a birthday present. She loved those bunnies more than anything, used to take them to neighbors' houses in a cage and let her friends pet them. But one day, while she and her friend Marisol were eating lunch in the alley behind their building, a neighborhood dog got into the cage and killed both bunnies, then sat there guarding their remains. Teresa came racing into the apartment, screaming her head off. Shy and his mom followed her back to the alley, and Shy saw.

His mom blew her nose, said: "Me and your sister were a wreck, Shy. We had to leave the room. And what'd you do?"

"Cleaned up," he said in a quiet voice.

"You shooed the dog away and scooped those bunnies into a box. Took your dad's old shovel and dug a hole in the empty lot next door. And you buried them. You were seven years old, Shy. Barely older than Miguel is now. I kept thinking, Where did my son learn to do this?"

Shy shifted uncomfortably in his chair. "They honestly think the medicine can work?"

"That's what the doctor told us," his mom said. "My point is, I don't want you beating yourself up about being away. You're working, Shy. You're helping out your mom."

"Email me updates, okay? Many as you can. I wanna know everything."

"I promise," his mom said. "Can we do this again tomorrow? I need to see my son's face."

Shy nodded. He kept picturing his little nephew lying in a hospital bed, the whites of his eyes having already turned red. It broke his fucking heart.

His mom wiped her face with tissues again, her eyes shifting off of Shy. "What happened to your room?"

Shy looked over his shoulder, saw Rodney cleaning up. "We're rearranging," he said, turning back to his mom. "Tomorrow between two-thirty and three, all right? And email me."

"I will."

"And I'm serious, Ma. Make sure you cash that bond."

"Be safe, Shy. I love you."

"Love you, too."

Shy closed out of the call and turned off the computer. Then he just sat there for a few seconds, thinking about what he'd just heard. All his problems on the ship seemed laughable now that he knew his nephew had Romero Disease. He pushed down the urge to punch the wall in front of him.

"You all right?" Rodney asked.

Shy took a deep breath and turned around, saw that Rodney was now cleaning up his stuff, too. "I been better, man."

"Sorry to hear about your nephew," Rodney said. "What exactly is Romero Disease, anyway?"

"You never heard of it?" Shy asked. Back home it was all anyone ever talked about.

"I've heard the name. And I'm pretty sure people have died from it, right?"

Shy shook his head, remembering all the shit he saw his grandma go through. "It's this awful disease going around back home," he told Rodney. "People's eyes turn red and their vision goes blurry. Then their skin gets so dry and brittle it starts flaking off. They die from fluid loss in like forty-eight hours."

"Jesus, dude." Rodney looked horrified.

Shy got up and grabbed his uniform shirt for the gym. He wouldn't allow himself to even consider Miguel not pulling through. "He'll be all right," he told Rodney. "They got medicine now."

Rodney stood there, hands on hips, nodding.

Shy looked at his clock. Two-forty-nine. "Anyways, I gotta get to the gym. Don't worry about the rest of my stuff. I'll pick it up later."

"I don't mind," Rodney said.

"Soon as I'm off, I'll go to Paolo's office." Shy pulled open the door, but just as he was leaving he heard Rodney call his name.

He turned back around.

Rodney cleared his throat. "You think whoever was in here will come back? Like while we're sleeping?"

Maybe it was because Shy's mind was so tweaked after hearing about Miguel, or maybe it was pure exhaustion, but Rodney's words made him feel choked up. Like if he breathed the wrong way or something he might start crying. And Shy hadn't cried since he was a little kid. He took after his mom that way.

"Nobody's coming in here anymore," he told Rodney. "I'll make sure of it." Then he turned and went out the door.

11

Names Have No Meaning Here

According to a few of the passengers crowding into the gym, the sun had completely disappeared behind thick gray clouds out by the pool, and sunbathers were migrating to other parts of the ship. This made the gym so busy during Shy's four-hour shift, he hardly had time to stress about Miguel. He handed out towels, Windexed the floor-to-ceiling mirrors, wiped down machines when they weren't in use, demonstrated how to adjust the sauna controls, spotted for a few guys in the free-weights section, and handed out complimentary bottles of Gatorade and water.

Shy had no idea it was the end of his shift until Frederick from

Denmark came walking in to relieve him. "Everything is good?" he asked Shy, stashing his backpack behind the gym's reception desk.

"Just crowded." Shy motioned toward the floor where a couple dozen passengers were sweating on treadmills and stationary bikes and elliptical machines—all of them glued to the little personal TVs in front of their faces. "We're running low on towels, but I already called down to Claudia. They should be on their way."

"Very nice."

Shy grabbed his stuff from the employee cubby, saluted Frederick and headed for the exit. As he pushed through the door, he ran right into Addison and Cassandra, the girls he'd met at his pool stand earlier.

They both looked at each other and started laughing.

"What's so funny?" Shy asked, glancing down at their tight workout gear. Girls this irritating shouldn't be allowed to have such smoking bodies. And guys with sick nephews shouldn't be noticing shit like that.

"Oh, nothing," Addison said.

"You work in the gym, *too?*" Cassandra asked.

"I do everything on this ship," Shy said, trying to keep a playful attitude. "Couple more voyages and I'll probably be captain."

They looked at each other again. "Ah, he made a little joke," Cassandra said.

"How adorable," Addison said, and then they both burst out laughing again.

Shy felt like a complete idiot. It was definitely time to get out of this convo and talk to Paolo. "Look, I gotta go handle a few things," he told the girls, giving them a sarcastic thumbs-up. "It was great talking to you."

He started past them, but Addison latched on to his elbow, saying: "Just so you know, Cassie decided dinner should just be you and her."

Cassandra shot her an exaggerated look of shock and said: "You lying little bitch."

"What?" Addison said. "I doubt my dad will be back by the weekend anyway. It'll be perfect. I'll post a bunch of pictures online—'Cassie and her pool boy.' Can you imagine everyone back home?"

They laughed at him some more, and Shy slipped her grip, still smiling, and told them: "Have an excellent workout."

"Ah, don't be all sensitive," one of them called after him—he couldn't tell which one. "We're just joking around."

Shy waved over his shoulder and started down a flight of stairs, hoping they both ate shit on the treadmills.

Paolo wasn't in his office.

Vlad and Kyle, the two security guys Shy found in the break room, said Paolo was meeting with the captain about the weather. They had no idea when he was coming back. Shy left the security wing and stood in the crew hall for a few minutes, trying to work out his next move.

He had an hour and a half before he was supposed to meet Carmen at the Destiny Dining Room. He could keep searching for Paolo, or he could try and get some sleep. He wished he could go talk to Carmen now, explain the news about his nephew, but she'd want no part of him rolling up on her cabin after what happened.

He decided to go talk to his boss, Supervisor Franco. Technically he was supposed to run all concerns by him first anyway.

Romero Disease

On the long walk to the other side of the ship, Shy thought about when his grandma started getting sick.

Her first symptoms had matched exactly with some new illness people were talking about on the news. The whites of her eyes were turning red. Her vision was blurring. She was so dehydrated her skin had become extremely dry and itchy and she was having trouble using the bathroom. Still, she refused to see a doctor.

"I've lived through sixty-seven years' worth of flus," she told Shy's mom. "I don't see what's so special about this one."

"That's the point," his mom pleaded. "I'm worried it's more than just the flu."

His grandma shook her head and went to lie down in her room.

Back then most people didn't know about Romero Disease. Shy only knew what his mom had mentioned after reading an article in the paper. A few dozen people had died in America, all of them from border towns in California like Tecate, San Ysidro, Otay Mesa and National City. What he didn't know yet was that *thousands* had already died on the other side of the border, in Tijuana, including a popular young governor named Victor Romero—which was how the disease got its name in the media.

The next morning, Shy's grandma collapsed in the kitchen while kneading dough for her sweet bread.

She didn't wake up until she'd been checked into the hospital for several hours, and she didn't recognize Shy or his mom or sister. She asked if they knew where she could find Jesus. She asked if the world had ended and they'd forgotten to take her on their space-ship. The whites of her eyes were now blood-red and her tan skin had turned yellow and papery and she couldn't stop scratching at her arms and legs.

They diagnosed her with Romero Disease and placed her in the special quarantine unit. After Shy, his mom and his sister tested negative for the disease, they were allowed to sit outside her room and watch over her through a thick wall of glass.

In the middle of that night, Shy heard an alarm go off and he lifted his head, saw his grandma scratching off chunks of her own skin. Blood all over the white sheets. His mom raced down the hall shouting for help. A group of nurses in full hazmat suits came and held down his grandma's flailing limbs. A doctor rushed in, stuck a long needle into her thigh.

Shy's mom and sister were crying hysterically as the three of them were pushed out into the general waiting area. Shy paced the room, unable to comprehend what was happening. Just a couple days ago, his grandma was fine. She was working on a scrapbook and watching Telemundo. Now she looked like something out of a horror film.

Thirty minutes later the doctor emerged shaking his head and looking at the ground.

He said he was sorry.

Shy went to knock on Supervisor Franco's open door but froze when he saw someone was already in there—the older black dude with the funky gray hair who was always writing in his leather notebook.

Franco looked up at Shy, said: "May I help you?"

"It's okay," Shy said. "I'll just come back later."

"Please. You can wait outside. We will be done here momentarily."

Shy stepped away from the door, leaned against the wall and let his warm eyelids slowly drop. As he listened to Franco's heavy accent, he tried to imagine his nephew stuck inside the same quarantine room as his grandma. But he couldn't. Miguel was too tough. Never even caught a cold. He remembered throwing around a football with the kid just a few hours before he left for his first voyage. In the alley behind their building. One of Shy's longer tosses slipped right through Miguel's little-kid hands, and the football smacked him in the face, split his lip. But Miguel didn't go down. Just looked up at Shy as blood trickled down his chin, got all over his T-shirt. He forced himself to smile at Shy, laugh even—though his eyes were filling with tears, too.

Shy felt a hand on his shoulder and opened his eyes.

The man he'd just seen in Franco's office was staring at him, holding his shoeshine kit. "How do you sleep standing up like that, young fella?"

"I was just closing my eyes," Shy said, wiping a tiny bit of drool from the corner of his mouth.

The man grinned. "Franco's on the phone now. Says he'll have to check back with you later."

Shy nodded.

Still no answers about the suit guy or their trashed room. Nothing to tell Rodney.

The man looked toward the window down the hall. "They're worried about this storm rolling in. Supposed to hit sometime tonight."

"It's an actual storm now?" Shy had yet to experience even a drop of rain in the time he'd spent out with the cruise ship. But he'd learned in training how badly storms affected the way passengers spent money. Which meant fewer tips. Less money to bring back home to his mom and sis.

The man set down his shoeshine kit and wiped his forehead with a handkerchief. "If it's as bad as they say, this boat's gonna get to rocking pretty good." He reached down into his kit, moved his notebook and some other books to the side and pulled out a gray wristband-looking thing, held it out to Shy. "Wear this when it picks up."

"What is it?" Shy said, turning the thing over in his hand.

"Something I made for seasickness. Be sure the white button in the middle is against your inner wrist. Same idea as acupuncture."

"Thanks," Shy said, shoving it into his pocket. He was pretty sure the nasty-looking band would never make it onto his wrist, but he didn't want to offend the guy.

"You're the one who saw the man take a dive, that right?"

Shy nodded. He glanced in Franco's office, saw him pacing back and forth, phone pinned to his ear. "Guess everyone knows about that now."

"And there's a man on board who's been watching you."

Shy stared back at him, shocked. "How'd you know that?"

"Always keep my eyes open." The man pointed at his kit. "The job puts me in a certain position of observation."

It baffled Shy that a shoeshine guy, someone he'd never given a second thought to, knew what was going on in his life. "You know who he is?" Shy asked. "Is he FBI or something?"

The man shrugged. "Don't know. But let me ask you something, young fella. Would it make sense for an FBI man to focus on just you?" He pointed at his own temple. "Think it through some."

Shy studied the man in front of him. Tired-looking eyes that never blinked. Wild hair. For some reason, Shy felt like he could trust him. He held out his hand and said: "I'm Shy, by the way."

The man grinned and gripped Shy's hand. "Shoeshine."

They let go and Shy pointed at the kit on the ground. "I know that's what you do on the ship. But what's your name?"

"Names have no meaning out here, young fella. I'm just an old man passing through." Shoeshine picked up his kit, gave a nod to Shy and started down the hall. He stopped in front of the small window and looked outside. "Oh yeah. Looks to be the real thing, all right."

Shy went to the window, too. Saw a dense ceiling of nasty-looking storm clouds rolling in. Blocking out the setting sun. The ocean was choppy and raw. A crooked pulse of lightning stabbed into the horizon in the distance.

"Best prepare yourself, young fella. The sea is fittin' to make itself known tonight." Shoeshine continued down the hall, his wooden kit dangling from his right hand.

Shy watched him for a few seconds, playing with the crazy wristband in his pocket. Then he turned back to the window and what was coming.

12
Storm in the Forecast

An hour later Shy was standing against the wall near the entrance of the Destiny Dining Room, waiting for Carmen—the ship now swaying underneath his feet. Most of the formally dressed passengers had already been seated for dinner, and the half-dozen hostesses moved from table to table, greeting everyone.

Shy scanned the restaurant, looking for familiar faces. He spotted the Muppet boy from the pool, dressed in a tux. He tried to imagine his nephew dressed like that, but all he could picture was Miguel in one of those hospital gowns, lying in his quarantine bed, alone. He spotted Addison and Cassandra, all done up, sitting with a few men in tuxedos. The gray-haired dude wasn't one of them. Shy then spotted the oilman sitting next to an empty chair, downing a glass of red wine.

Just when Shy started thinking Carmen was a no-show he heard the ding of the elevator and looked up. The doors slid open and Carmen came walking out in a long black dress and heels and his stomach instantly filled with butterflies.

"Don't tell me I missed the proposal," she said.

Shy shook his head. He couldn't stop staring. She looked more beautiful than ever.

"What?" Carmen asked.

"Nothing." Shy rubbed the stubble on his chin. "You just look real nice is all."

Her dress was cut low in front, showing an unfair amount of cleavage. It hugged in tight on her waist, then stretched out over her curvy hips. Carmen had to dress up whenever she emceed karaoke nights, but tonight she'd taken it to a whole other level.

"You're not allowed to say that," she told him. "It's rule number one of our new rules."

"Seriously? I can't say you look nice?" Shy pushed off the wall, feeling frustrated. "You know what, then? Maybe rule number two should be you're not allowed to dress like that around me."

"Like what?"

"Come on, Carm." He pointed up and down her sexy dress.

She rolled her eyes with a slight grin. "How you think I pull in all them tips at karaoke? It's more than how I announce some fool's song he's about to do."

Shy shook his head and looked away. If he didn't change the subject they were gonna end up in some kind of argument. And he didn't want to argue with Carmen. Not tonight, when he needed to talk to her about his nephew. "Anyways," he said, motioning toward the oilman's table. "Kind of weird his girl isn't here yet. Seems like they'd have shown up together, right?"

"I bet she's still in the mirror, trying to do her makeup extra-perfect. Women can sense when something big's about to happen."

Shy nodded, wondering if Carmen had sensed anything last night, before they hooked up. And what would it mean if she had and then leaned in on him anyway? Weren't actions supposed to speak louder than words?

He was startled out of his head when the ship emcee came on over the loudspeaker—which never happened at night: "*Attention, ladies and gentlemen. As many of you already know, there's a major storm in the forecast. As a precaution, all outside decks will be closed for the evening.*"

A collective groan passed through the dining room. Shy wondered if this meant he wouldn't have to work. Maybe he'd be free to keep checking Rodney's computer for an email from his mom.

"*Tomorrow morning they will be reopened, weather permitting, at their regularly scheduled times. We apologize for any inconvenience this may cause, but we'd like to assure you that all indoor programming will be running as usual, including the big poker tournament in the Grand Casino. We'll be issuing free bar tickets to the first fifty passengers who sign up.*"

Soon as the emcee's voice was gone, the hum of conversation picked back up. A hostess named Toni walked toward Shy and Carmen, looking beyond stressed. "You guys," she said, "I'm kind of freaking out right now. I've never been in a storm."

"Same here," Shy said.

"You just can't overthink it," Carmen said. "Trust me, your mind can build shit up way worse than it really is."

"I think it's already happening," Toni said.

"What I don't understand," Shy said, "is how these people can eat with the ship swaying like it is."

The girls nodded and then Toni held out her arms for Carmen and they hugged. "Love that dress on you," she said as they separated.

"She hates people telling her that," Shy said.

Carmen shot Shy a dirty look and turned back to Toni. "Thanks, girl. I borrowed it from your roommate."

"I know. Meagan stopped by earlier. She also told me the big news. I didn't know you were getting married."

"Brand-new." Carmen gave Shy a little sideways glance. "Still feels weird to say I have an actual fiancé."

Shy took a baby step back, tried to act like he wasn't listening. Maybe he should feel more guilty about hooking up with someone who was engaged. 'Cause he didn't feel guilty at all. Not about that part. Maybe it meant he wasn't a good person.

"Tell me about it," Toni said. "I just got engaged, too."

"Are you serious?" Carmen said. "Congratulations!"

Shy watched as they grabbed each other's elbows and jumped up and down. When the mini-celebration ended, Carmen said: "Where'd he do it?"

"A steakhouse in Newport Beach. With my parents."

"Ah, that's so respectful."

"You?"

"Brett took me to the boardwalk in Venice. We were walking together, holding hands, watching all the weirdos, and out of nowhere he drops to one knee and takes my hand. I was so shocked I didn't even give him time to ask. I swiped the ring right out of his hand, shoved it on my finger."

Shy felt like gagging. He wondered if he should throw on Shoeshine's homemade wristband-thing to keep from getting sick. He took another baby step back.

Toni laughed. "That's so like you, Carm."

"I grabbed Brett's cell," Carmen said, "and called Mami. She was like, 'Oh, *mija*, it's so wonderful. My baby's marrying a lawyer!'"

"There's a mother who's got her priorities."

"Believe me," Carmen said. "She was ten times more excited than me. Like it was her lifelong dream coming true."

82

Shy cleared his throat, said: "Is this trip, like, sponsored by Kay Jewelers or some shit? All anybody can talk about is getting married."

"Don't be a hater," Carmen said, trying to act mad.

Shy looked into her big brown eyes. Seemed like ten years ago that he'd held her face in his hands, stared into those eyes from only a couple inches away. He wished he could do it again. Right now. In front of everyone.

Toni was patting Shy on the back, saying: "I'm sure it's lots of fun hanging out with all your little high school girlfriends. But one day—trust me. You'll fall in love, too. And you'll wanna spend the rest of your life with that person."

"From what I heard, he might've already met her." Carmen winked at Shy. "Frederick from Denmark told me all about you and some skinny blond chick flirting outside the gym."

"Wait, what?" Toni said. "Shy's moving in on a passenger?"

Shy was shocked Frederick even knew about that stupid little exchange. "Sounds like you got some bad intel," he told Carmen. "More like those chicks were capping on me about working at the pool."

"That's how the blanquitas like to flirt, dummy." Carmen grinned a little and gave Shy a quick shot in the ribs. "You should go for it, dude. Isn't that every Otay Mesa guy's wet dream? To land an anorexic blonde?"

The girls started laughing.

"Whatever," Shy said. He was getting a little tired of people laughing at him. Before he could think up some kind of comeback about Carmen and rich law school dudes, the ship emcee came back on over the loudspeaker:

"Ladies and gentlemen, we've just learned some unfortunate news. The storm is advancing toward our location more rapidly than we'd originally anticipated. As a precaution, the captain is asking that we evacuate all large dining areas at this time."

Everyone in the dining room fell completely silent, staring at each other.

Shy was suddenly having a hard time getting a deep breath.

"The smaller cafés and shops will remain open. And staff members will be available for full cabin service. We sincerely apologize for any inconvenience this may cause, ladies and gentlemen. But I repeat: we must close all large dining areas, effective immediately. Thank you for your cooperation."

Shy turned back to Toni and Carmen, whose grins had vanished.

"I've never heard of them clearing the dining rooms before," Carmen said. "Do you think something could actually happen to the ship?"

"There's no way," Shy assured her. Secretly, though, he was worried about the exact same thing.

"What am I supposed to do?" Toni said. "Just tell them to leave? This is so scary." She hurried after another hostess, who was walking out onto the dining room floor.

Shy watched the buzzing passengers get up from their tables and start moving toward the exits. He spotted the oilman, still sitting in his seat, gripping an empty glass of wine. Now all the seats around him were empty.

Someone grabbed ahold of Shy's arm.

He was surprised to turn and find Supervisor Franco standing there. "Come with me," his boss said. "There is much to do before we pass through the eye of this storm."

"But they said Lido's closed, sir."

Franco shook his head. "Not for us, it isn't."

Shy turned and found Carmen staring at him.

It was the first time he'd ever seen fear in her eyes.

13

LasoTech

They moved quickly through the atrium, past packs of well-dressed passengers hurrying back to their cabins, past one of the live orchestras breaking down their instruments, Franco listing all the things that had to be done before the actual storm hit: ". . . and every deck chair must be put into supply room. Every umbrella. The towel stand and busser stations. All tables and chairs of the café."

Shy nodded, trying to concentrate on what he was hearing. But seeing worry on his supervisor's face made him worry, too. What if the ship was in actual danger?

"Heavy covers on the pool and Jacuzzi. The main stage must be locked completely. Everything just like in training, you understand. Ariana is in charge."

"Yes, sir," Shy said, trying to remember what they'd gone over during training. He should have listened better. But it never crossed his mind that something might actually happen.

They moved past Shoeshine, his head down as he worked a man's shoe with his rag. Shy glanced at the guy sitting in the chair, reading the ship's daily bulletin, sipping a cocktail. He didn't seem scared at all. Neither did Shoeshine. Shy tried to decide how scared *he* was. The ship was huge, seemingly indestructible. But maybe it wasn't. Maybe his grandma had been right to worry.

Franco stopped a few feet from the Lido Deck door and turned to Shy. "When you are finished here, please, Shy, you must do special task for me. Take down all umbrellas on Honeymoon Deck. Baby trees, too. There can be nothing left outside."

"Yes, sir," Shy answered, remembering this part of training. They'd only practiced clearing the Honeymoon Deck during the emergency phase. Which meant the storm was an emergency. And Shy should be scared.

Franco keyed open the supply closet near the automatic glass doors, reached in for a yellow slicker. He handed it to Shy, saying: "I'm trusting the Honeymoon Deck only for you because it may be dangerous winds up there. And I know you will be extremely care-ful."

"I'll be careful," Shy said, slipping into the slicker.

Supervisor Franco took Shy by the shoulders and looked into his eyes. "This storm is making you afraid?"

"A little, sir." Shy glanced over his supervisor's shoulder, saw a couple dozen staff members already rushing around the Lido Deck in the rain. Carrying chairs and tables. He spotted Ariana, Franco's second in command.

"Believe me," Franco said. "I have been in worse storms and everything is okay. Okay?"

Shy nodded, trying to decide if this was something his supervisor was supposed to say or if he genuinely believed it.

Franco patted Shy on the back, said: "Everything we do is for precaution, you understand. The weather report says it will be sunny again by morning. So only this problem is for tonight." He forced a smile.

Shy knew it wasn't the best timing, but he had to at least bring up what happened to his cabin. "Sir, can I ask you something?"

"Yes, of course."

"The reason I stopped by your office earlier—"

Franco raised a hand to cut Shy off. "Yes, yes, I understand about this, Shy. A man from LasoTech entered your room this afternoon. I'm sorry I did not explain, but we were not expecting weather. Don't worry, he found nothing."

"What's LasoTech?" Shy asked. "And what were they looking for?"

"It is a main sponsor for Paradise Cruise Lines. Tomorrow we will talk more, okay? For now we must hurry."

Shy stepped up to the glass doors, watched them slide open, then he stepped out into the growing wind and rain. He was surprised Franco knew what had happened in his cabin. Why hadn't he said anything earlier, when Shy was outside his office? And why would a company go through his and Rodney's stuff?

The sky was dark gray. The wind pressed Shy's slicker against his body. He squinted and made his way to the two closest chairs. He folded up the head and feet, tucked one under each arm, and started for the large storage room. He had to put Franco's words out of his head. He could worry about it once he got back inside. For now he needed to concentrate on securing the deck.

14
Hidden Islands

Franco was right about the wind near the top of the ship. It was far more powerful. Shy had to lean into it in order to move out onto the Honeymoon Deck. The rain was now falling at an odd angle, pelting him in the face under his slicker hood. He cupped a hand over his eyes and went right up to the railing and peered over the side.

In the morning the sea had been perfectly calm and beautiful, like a postcard. Now it was a thousand hostile waves crested in white foam and crashing into one another. The massive ship moaned as it pitched and surged under Shy's shell tops—the bow bucking slowly into the air and then falling, bucking and then falling. Thick black clouds hung so low in the sky it felt like the ship was traveling through a rain tunnel.

Shy watched it all in awe for several minutes, the world lining up exactly with his insides. He'd never been a true believer like his grandma, but he closed his eyes now and asked whoever might be listening for Miguel to be okay. And his mom and sis. And himself.

Please, just let me get back to them.

I have to get back to them.

Then Shy pushed away from the railing and set about his work.

Conditions improved slightly as he moved the last of the baby palms back into the supply room. But his stomach was a mess. His legs felt flimsy and unfamiliar. He broke down the first two umbrella poles slowly, feeling so queasy he thought he'd be sick at any second. He dragged them, one in each hand, into the supply room, placed them on the storage racks, then leaned over, hands on knees, and pulled in deep, even breaths.

In the morning it had been wine.

Now it was the relentless motion of the sea.

Shy remembered the wristband Shoeshine had given him and pulled it out of his pocket. He still didn't think the raggedy-looking thing would do him any good, but he slipped it onto his wrist anyway. Just in case. Forced himself upright again, warm saliva pooling in his mouth.

As he moved out of the supply room this time, he spotted two people standing near the railing. Long pink and black raincoats provided by the ship. One of the women staring out over the ocean through binoculars.

"Excuse me," he called out to them. "The Honeymoon Deck's closed."

The two figures spun around.

Shy couldn't see much of their faces under their oversized hoods, but he saw the wet blond hair of one. The green eyes. And he knew it was Addison. Which meant the other one was her friend. He moved toward them, wondering why they'd come out into a storm like this when they didn't have to.

"We're not hurting anyone," Cassandra said.

Addison's eyes looked glassy, like she'd been crying.

Shy motioned toward the binoculars in her hands, told her: "I'm sorry, but nobody's supposed to be outside right now. Captain's orders."

"Just back off," Cassandra snapped at him.

Addison glared at him, fresh tears streaming down her cheeks.

Shy stared back, pissed off now on top of being queasy. Soon as he got off this stupid ship he was done dealing with rich girls.

Cassandra rubbed Addison's arm as they both turned back to the frenzied ocean, ignoring Shy. What was he supposed to do, drag them away? And why the tears? He looked around, saw that they were only a few feet from where he'd tried to keep his grip on the comb-over man. And what would he do if the wind blew one of them over the side? Would he try and play the hero again? Didn't work out too well the last time.

Shy swallowed, deciding he had to play it another way. "What are you looking for, anyway?" he asked.

They ignored him.

"Maybe I could help."

Cassandra turned to him, her face softer now. "Her dad's out there somewhere," she said. "He works on one of the Hidden Islands."

The Hidden Islands?

Other than Hawaii, Shy had never heard of any islands out here, in the middle of the Pacific. And Hawaii was still a couple days away.

The rain picked up again, all three of them pulling their hoods farther over their eyes. Densely packed drops battered their slickers and the deck around their shoes. A sudden gust of wind made the girls hold on to the railing.

"For real," Shy said. "You guys gotta go inside. It's dangerous."

Addison spun around and faced Shy. "Why does my dad have a picture of you?" she shouted over the pounding rain.

"Of me?" Shy said, confused. "What are you talking about?"

Addison lowered her binoculars and cried harder.

"She found your picture in her dad's cabin," Cassandra said, holding Addison. "You're in a cemetery."

Shy just stared back at them in shock.

It had to be a mistake.

Thunder pounded so violently overhead all three of them flinched.

"Come on, Addie," Cassandra said, leading her away from the railing.

"Who are you?" Addison barked at Shy as they moved past him. "Tell me who you are!"

"I'm nobody!" he shouted back. He'd probably get in trouble for snapping at a passenger, but he didn't even care anymore. The girl was talking crazy.

"I'm nobody!" he shouted again. "All right?"

Soon as the girls ducked back inside the ship, out of sight, Shy spun around and leaned over the railing and got sick.

He heaved several times before spitting and wiping his mouth. Then he just stood there, staring out at the frantic ocean, trying to make sense of what the girls were talking about. A picture of him? In a cemetery? How could Addison's dad have a picture of him?

When Shy finally turned back around, he found a man standing out on the deck in the rain, dressed in a yellow Paradise slicker, watching him.

Shy knew right away he wasn't part of the crew.

15

A Few Questions

"You can't be out here!" Shy shouted over the storm.

The man didn't move or say a word, just kept watching Shy.

Rain flooded the deck as Shy started breaking down the two remaining umbrellas. He pretended to be so occupied with his task he didn't have time to worry about the man. Secretly, though, his heart was beating in his throat. He wanted to get this over and be done with it, but not now. Not during a storm, after he'd just gotten sick.

A streak of lightning stabbed into the sea not far from the ship. Thunder roared.

Shy hurried the poles across the deck, addressing the man again: "You have to go inside, sir!"

The man nodded.

Inside the supply room, Shy stacked the umbrella poles on the storage racks, then fumbled for his keys and started back toward the door, thinking only about getting inside the ship, everything would be fine once he got inside the ship.

When the man stepped into the doorway of the supply room, Shy stopped cold, said: "Sir, nobody's supposed to be out here. I need to lock up."

The man stepped aside, and Shy hurried out of the supply room, pulled the door closed and locked it. The man followed Shy into the vacant Luxury Lounge, where he started unzipping his wet slicker and said: "It's Shy, am I right?"

Shy tried to hide the fact that he was so nervous he was having trouble catching his breath. "Who are you?"

"I'm Bill," the man said, pulling off his slicker. Sure enough, he was wearing a black suit.

They both stumbled a little as the ship pitched more dramatically, Shy holding his hand out against the wall for balance.

"I want you to understand right up front," the man said, "there's no trouble here. At least there doesn't have to be. I just need to ask you a few questions." He had curly black hair. A mole on the right side of his nose. He smiled like this was an everyday kind of conversation for him.

All Shy could think about was how this was the man Kevin had warned him about. The man who'd been watching him. But this wasn't the time for questions. Didn't the man understand the ship was getting pummeled by a storm?

Shy watched him calmly pull a small pad of paper and a pen from his pocket. "Now, it's my understanding that on the previous voyage, you witnessed a man jump overboard. Right out there, in fact." He pointed through the glass doors, toward the Honeymoon Deck. "Is this correct, Shy?"

"Yeah . . . ," Shy said, hesitating. He didn't understand why the man wanted to have this conversation now. Couldn't he wait until morning? Shy glanced over his shoulder, saw that the hall door was open.

"Tell me about it," the man said.

"Like I explained to everyone else," Shy answered, pulling off his wet hood. "I gave him a bottle of water, then I helped these two older ladies. A few minutes later I saw him climbing over the railing and ran over and grabbed his arm, tried to pull him back up. But he was too heavy. That's it, I swear."

The man looked up from his pad. "We have no doubt this was a suicide. I'm not here to ask questions that have already been answered."

Shy wondered what "we" the guy was referring to. Had to be the company Franco had mentioned, LasoTech.

"All I need to know," the man went on, "is what was said in those last few minutes. Because we have, in fact, spoken to the two women you referenced in your official police statement. They both claim that when they walked outside, you and Mr. Williamson were engaged in a conversation."

Fear shot through Shy's body.

Throughout the many hours of questioning that followed the suicide, Shy had never mentioned speaking to Mr. Williamson. It had never occurred to him that the two old ladies might have said something about it. So, what now? Did he add new information to his story? Wouldn't that make people even *more* suspicious?

"What were you and Mr. Williamson discussing, Shy? What was he sharing with you?"

Shy stared at the floor in front of him, the ship moving as erratically as his thoughts. Why was he so worried, though? It's not like he had anything to hide. "He wasn't making any sense," Shy finally answered. "That's why I never brought it up."

The man nodded. "Maybe it will make sense to me. Try to remember his words."

"He called himself a coward," Shy said. "I remember that. And he asked me where I was from."

The man wrote all this down. "And where did you tell him you were from, Shy?"

Shy shrugged. "I don't get why any of this matters, sir."

"Please," the man said. "Call me Bill. And it matters because my client needs to know everything that was said, no matter how irrelevant it may seem to you. Now, where did you tell him you were from?"

"Otay Mesa. In San Diego."

The man nodded and wrote this down. "And how did Mr. Williamson respond to this?"

"He said he knew it was by the border."

"And after that?"

Shy knew he was explaining things out of order, but his conversation with the comb-over man didn't make any sense no matter how he told it. "He said he had a bunch of vacation homes. And when I congratulated him, he got mad. I'm pretty sure he'd had a lot to drink."

The man nodded, still writing.

"And that's it," Shy said. "Then those two ladies came outside."

The man looked up from his pad of paper. "There's nothing else, Shy? You're sure?"

"There's nothing else," Shy lied. He glanced over his shoulder again, at the open door to the hall.

The man put away his pad of paper and his pen and walked over to the window. It was raining so hard you could barely even see the water now. "Rough storm," he said. "I understand it will be over by morning, though. And we'll be on our way to Hawaii." He turned back around, said: "You ever been to Hawaii, Shy?"

Shy shook his head, feeling overwhelmed by everything. The storm. The questioning. The memory of the comb-over man falling.

Addison crying and asking who he was. He looked over his shoulder at the door again.

"One of my favorite places on earth," the man continued. "My wife and I go every year. We like to walk the beach early in the morning." Bill turned to Shy. "You'd like to enjoy Hawaii, too, wouldn't you?"

Shy stared at the guy, trying to figure out if he was being threatened.

"I still have a few more interviews to conduct," Bill continued. "And if your story doesn't check out, I'll be forced to find you. Do you understand what I'm saying, Shy?"

"I gotta go," Shy said, backing away. "I gotta get back to work."

The man's face grew cold and he pointed at Shy. "Don't walk away from me, Shy."

Shy shrugged, then spun around and hurried out the door, into the hall. Before ducking down a flight of stairs he looked over his shoulder, saw that the man was still pointing at him.

16
International News

First thing Shy did when he got back to his cabin was lock the door and log on to Rodney's computer.

Still no email from his mom about Miguel.

He wondered if the lack of communication was a good thing or a bad thing as he pulled off his wet shoes and socks, his shirt. He collapsed onto his cot and closed his eyes, the backs of his lids stinging hot with exhaustion, the storm shifting everything around in his room.

If he could just fall asleep.

Then everything would be okay.

He'd wake up rested and the storm would be over and his thoughts would be clear again. He'd Skype with his mom, and she'd tell him the good news about Miguel. The medicine was already working.

He was going to make a complete recovery. And then Shy would go meet with Franco about the man in the black suit. Bill. And he'd find out who exactly he was and what he wanted.

Everything would be okay if he could just fall asleep.

But Shy couldn't shut off his stupid mind.

There was too much to worry about: the surging storm and the questions about the comb-over man and Miguel lying in the quarantine unit and even the look on Addison's face when she asked who he was. He tossed and turned for almost an hour before finally sitting up and deciding he needed to go find Carmen.

He slipped his feet into fresh socks and a backup pair of shell tops, pulled on a new shirt. He left the cabin hoping Carmen would forgive him, at least for tonight. She could go right back to being mad in the morning if she wanted, but right now he seriously needed her.

The ship was lurching so violently now it was impossible to walk straight. Shy found himself stumbling up the stairs like a drunk, holding on to the railing and the walls. As he staggered down the hall, though, he realized he was no longer nauseous. He cracked up a little in his head, amazed that Shoeshine's wristband was actually keeping him from feeling sick. It was the one positive in the entire night.

Shy popped his head into the Normandie Theater. An older-looking comedian was telling bad *Titanic* jokes to a small, scattered crowd. The Grand Casino was nearly empty, too. The colorful strobe lights still flashed and dealers manned their tables. Cocktail waitresses were huddled near the bar. But only a dozen or so passengers were playing in the poker tournament.

Shy kept looking over his shoulder as he moved through the ship. He was sure he'd spot the suit guy following him at some point, but there was never anyone there.

He ducked his head into a few of the clubs. House music or hip-hop still blaring, but the dance floors all deserted. He found Kevin in Blue Water Disco pouring drinks for two women sitting at the bar. Kevin looked up and they waved to each other; then Shy continued toward the front of the ship.

It was eerie seeing all the hot spots empty this early in the night. Usually passengers were everywhere, drinking and gambling and eating, dancing in the clubs, soaking in the Lido Deck Jacuzzi. But tonight even the main promenade was quiet. Everyone apparently waiting out the storm in the comfort of their own cabins.

Eventually Shy made his way to the Karaoke Room, where Carmen, still wearing her fancy dress and heels, was standing on the stage, watching a news report on TV.

She was the only person in the room.

"What, nobody showed up?" Shy called to her from the door.

Carmen shut off the TV and spun around. "Hey," she said. Even though she was smiling she seemed upset—because of the storm, he assumed.

"You okay?" he asked.

"Of course I'm okay." She kneeled down, started packing up her things. Over her shoulder she told him: "A few people wandered in earlier, looked around, then wandered back out."

Shy leaned against the wall for balance. "What were you just watching?"

Carmen ignored his question.

She stood up, locked her equipment in a trunk on the right side of the stage, picked up her bag and moved cautiously down the stage stairs, toward Shy. "This storm's tossing us all over the place. Doesn't exactly make people feel like singing."

"Doesn't make 'em feel like doing anything," Shy said. "You seen it out there? There's nobody."

The ship jerked violently as if on cue, and Carmen grabbed Shy's arm to keep her balance. "I'm not gonna lie," she said, "it's messing with me a little, too. And I never get seasick."

"Try this," Shy told her, pulling off his wristband. "That guy Shoeshine made it."

Carmen stared at it, frowning. "Shoeshine? Nah, I think I'm good."

He smiled. "It really works, I promise. You just line the button up with the inside of your wrist."

She looked at Shy, her glassy eyes creating a tiny ache in his chest. She'd definitely been crying.

"Fine," she said, taking the wristband and slipping it on. "But if I get scabies or some shit . . ."

Shy watched her position the button.

She looked at him again, but all squinty-eyed this time, like she was trying to figure something out. "What's going on with *you*, Shy?"

He shook his head. "Just this storm, man."

"Nah, it's more than that," she said. "I maybe haven't known you that long, but I can tell when something's up."

Shy shook his head. But the fact that she could read his mind made the chest ache grow heavier. It felt like things were normal between them again, like before they messed around.

"Spill it," Carmen said.

Shy could feel everything bubbling up inside him, like a shook-up soda. He knew the second he opened his mouth it would all come spewing out. He stared at her heels for a few seconds, concentrating on the movement of the floorboards and trying to think how to put it. He looked back at Carmen, said: "Me and my mom finally did that Skype call. The one I told you about."

Her face grew serious. "And?"

He shook his head.

"Shy? Is she okay?"

Seeing Carmen look so worried about him made Shy feel overwhelmed with emotion, to the point that he couldn't speak.

"Oh my God," Carmen said. "She's sick, isn't she?"

He shook his head. "My nephew."

Carmen dropped her bag and covered her mouth. "What's happening, Shy? For real."

"I don't even know." Shy's throat felt so tight his words came out flimsy.

"When you came in I was watching an international news channel," she said. "The guy said this Romero shit has spread all the way up to Oakland now. They even did a profile on some Beverly Hills CEO's wife who got sick."

So this was why she was upset. It was more than just the storm.

"But here's what pisses me off," Carmen said. "Why isn't it international news when it hits where *we* live? Why isn't there a profile about my dad? Or your grandma?"

Shy shook his head. "They got Miguel on that new medicine, at least. But I swear, Carm. It's messing with my head."

They were both quiet for a few seconds, looking at different parts of the floor. Then Carmen picked up her bag and grabbed Shy by his forearm. "Come on," she said. "We're going to my room."

Shy looked at her, surprised. "Your room?"

She nodded. "You heard me. This is an emergency."

They left the Karaoke Room together, Carmen walking slowly and cautiously in her heels, Shy trying not to overthink where they were going, or what it meant.

17

A Sliver of Carmen

Carmen bought them each a slice of pizza at the crew cafeteria; then she led him back to her cabin, where she cued up more Brazilian music on her laptop and kicked off her heels. "First off," she said, "you remember how I made up rules for us, right?"

He did.

She pulled out the desk chair and pointed for Shy to sit. "Well, the second one is this: no more of your cheesy hand-holding tests." She sat on the side of her cot, as far away from Shy's chair as possible. "Especially in my room. The only reason you're in here right now is so we can talk about your nephew. Got it?"

"Got it," Shy said, taking a bite of his slice. He felt guilty, though, like she might think he was using Miguel's condition to get close to her. But that's not how it was.

He pointed at her laptop, said: "Mind if I check my email real quick?"

"Go 'head."

Shy logged on. His in-box was still empty, though, so he logged right back off.

"Nothing?" Carmen said.

Shy shook his head and sat back in the chair, picked up what was left of his slice. As they ate, Shy noticed that the ship was a little calmer now. "You think we're past the bad part of the storm?"

Carmen shrugged. "It's definitely not thrashing around as much." She wadded up her paper plate, adding: "You were right about this wristband, by the way. I can't believe I was able to eat something."

"Maybe Shoeshine's a genius," Shy said.

Carmen laughed a little. "I don't know about that. But he's definitely mysterious. One time I saw him shooting a damn bow and arrow off the back of the ship. Middle of the night."

Shy decided "mysterious" was the right word. "I saw a bunch of books in his bag earlier. I think one of them had to do with science or something. Where's he even from, anyway?"

Carmen shrugged. "Vlad from security said he spent half his life in prison for a crime he didn't commit. This girl Jessica who works in the spa said he was never in jail, he worked on a cattle ranch. Someone else told me he used to be homeless." Carmen shook her head. "Who knows, right? You can't trust none of these fools."

She got up and lowered the music some. "Anyways, I want you to back up and tell me everything about your nephew."

Shy threw away his plate, too, and sat back down.

He told her how his mom and sis had taken Miguel in as soon as the whites of his eyes turned pink, and how the doctors diagnosed him with Romero Disease on the spot and got him on meds. He told her how expensive everything was going to be because his sister didn't have insurance, how he told his mom to cash the bond he

103

won at a halftime shooting contest and how there was a selfish part of him that was actually stressed about losing the money, and he hated that part of himself.

Carmen shook her head and said how sorry she was, and then she told him more about the news program she'd been watching when he walked in. "I guess they're doing all this research now and coming up with treatments. Did you know they found out it can spread through water? Or how about that you have to get on those meds within twenty-four hours or you're done."

"That's what my mom told me."

"When it was just in our neighborhoods they didn't research shit."

Shy shook his head. He was starting to understand that some people's lives mattered more than others. Back home, that thought never would've crossed his mind. But working on a cruise ship made him notice things.

"When I win the lottery," Carmen said, "I'm gonna build state-of-the-art hospitals, all along the border. So future kids like us won't have to know what it feels like to lose family for stupid reasons."

"You could name 'em after your dad," Shy told her.

"And your grandma," Carmen said. "But not your nephew. 'Cause that medicine's gonna make him better."

"Man, I hope you're right," Shy said.

It went quiet between them for a few seconds, and Shy thought of something. He'd give back every single second of him hooking up with Carmen last night, as long as he knew they'd keep being friends after the voyage ended. She was way more than just some girl you messed around with.

"Anyways," Carmen said, standing up. "I'm gonna change into sweats. You can stay if you wanna keep checking your email or whatever."

"If it's cool," Shy said. "Just kick me out whenever you're ready to crash."

Carmen went to her dresser, pulled a pair of sweats and a sweatshirt and her toiletry bag. On her way to the bathroom she stopped and patted Shy on the shoulder. "Sorry you have to deal with this disease again," she said. "It's bad enough when it's an adult. But a little kid?"

He locked eyes with her and nodded.

She took her clothes into the bathroom, and Shy just sat there staring at the door as she pulled it closed behind her. He felt nervous being in her room this long. He honestly wanted to respect her whole fiancé situation. But at the same time, he didn't want to rush off either. Talking to Carmen was making him feel way better.

He got up and went back to her laptop. Checked his email. Nothing.

His thoughts drifted back to the man in the suit as he browsed through Carmen's music on iTunes. Maybe he should have stayed longer, heard everything the guy had to say. But then he'd started tossing out threats—Shy hadn't even done anything wrong. That's when he'd had enough. Hopefully Franco would be able to explain everything in the morning.

Carmen had a ton of world mixes. Some angry chick stuff. Finally he stumbled into some hip-hop he dug and put it on and the beat filled the tiny cabin.

Carmen cracked open the bathroom door and mumbled over her buzzing toothbrush: "I know you didn't just mess with my music, Sancho."

"Just switching it up for a sec," Shy said.

Through the crack in the door, he saw her rinse out her mouth, then tap her electric toothbrush against the miniature sink. "Why do you settle for generic American hip-hop?" she called out over her shoulder as she took out her contacts.

"It's *your* music," he said.

"Brazilian beats are way more raw," she said.

"I don't even know what they're saying, though." He went back to scanning through her library.

"It's not about the words, Shy. It's about the feel."

When he looked toward the bathroom again, he saw her slipping out of her long black dress, and he froze.

His mouth fell open.

He knew he shouldn't be seeing what he was seeing, but he couldn't tear his eyes away. Her skin was perfectly brown and soft-looking and she was spilling out of her bra, and she had on a black thong that was barely any material, and all over she was thick except her slim waist and stomach, and she had a tattoo just beneath her belly button, words written in script, too small to make out, and for the first time in Shy's life a girl was making his heart pound so hard inside his chest he wondered if he was having a heart attack and he wondered if this was how love felt.

Their eyes met in the mirror for a fraction of a second. He quickly cut away and stared back at her computer. He heard the door click shut.

Shy didn't move for a while.

He just stared at her computer screen and concentrated on the feel of his breaths going in and out of his lungs.

It definitely wasn't the time to be checking out Carmen. Not when she was being so nice to him. And so supportive about his nephew. If she wanted to be just friends, then he did, too.

But damn.

That perfect sliver he'd just seen of her body.

He couldn't get it out of his head. Couldn't stop imagining himself getting up and going to the bathroom door and knocking, her letting him in.

He had to leave.

Now.

Shy stood up and started toward the cabin door, but just then Carmen came out of the bathroom.

She had on a Chargers shirt and a pair of Adidas sweatpants, and they both started talking at the same time:

"Listen—"

"Here's the deal, Shy—"

They looked at each other.

"I just wanna say—"

"Last night—"

Carmen put a finger to her lips, said: "Let me get this out first, then I'll listen to whatever you have to say, okay?"

"Okay." Shy's heart wouldn't stop pounding.

"I've been thinking a lot about last night," Carmen started. "About why I did what I did. And I'm gonna be honest with you, Shy. There's maybe a few little feelings on my side." She took a deep breath and shook her head, went and sat on the edge of her cot.

Shy stayed by the door.

"I mean, you're definitely a little corny. And you go to the dumb high school back home. But still. You're from the neighborhood, you know? We get each other without any words. And it's not like you're hard to look at." She paused for a few seconds. "What I'm trying to say is, you got a little something, all right? But I made a commitment to Brett. I'm getting married in a few months. Jesus, I'm getting *married*."

"I wanna respect that, Carm."

"I know you do. But maybe it's not just you I'm worried about. I don't even know what I'm doing."

Shy didn't know how to respond to that so he just stood there, waiting for her to talk again.

"Sometimes . . . I don't even know, Shy. I got all this doubt going through my head. Like, am I messing up here? Am I doing this for the right reasons?"

Shy shoved his hands into his pockets, said: "Everyone probably has those thoughts."

Carmen looked up at him. "That's what my mom says. But I don't know."

It was super awkward now, and Shy decided he should break the tension somehow. He forced a little grin and told her: "Man, it's just too bad your guy doesn't have a cooler name. 'Brett' sounds kind of soft, don't you think?"

"Oh, 'cause 'Shy' is so gangster," Carmen fired back.

They both smiled and Carmen said: "Come give me a friendship hug, all right? Then I'm kicking your ass out of here so I can go to sleep."

Shy was just starting to move toward Carmen's open arms when the ship jerked violently.

They stared at each other, neither saying a word.

Heavy footfalls shook the ceiling above them.

Doors opened and closed in the halls.

"Shy?" Carmen said.

He opened his mouth to answer, but before he could get any words out there was an explosion of deafening sound. They both covered their ears and stared at each other, Carmen's face filling with worry.

The ship alarm.

Shy threw open the cabin door and looked down the hall. Other doors were opening, people gathering in groups, looking at one another, confused. Shy spotted the man in the black suit, Bill, hurrying away from Carmen's cabin. Like he'd been listening to their conversation through the door. But why? That seemed as bad as breaking into his cabin.

Shy refocused his attention on the alarm and the panic rising in the hall. Maybe the ship had reached the eye of the storm. Or maybe it hit something or there was a fire in the engine room or pirates had stormed the captain's quarters.

He saw Carmen rush over to her tiny porthole and look outside. "I can't see anything!" she shouted, turning back to him. "Can you see anything?"

Shy hurried to her side, but all he saw was a thick blur of rain and choppy waves crashing into each other.

No fire.

No smoke.

No other ships.

The alarm continued as they hurried back to the door, ducked out into the hall. More crew members now gathered there, everyone looking around and shouting over the earsplitting sound. Shy's throat tightening, his eyes darting every which way.

Then the alarm cut off.

Just as abruptly as it had started.

The ship emcee's voice came over the loudspeaker:

"Ladies and gentlemen, this is an emergency. All passengers and crew members should secure a life jacket from the closet of your cabin and proceed directly to the appropriate muster station. I repeat, all passengers and crew members must secure a life jacket and proceed directly to their muster station."

Shy and Carmen turned to each other.

He saw in her terrified eyes that this was something serious, and he knew immediately his life would be forever changed.

18

Order in the Normandie Theater

The alarm was blaring again as they raced up the stairs toward the Normandie Theater. Shy's heart pounding inside his chest and throat, his thoughts all half formed. They were in trouble. He knew that. And he had to get to his and Kevin's assigned muster station, the balcony area of the theater.

Just yesterday, he'd met with his group of passengers and led them through all the emergency procedures and marched them out to the lifeboats—but never once had he considered that there might be an actual emergency.

He glanced at Carmen, her anxious stare fixed directly ahead as they hurried through the hall. Life-vested passengers all around them now, wide-eyed and clinging to one another, shouting over the alarm.

Carmen broke off from Shy, hurried toward the stage level of the theater, her own muster station.

Shy continued across the corridor, toward the far staircase. He had to get to the third floor. Check on his group. Then he could think. And Kevin would be there, too. But he was slowed by a mob near the elevators. They turned on him with their questions, yelling over one another, the blaring alarm drowning out almost every word.

During training week they'd spent three full days on emergency procedures. Drilled every possible scenario, again and again. But now that it was happening for real, Shy felt totally unprepared.

"I'm sorry," he told them.

"I don't know anything," he told them. "We have to wait for another announcement."

It wasn't good enough.

The mob kept shouting at Shy and pressing in on him until he couldn't take it anymore. He shoved past everyone and broke for the far stairs, climbed two at a time.

Kevin was on the next floor up, barking directions at passengers: "All guests must go to their muster stations! Let's move it, people! This is an emergency!"

Shy ran up a final flight of stairs, stepped into the hall just outside the theater and repeated Kevin's exact words to all passengers who were lost. It helped Shy as much as it helped them. Gave him something to focus on. A job. No time to think about the storm or what the ship alarm meant or the supposed eighteen feet of steel keeping them afloat.

Each passenger carried a ship card, which was like a credit card they used for everything on board. Shy flipped over the cards of lost passengers, directed them to the right muster station based on the color code on back. Some of the things he'd learned in training were actually returning to him.

All around were panicked faces, the ship pitching aggressively again, and sometimes a man or woman getting sick right there, in the middle of the hall, and the other passengers stepping around him, over him, through him, and it was all so chaotic and over-whelming, but Shy no longer had time to think about his own fear because he had a job.

Take a card.

Flip it over.

Shout the muster station name and point a direction. "Go!"

He spotted the foul-mouthed Muppet boy sitting against the far wall, rocking back and forth, alone. The kid wasn't cursing now, he was crying and calling for his mom. Shy grabbed him by the shirt, lifted him up. "What's your mom's name?"

"Barbara!" the boy shouted.

"Barbara what?"

"Barbara Pierce!"

Shy dragged the kid into the theater and called this name, over and over, "Barbara Pierce! Mrs. Barbara Pierce!" above the crowd noise and the alarm and the kid's continual sobbing, until a woman downstairs, in Carmen's section, started waving her arms frantically and screaming the boy's name: "Lawrence!"

Shy led the boy to the stairs, made the handoff, watched the mom wrap her son in a tight bear hug, her face wet with tears and relieved, and right then Shy decided something: This was what he had to do. Help people. Because when he helped people, he didn't try to guess what was happening and he didn't worry. He just acted.

He turned back to his muster station and shouted for everyone to line up, recalling many of the faces from yesterday's departure, when he'd led them through the safety rules and marched them to the lifeboats off the Lido Deck—back when the lifeboats seemed like nothing more than decoration and all the faces he saw were full of excitement. The faces he looked at now were frantic and bloodless and lost.

"What's happening?" they shouted at Shy.

"Where's the captain?"

"We need to speak to the captain!"

"Why aren't they telling us anything?"

"Please!" Shy shouted back, feeling more in charge now. "Right now we gotta line up! Like yesterday! Come on, guys, let's go!"

The alarm cut out again.

Every passenger stopped in their tracks.

The entire theater went perfectly silent for a few long seconds, everyone looking around at each other, looking at Shy, but soon the quiet was broken, and the hum of conversation picked back up, the ship still bucking underneath them.

Shy moved to the balcony to see what was happening. The theater curtain opened and the movie screen lit up, but all it showed was static.

He spotted Carmen, standing off to the side of the stage with Vlad, one of the security guards.

Just the two of them.

Vlad talking and Carmen listening.

Her face suddenly fell and she grabbed at Vlad's uniform shirt and let out a piercing scream that filled the entire theater.

Everyone turned to her.

Shy leaned over the railing and shouted Carmen's name.

She didn't look up, but covered her face and dropped to her knees, sobbing.

19
The Big One

The ship emcee came on over the intercom again, his normally enthusiastic voice now slow and measured: "*Ladies and gentlemen. There has been a major earthquake east of Los Angeles.*"

Shy looked around at the gasping crowd.

"*A catastrophic earthquake. We're still gathering information at this time, but we've been informed that its size is beyond anything previously recorded on the Richter scale. The epicenter appears to be near Palm Springs, but the effects are much more widespread, reaching all the way into Mexico.*"

Shy gripped the railing.

If the earthquake affected Mexico, it affected San Diego, too. Which meant Otay Mesa.

His body went cold as he thought of his family.

"We have been advised to discontinue the voyage until we regain satellite connection. Again, ladies and gentlemen. Approximately thirty-five minutes ago, a catastrophic earthquake hit California and we have been advised . . ."

Shy only caught bits and pieces of the rest of the announcement. Something about connecting to a news feed. About passengers remaining in their muster stations and the threat of rough seas. Mostly, though, Shy tried to make sense of his own jumbled thoughts.

An earthquake in California.

Off the Richter scale.

It was the "Big One" everyone had always talked about.

And how bad was "catastrophic"? Did that mean everyone was dead? Was his family dead? Had all the buildings been leveled? He tried to imagine his street back home. His high school and apartment complex. The hospital where his mom and sister sat waiting for the medicine to fix Miguel.

Shy's breathing started going way too fast, like he was hyperventilating. Because his thoughts now turned to the ship. All the way out here with no protection. The storm tossing them around and the waves growing and what did the emcee mean by a threat of rough seas? Wasn't it rough already?

Shy kneeled down and tried to calm his breathing but he couldn't. They had to hurry and get to Hawaii. Or turn around and go back home. They couldn't just sit out here in the middle of the ocean; they had to *do* something.

Soon as the announcement ended, the hysterical voices of passengers were all around Shy and people were crying and anxiously punching numbers into useless cell phones and holding each other and shouting demands at Shy and Kevin, and all Shy could do was stand up and ask everyone to remain calm and line up, like they did when he'd led them through the safety exercise, but how could anyone be calm after what they'd just been told?

Shy imagined his mom.

His sister and Miguel.

His grandma.

But he no longer needed to worry about his grandma, because his grandma was dead.

And would he be dead, too, if he was back home? Had the cruise ship saved his life? Maybe the captain was right to have them sit out here and wait. Maybe there was nowhere else to go.

Shy helped herd all the passengers into theater seats, and then he hurried back to the balcony. Carmen was still there, now huddling against the wall and crying into her hands. He leaned over the railing to call down to her, but just as he opened his mouth, the giant movie screen flickered into a grainy picture above the crowded stage.

Everyone turned to it.

Carmen pulled her hands away from her face, looked up.

A mess of war-zone-like footage came into focus. Shot from a helicopter. It was hard to tell what they were seeing at first, but gradually it became clear.

The words "San Francisco" appeared at the bottom of the screen, but it didn't look like San Francisco. It looked like a foreign city that had just been bombed. Or CGI in a movie. Leveled buildings reduced to hills of concrete and protruding metal stakes. Thick clouds of dust rose off the wreckage and smoke billowed from fires that burned over the caved-in streets. And everywhere the camera went it showed overturned cars, motionless bodies pinned underneath or hanging out of busted windshields. And in the background the Golden Gate Bridge was no longer a bridge but a mess of hanging cables and two crumbled sections that ran straight down into the bay.

The audio kept cutting in and out, but Shy was able to make out some of the information as they cut to footage of other devastated sections of San Francisco.

It hadn't been just one earthquake but several, leveling the entire coast of California and Washington and Oregon and Vancouver, and they were already estimating over a million deaths.

There had been four major quakes, the two most devastating centered just outside Palm Springs and along the Cascadia Subduction Zone off the coast of Washington State. The most powerful offshore quake had struck just west of Morro Bay, which Shy knew was in California. What he didn't know was how far out into the ocean "offshore" was.

Shy was so stunned by what he was seeing and hearing his whole body started shaking.

The picture cut out for several seconds, and when it came back they were showing aerial footage of Riverside, where a huge chasm had opened up along the 91 Freeway, massive fires burning on both sides, but there were no fire trucks on the scene, the red-eyed reporter explained, because all the firehouses within a hundred-mile radius had been taken out by the earthquake. And then a shot of downtown Los Angeles, where only a few buildings still stood and everywhere small fires burned and the Santa Monica Pier had collapsed into the ocean and the famous Ferris wheel had snapped in half and lay crushed on its side, people trapped underneath, and the beach stretched out incredibly far now, the tide so low it didn't even look real. Shy remembered seeing footage of a beach in Thailand that had looked like that just before it was hit by a tsunami. Did that mean they should expect a tsunami?

Shy's legs grew so weak he had to squat down and hold on to the railing.

The Hollywood sign had missing letters and those that remained were in flames, and the 405 Freeway was full of gaping holes, people stranded on concrete islands, waving for help from the tops of cars, and hundreds of yachts from the marina were beached and lying useless on their sides.

It was definitely the "Big One."

What Shy had been hearing about ever since he was a little kid. The crowd inside the theater, realizing the same thing maybe, grew so hysterical it was no longer possible for Shy to make out any of the audio, but he could still see.

The picture cut out for a few seconds, and when it came back it was an aerial shot of a huge black smoke cloud smothering all of Orange County, and in the gaps of the smoke you couldn't see houses or buildings but flames. A shot labeled "Seattle" showed the Space Needle in pieces in front of leveled downtown buildings, fires raging up and down every street, and the famous marketplace had been ripped from its foundation and heaved into Elliott Bay.

Shy's throat closed up completely when the Mexican border flashed onto the screen, a stretch just east of the ocean that he didn't recognize right away because there was no longer a physical border, there was only fire and rubble and a few tiny dots that were people wandering aimlessly, and border patrol trucks abandoned with their doors still open. And then they cut to a part of San Diego just north of Otay Mesa engulfed in flames, Shy's heart pounding and his body shaking, and then the picture cut out again and this time it didn't come back.

The entire theater was in a frenzy.

People shouting and crying and holding each other.

Shy glanced down at the stage, searching for Carmen, but she wasn't there anymore.

He looked all around, finally spotting the back of her head as she hurried toward the theater exit. He motioned to Kevin that he'd be back and then he took off after her.

20
Caught in the Ship Spotlight

Shy raced down the stairs and into the hallway, his mind flooded with all the awful things he'd just seen. Fallen buildings and fires and dead bodies. He had no idea how to process any of it.

He stopped in the hall, spun around searching for Carmen. It was all that seemed to matter now. Just find Carmen. Make sure she's okay.

He shouted her name.

Nothing in return but the sound of the storm and the movement of the ship.

Then he spotted the glass doors sliding closed on the other end of the hall. Doors that were supposed to be locked because of the storm. And only crew members knew the code that opened them.

He took off in that direction, punched in the code and hurried through the doors himself, back out into the storm.

"Carmen!" he shouted over crackling thunder.

The rain was lighter now, but the wind was the strongest it had been all night. He had to lean into it to get all the way out onto the deck. He moved cautiously around the covered pool and Jacuzzi, eyes darting every which way, the destruction he'd just seen still stuck in his brain. And Otay Mesa. His family.

He climbed up onto the stage, moved through the empty outdoor café, searched behind every bar and busser station, every doorway, sprinted up and down every stairwell.

But there was no sign of Carmen anywhere.

He needed to get back to his group of passengers in the theater. It wasn't right to leave Kevin in charge of everyone.

An awful thought crept into Shy's head, and he hurried to the ship railing and peered over at the ocean below. It was even rougher now. Choppy whitecaps and aimless head-high swells that crashed into the side of the ship from every angle. Streaks of lightning flashing from above.

Carmen wouldn't jump, though, he promised himself. Even if she knew her entire family was gone. She wouldn't do that.

As Shy pushed away from the railing, a different voice came over the PA system:

"*Ladies and gentlemen, this is your captain speaking. I need every passenger and crew member to remain in their muster station, sitting down, with their life jacket securely fastened. We will be encountering extremely rough seas ahead. I repeat, this is your captain speaking. All passengers and crew members must be seated with their life jackets securely fastened. We are working to regain satellite contact and get more information, but our immediate concern is for your safety.*"

Shy continued around the deck, looking for Carmen and trying to decide what the captain meant by "rough seas."

On the other side of the deck Shy found Paolo and several emergency crew members prepping the lifeboats. Paolo turned to Shy, shouted: "Why are you out here? You need to be inside with your group of passengers! Get back to the theater!"

"How come you're doing the lifeboats?" Shy asked.

"Standard emergency procedures! Now go!"

Shy backed away, watching the emergency crew climbing in and out of the boats. Near the glass doors he bumped into someone and spun around.

Vlad. "You shouldn't be out here!" he yelled.

"Just tell me why they're doing the lifeboats," Shy said.

Vlad looked toward Paolo and his crew, then turned back to Shy. "The problem is our location!" he shouted over the storm. "We're too close to the Hidden Islands! The water is very shallow!"

"What does that mean?" Shy asked.

"And this wind!" Vlad shouted. "They're worried how the ocean will react!"

Vlad looked back at Paolo again, then pulled Shy down the ship a ways, just outside the sight line of the emergency crew. He clicked on a high-powered spotlight and shined the beam on the raging ocean surface. "Watch the sea life!"

At first Shy only saw furious whitecaps and waves, but then a heavy swell rolled past and in the light he spotted a pod of dolphins racing past the ship, in the direction of the wind.

"They're trying to get away from something!" Vlad shouted. "Don't you get it? It's likely we'll encounter a tsunami!"

The word was a punch in Shy's stomach.

But the scared look in Vlad's eyes was even worse. It told Shy the ship was in serious danger.

Just then they heard the deep revving of the massive engines, and the ship slowly started moving again—not away from whatever the dolphins were fleeing, but toward it.

Vlad's eyes grew even bigger as he stared into the wind. "Oh my God."

"What?" Shy shouted.

He looked again, but didn't see anything.

"They're trying to make it over!" Vlad shut off the spotlight, spun around and started toward the glass doors.

"Everyone inside!" Shy heard Paolo shouting. "Now! Let's go!"

Shy followed Vlad, looking over his shoulder at all the emergency crew members leaping down from the lifeboats, racing across the deck toward the doors.

Shy's last thought before ducking back into the ship with everyone else was of Carmen and how he still hadn't found her.

21
A Wall of Water

When Shy made it back to the Normandie Theater and his group of passengers, he found everybody seated except for Kevin, who was standing in front of a window. Shy made a beeline to the railing and scanned the lower theater for Carmen, but she wasn't there either, so he hurried up to Kevin, saying: "There's gonna be a tsunami." He looked over his shoulder, making sure none of the passengers had heard him.

Kevin stared back at him wide-eyed and pointed out the window.

Shy saw it now.

The slight rise in the distance.

It was subtle and far away, but the ship was moving directly toward it.

"What if we don't make it?" Kevin said. He looked terrified.

Shy turned to the crowded theater seats, thinking for the first time that he might die out here, in the middle of the ocean. His heart climbed into his throat, and he felt like he was about to gag or faint. Dying had never crossed his mind in a real way before. Not like this.

A pack of passengers were now gathered at the balcony railing, and Kevin was moving toward them and shouting: "Sit down, please! Everyone needs to be sitting down!"

Shy hurried to his group, making sure they were all secured in their life jackets, and he double-checked his own jacket; then he sat himself in one of the theater chairs and gripped the armrests and closed his eyes and told himself they'd be okay, they'd be okay, they'd be okay, the ship was huge, the bottom indestructible like he'd told his grandma. All they had to do was sit in their muster stations like the captain said, because the captain had probably seen it all and knew what he was doing.

Shy clasped his hands together as if to pray, but he didn't know how to pray because he never went to his grandma's church, and he was making shit up when he told her the bottom was eighteen feet thick and made of pure steel, he had no idea how thick it was, or what it was made of, and what if this was his punishment for lying or for not going to church?

Shy was up again, moving through the balcony seats to check the rise on the ocean through one of the windows.

It reached higher now.

And it was closer to the ship.

And they were charging right at it.

He heard voices over his shoulder and turned around. Scattered passengers were now gathered at the window behind him. They were at every window. All of them pointing at the rise and holding each other and panicking. Kevin was shouting for them to get back to their seats, but nobody was listening.

Shy tried shouting, too, but all the screaming drowned him out, so he went to the railing to look for Carmen again, his heart slamming inside his chest, his breaths too fast, because they were only seconds away from living or dying. He understood this. And what if Carmen was outside somewhere? What if she didn't know what was coming?

He circled his group of passengers again, pleading for everyone to sit down.

Some did, but most of them still crowded the windows trying to get one last look, and Shy shoved his way to the window where Kevin stood and peered outside.

He froze.

A massive wall of water, almost twice the height of the ship and climbing still, and coming directly at them. It was clear they had no chance of making it over, but the ship continued plunging forward.

Everyone at the windows was screaming, even men, and Shy realized he was screaming, too, and a heavyset middle-aged man slumped to the ground holding his chest, and Shy's entire body started to tingle and he lost all strength in his arms and legs and had to hold on to the window to stay standing as he stared at the cresting wave—this beyond all his understanding except it was the end of everything, and no person could change this fact, and no God, and the wave was directly in front of them now, and all Shy could see through the window was the roaring wall of ocean water.

He turned to run just as it slammed into the ship and all the small windows exploded with glass and water, and the floor shot straight up, and he found himself in the air—and in his slow-motion flight Shy saw bodies thrown from chairs, bodies crashing into other bodies, into walls, bodies toppling over the theater railing, falling onto the stage, onto chairs, onto the backs of other passengers, the ship alarm once again blaring in Shy's ears, and the spray of cold ocean salt water in his nose and mouth and eyes, blinding him, and then he was somehow slammed headfirst into a chandelier and was lost. . . .

22

Gaps in Consciousness

Shy came to in front of the open balcony door as the ship was slowly starting to right itself. Fallen passengers lay all around him, battered and twisted, faces frozen in shock or facedown, ocean water raining down on all of them from a gaping hole in the theater ceiling, and everything smelled of brine and seaweed.

He looked down at himself, saw that he was covered in blood and searched in a panic for where he was hurt—then he saw the woman lying next to him, her throat pierced by a thick shard of glass. She was choking on her own blood, coughing, her wild eyes staring directly at him as she vomited more blood into his lap.

Then her eyes slowly emptied out and her head slumped to the side, and when Shy went to reach for her, he was lost.

* * *

He came to in fits and starts after that.

At first everything he saw was frozen, like a photograph. Not a person moved and rain hovered in the air above him in sparkling droplets, and there was no sound other than the deafening roar of his own heart.

He saw a limp pile of bodies facedown in a pool of pink ocean water, and he saw a man holding a woman's bloodied face in his hands and crying, and he saw Kevin's body in front of the railing, an arc of thick blood spewing rhythmically from his forehead, and he saw a small girl standing against the far wall in her dinner dress and life jacket, eyes squeezed shut, hands reaching for some imagined person.

He turned back to Kevin, telling himself he had to do something to stop the blood, and he crawled over to Kevin's still body, shouting his name, but he couldn't hear his own voice. Shy ripped off his life jacket and his overshirt, tore it in half and tied it around Kevin's head like a tourniquet. He pulled tight and then refastened his life jacket and shook Kevin's shoulders, shouting: "Wake up! Kevin!"

But he still couldn't hear his own voice.

Couldn't hear anything.

And Kevin wasn't waking up.

Shy kept shaking Kevin and yelling so hard that all the blood rushed to his head and he was lost.

He came to with ocean water pouring down onto his face, and him gulping for air, swallowing salt water and sand and gagging, until he rolled away coughing and vomited.

He was on the theater stage somehow with no recollection of getting there. And no Kevin. All around Shy were lifeless bodies submerged in a foot of water, drowning if they weren't already drowned, theater seats ripped from their foundation, floating, the roof half caved in and the air thick with smoke and salt and mist,

127

and the man in front of him was looking down at his bare thigh where a thick ragged bone had pierced through the skin.

Shy watched this man try to straighten the shattered bone in his shock, and it occurred to Shy that the man would soon bleed to death and that the man was Supervisor Franco.

Shy came to on his knees, at the front of the stage. He was crawling over his dead supervisor, over a drowned woman, and then tumbling down the stairs onto his back, where he stared up at the sky from which rain no longer fell, only hovering smoke and dew and odd salty droplets that traveled in slow motion toward him, dotting his forehead, his nose, his lips, his eyes, and he could see the faint outline of the moon through the thinning storm clouds in the sky, oblivious to all that was happening and people dying, and he breathed and tried to understand, but his mind grew so overwhelmed he was lost.

Shy was on his knees again, trying to get to another window. He could no longer feel the hum of the engine and he couldn't hear anything and the air now smelled like burning plastic.

He rose to his feet, staggered through the silence, over drowned and broken bodies, looking back once more at his dead supervisor, and then he climbed the stairs to the balcony and carried himself to the first blown-out window, where he saw a second great rise of water in the distance, speeding toward them, this one so high above the ship it left no room for sky or moon or stars, and Shy opened his mouth to scream but no sound came out, and then there was another tremendous collision, this one soundless and so vicious he felt ship steel ripping and the walls caving and everything turning over, and he was hurled into the air again, only this time he was lost before he landed.

23
The Dead

Shy opened his eyes to darkness.

His vision slowly adjusted, and when it did he saw that he was outside the balcony door, a wall inches from his nose. When he turned his head he realized that the ceiling had collapsed and he was trapped underneath. No, not trapped underneath, more sheltered within. The ceiling and wall had formed a sort of teepee over him, saving his life.

He felt all around his body: head, arms, legs, feet. Everything still there and uninjured. The only pain was in his chest when he took a deep breath.

He breathed shallow as he pushed out from under the wreckage, then stood looking at the collapsed ceiling—a little to the left or right and he'd have been crushed. He was lucky to be alive.

Moving back into his muster station, Shy wondered how long he'd been knocked out, because it all looked so different now. Ocean water flooded everything and the entire theater seemed off—the ceiling now more of a wall and the stage at an odd angle. He could hear again, too, and what he heard was the groaning of the ship's foundation and a few passengers crying or calling out names.

Something deep inside the bowels of the ship snapped, and the front end of the theater dropped several feet. Shy held on to the balcony railing in shock, knowing only that the cruise ship was ruined and that something impossible would be expected of him.

He struggled through cold, knee-high water, one of his shoes missing and his chest burning with every breath. Something was wrong with his ribs. He glanced down at his life jacket. Ripped straight through. Blood dribbling out the bottom. He reached up to unfasten it, but then thought better of it and kept moving.

At first Shy turned over each body he passed, but none of them could be helped because none of them were alive.

There was no sign of Carmen or Kevin or Rodney or Marcus. For a while he wasn't sure if he was alive either. But he had to be alive because he was walking and breathing. Painfully. And he was seeing these bodies facedown in the water, bodies missing limbs and gashed open and covered in bright red blood.

The only dead person he'd seen back home was his grandma. And even after how sick she got, she looked almost peaceful inside her wooden casket—the makeup they'd used made her look nearly like herself again. But this death was different. It was fresh and ugly and vicious.

He stopped turning over so many bodies.

Shy spotted the back of Carmen's head near the stage, sticking out from under the fallen curtain. He rushed down the angled steps toward her, turned her over, but it wasn't Carmen. It was a middle-aged woman he'd never seen before, and the woman was dead. He lowered her head back into the water and moved on.

More fallen passengers to climb over.

Shy found himself pounding the heel of his hand against his own forehead, trying to think, trying to wake himself up, but he couldn't think or wake up.

They'd been hit by two giant waves. He knew that.

And all around him people were dead.

And the ship was sinking.

But his brain refused to process anything beyond these facts, like all of it was happening to someone else, his space self or a complete stranger.

He shoved debris out of his way: splintered paintings, fallen statues, potted plants, jagged shards of shattered mirrors, chunks of the ceiling and the walls and the stairs. Empty life jackets. Motionless bodies.

"Carmen!" he began shouting through the theater.

"Kevin!"

"Rodney! Marcus!"

Over and over he shouted their names, but there was never an answer. Only a handful of people still seemed even conscious, some just sitting in the water, dumbfounded, others searching for loved ones or stumbling toward the exit like Shy.

Outside lightning flashed, and in that second of illumination, Shy saw how badly the ship had been damaged. The back half already sinking into the ocean and the front twisted on its side and raised slightly above the water. All the windows blown out and no trace of the glass atrium ceiling. The control room flattened and battered and the bridge ripped right down the middle. Seaweed and ocean water pooled in every corner of the Lido Deck.

Thunder pounded, followed by more lightning.

There were hundreds of passengers already lined up near the life-boat launch site in the dark. A few emergency team members loading them aboard. Many of the boats were missing, either already launched or ripped away by the waves.

Shy tried to take deep breaths to calm himself down, but each deep breath felt like a knife in his chest.

And he didn't know where he was supposed to go.

Or what he was supposed to do.

He spotted Marcus with a group of crew members on the Lookout Deck, near the life raft pods. Shy knew the rafts were a last resort, because they were so much smaller and less equipped for survival. It meant some of the lifeboats had been lost.

He headed for the rafts in almost a crawl to keep from slipping on the angled deck. The passengers near the lifeboats were in a disagreement about whether the vessels should be lowered into the storming ocean now.

"You can't expect us to survive these conditions!" one passenger was shouting. "Look at it out there!"

The ocean was still raging below them. Whitecaps everywhere and sometimes a twenty-foot wave that would crash into the broken ship.

"This thing's going to sink!" another passenger shouted. "And there are fires, too! Don't you get it? The lifeboats are our only chance!"

"They're designed for rough seas," a crew member tried to explain.

"But we still have time! We should stay on the ship as long as possible. Radio for help!"

"There *is* no help!" a woman shouted. "Didn't you see what happened to California? All the help will go to them!"

Shy didn't know who was right or wrong, just knew he had to do something. He joined in with the emergency crew, trying to calm everyone down as others continued prepping the lifeboats for launch.

"The captain said it himself!" a man shouted. "There's no radio communication! They won't even know we're out here!"

A tall passenger fought his way up to the front of the line with his wife and kid. He grabbed the shoulder of a crew member, said: "You need to get premier class off this ship first! We paid for that right!"

This sparked a new debate, about who should be loaded onto the lifeboats first: women and children or premier class.

Shy listened to them go back and forth, and he watched the passengers already loaded up in the lifeboat stare over the side at the choppy ocean, most of them holding on to each other or gripping the sides of the boat. One woman slipped trying to get in, and Shy watched her fall violently back onto the angled ship deck, headfirst, and roll against a closed door where she didn't move.

A group of people hurried to her. Everyone else stared. A man lowering himself from the boat, her husband maybe, started screaming. He ran to her, kneeled down and picked up her head, then looked up into the sky, shouting: "No!"

Shy pushed away from this group of passengers and continued toward the emergency rafts, slipping several times along the way. As he climbed the angled stairs, he heard a rise in commotion behind his back. A fight had broken out. Two passengers shoving each other while emergency crew members tried to separate them.

At the top of the stairs, Shy looked over the ship again. From this new vantage point he saw how much the back half was already sagging into the ocean. It didn't look real or even possible. Several lifeboats on that end had been forced underwater, empty. The front half of the ship reached up into the sky and leaned slightly to the side. Smoke billowed out from inside the ship, and Shy realized that fire was as much of a threat as sinking.

Lightning pierced the ocean right next to the ship. Thunder so loud he ducked for cover. He was overwhelmed and scared beyond understanding, but he forced himself to focus on crawling forward, on getting somewhere, to the rafts and Marcus, that was all he had to think about.

24

Sweep of the Destiny Dining Room

A group of Paradise crew members were huddled together, working to open the hard-shelled canisters that held inflatable life rafts. The first of them to look up was Kevin, Shy's bloody shirt still wrapped around his head.

"You're here!" Kevin shouted over the storm. "I looked all over the theater! What happened?"

"I don't know," Shy said. He pointed at Kevin's head. "You were knocked out."

Kevin touched the shirt on his head. "This is yours, isn't it?"

Shy nodded. He looked at Marcus, too. And Vlad. "How long since the second wave hit us?" he asked.

"Half hour," Kevin said.

It seemed impossible that he'd been out that long. Thirty minutes was a big chunk of time to be unaccounted for. But he understood how lucky he was—he'd eventually come to, while others hadn't.

Paolo called out to the entire group: "We get these rafts prepped first, men! Then we double back through each station in teams, helping only those who can be helped! There isn't much time!"

Shy kneeled beside everyone in the dark, his eyes fixed on what was framed by the two flashlights, his mind stuck on the last of Paolo's words: "There isn't much time."

They got the first pod open and Marcus held it as the raft filled automatically with carbon dioxide. It grew big enough to fit a dozen people. Paolo had already explained that all the lifeboats on the other side of the ship were trapped underwater and useless. And Shy had done the math in his head. Seven lifeboats and five rafts. It wouldn't fit even a quarter of the passengers and crew members. But then, how many of them were still alive?

Paolo capped the raft, pulled out the handles and made sure the emergency compartment was fully stocked. Shy studied the contents, knowing that he would likely need this stuff in order to survive: water, dry food, fishing kit, hand and smoke flares, radio signaling device, tarps, blankets, small basic tool kit and water dye.

Paolo tapped Marcus and another guy, shouted: "Drop the raft at the launching site and do a sweep of the theater! You've got fifteen minutes!"

They each took a side and carried the raft above their heads, half crawling down the angled stairs.

Before they cracked open the second pod, Shy heard a loud creaking sound coming from the back of the ship. An explosion followed, and they all spun around to look. Bright flames shot up into the dark sky, illuminating clouds of black smoke. Screams came from the line of passengers waiting to board the lifeboats. Shy looked down at the raging sea, then back up at the burning and sinking ship.

They were all going to die.

He repeated this fact in his head, again and again. Calmly, though, in his shock.

The second raft filled with carbon dioxide. Paolo did his safety checks and tapped Kevin and Shy this time, told them to drop off the raft and do a sweep of the Destiny Dining Room.

They both took a handle, lifted the raft over their heads and started cautiously across the Lookout Deck. When they got near the bottom of the stairs Shy scanned the line of passengers and spotted Carmen climbing into one of the lifeboats.

"Carmen!" he called out to her. When she didn't hear him, he turned to Kevin, told him excitedly: "Carmen just got on one of the boats! She's alive!"

Kevin nodded and they dropped the raft off at the launching point, secured it just behind the one Marcus had carried down. They moved back inside the ship, into the Destiny Dining Room, passing the empty hostess stand where they split up. Shy took the rear of the huge restaurant, Kevin stayed up front.

The place looked like it had been hit by a tornado. Fallen ceiling slabs, tables and chairs scattered and on their sides, thick smoke hovering above the flooded floor where motionless bodies lay. It was strange how numb to death Shy had already become. It hardly slowed him down. As he sloshed through the water, he recalled the jealousy he'd felt in this dining room earlier. Carmen and Toni talking about their engagements. Carmen's man kneeling on the boardwalk. It all seemed so ridiculous now.

He headed straight for the kitchen, the source of the smoke, looked through the swinging-door windows. Three kitchen workers were inside, aiming extinguishers at a roaring fire—the white foam hardly containing it at all.

Shy pushed through the doors, shielding his nose and mouth with his shoulder. "Paolo wants everyone up top!" he shouted in a muffled voice. "Now!"

The three of them turned around.

Shy was overwhelmingly relieved to see that one of them was Rodney.

"Shy!" Rodney shouted, tears streaming down his face.

"Rod! You need to go get on one of the lifeboats, man! There aren't many left!"

"Everyone's dead, Shy!"

"Go get on a lifeboat!" Shy shouted back at him. "Hurry!"

Rodney dropped his extinguisher, grabbed the others by their shirts and all four of them hurried out of the burning kitchen. Shy told Rodney he'd meet him on the Lido Deck as soon as he found Kevin. Rodney hugged him, then pushed away and sloshed through the water toward the exit.

Shy scoured the back half of the dining room for survivors with a new determination. Carmen and Rodney were still alive. But soon the air grew thick with smoke, which was now spewing out from underneath the kitchen doors. Shy had trouble breathing, and whenever he coughed it felt like a knife digging into his ribs.

Kevin shouted his name from across the dining room, but just as Shy started toward him, stepping over bodies along the way, he heard a second voice. "Help me."

Shy stopped in his tracks, looked all around, saw nothing.

"Help me. Please."

"Where are you?" Shy shouted.

"Here."

The heat from the fire in the kitchen grew more intense. A thick layer of smoke had gathered near the ceiling. Shy saw a man and woman, completely submerged in water, holding hands. He saw a motionless woman slumped against the wall holding her stomach, covered in blood.

"Shy, let's go!" Kevin yelled again.

Just then there was a massive explosion in the kitchen. A burst of flames shot through the doors, started eating at the restaurant walls and ceiling. When Shy turned to run he saw a hand reaching up from behind a fallen chandelier.

It was the man who'd been following him all around the ship. The man in the black suit, Bill. "Help me," he pleaded. "Please."

Shy froze.

The fire raged across the entire back half of the dining room now, smoke burrowing into his lungs. Shy flashed through Kevin's warning, his and Rodney's trashed cabin, the man's threats in the Luxury Lounge. But Shy couldn't just leave someone.

He reached down and grabbed the man's hand and pulled, but the man's leg was trapped under the chandelier. He couldn't move. And Shy couldn't lift him. The water now up to the man's chin.

"Please," he begged.

Shy slipped his hand out of the man's grip and tried lifting the chandelier, but it was too heavy. Kevin was beside him now, gripping the chandelier, too. Together they strained, Shy's chest killing him as he coughed, and Kevin shouting for the man to push.

Finally the three of them moved it enough for him to slip his leg free. The man got to his knees quickly, but when he tried to put weight on his leg he toppled back into the water.

Shy and Kevin lifted him, threw his arms over their shoulders and started dragging him through the restaurant. Flames crackling at their backs, running across the ceiling and walls in front of them now, the intense heat blistering Shy's skin, singeing his hair.

The front exit was on fire, the doors closed and covered in flames. Shy looked back at the rear exit, but it was even worse.

"Carry him!" Kevin shouted. "I'll do the doors!"

Shy coughed as he watched Kevin hurry awkwardly through the knee-high water. He struggled to stay standing with the man weighing him down.

Kevin led with his shoulder and crashed through the double doors, collapsing into the water on the other side. Shy followed, half carrying, half dragging the man, both of them diving through the flames, everything going silent for Shy underwater.

He quickly raised his head up and sucked in a smoky breath and started coughing uncontrollably as he and Kevin pulled the man toward the warped stairs.

25

Launch of the Lifeboats

Through the darkness outside, Shy saw the outline of several life-boats already on the ocean, whitecapped waves thrashing them around. A line of passengers and crew jockeyed to get on the two remaining lifeboats, as both ends of the sinking ship were now on fire.

Shy and Kevin helped the man up the uneven stairs to the closest lifeboat, pushed him through the line of shouting passengers. "Vlad!" Kevin yelled. "Make sure he gets on the boat! His leg is hurt!"

"We just reached capacity!" Vlad shouted back. "We're lowering it now! Get him on the next one!"

Shy and Kevin turned toward the other boat, a crowd already pushing and shoving in front of it. Shy knew he should be fighting, too. The lifeboats were ten times safer than the open rafts. Especially in these conditions. But there was no room left. And he was crew.

"I'll get off!" someone shouted from inside the lifeboat in front of them.

Shy watched the guy climb over the other seated passengers and jump down onto the deck. It was the guy Shy and Kevin kicked out of the Jacuzzi on the first night of the voyage, Christian. He was actually giving up his seat.

Christian asked about the man's leg, explaining he was a doctor, then he helped boost him onto the boat. Shy scanned the rest of the faces on board, looking for Carmen or Rodney, but they weren't there. He was sure he'd seen Carmen climbing into one of the lifeboats, though. Maybe hers had already launched.

Kevin and Shy started cautiously down the slanted deck toward the raft-launching site, Christian following closely behind them. But when they arrived they found Marcus and Paolo shouting for them to hold on and pointing toward the ocean.

Shy spun back around, saw another huge wave. This one only half the size of the previous two but big enough to lift one of the lifeboats and slam it against the side of the ship. Pieces of shattered boat flew into the air and flailing passengers spilled out into the stormy sea.

The cruise ship creaked and shifted under the power of the wave, the water just failing to reach as high as the Lido Deck.

Shy stared down at the battered lifeboat, scared to death that Rodney or Carmen might have been aboard. The top half ripped completely away. Paolo now explaining that they had to be close to the islands. Otherwise the waves wouldn't be breaking the way they were.

"I don't see any land!" Kevin shouted.

"We will by morning!" Paolo answered. "We just have to make it through the night!"

"If a boat can't make it," Marcus said to Shy, "how will a raft?"

Shy had no answer as he scanned the water, looking for Carmen's head. But it was too dark to see anything more than shapes.

The final two lifeboats were being lowered toward the ocean, several passengers staring out of the opening, looking down at the people floating on the water or back up at the burning ship.

Paolo loaded the few remaining passengers and crew onto rafts, one after the other. Shy looked around as he moved with the line. The sinking ship. The lifeboats getting tossed around on the ocean's surface. A group of passengers trapped up near the burning bow of the ship, leaping off, one by one, screaming as they fell past the raft launch site, into the raging water.

Shy was shoved onto one of the rafts by the crew member behind him, bodies quickly filling in around him, and then the raft slowly lowering down the side of the ship. When it reached the end of its launch rope, the raft plunged toward the sea, Shy gripping the handle beside him, yelling like everyone else, weightlessness like a knot in his stomach, his gaze fixed on the life-vested bodies below, on the stripped ship parts and swirls of ship fuel, and then he shut his eyes as tight as he could and braced for impact.

26
Power of the Sea

The raft slammed headfirst against the surface of the water, Shy's grip ripped away from the handle and he was thrown into the freezing black ocean. He kicked and reached frantically with his hands, choking on salt water, coughing out the last of his air as he was completely submerged.

Soon as his head poked back through the surface, he gulped in a desperate breath and coughed and looked all around in a panic. Heavy swells rolling past like moving mountains, lifting him, then dropping him, then lifting him again. Thunder pounded in the distance. A small wave broke over his head and he swallowed more salt water and gagged.

He wiped his stinging eyes with the back of his wrist and spotted the raft floating upside down, half a football field away, a handful of life-jacketed people already swimming for it. He'd turned to look back at the sinking ship when someone grabbed on to the back of his jacket and started pulling him toward the raft.

Shy spun his head back around, found Christian.

He couldn't process anything except that he was in the massive ocean now, freezing-cold, whitecapped waves cresting all around him.

Lightning lit up the night sky and for a fraction of a second he saw all the survivors thrashing around in the water near the ship.

Shy shook free of Christian's grip, turned onto his stomach and started swimming for the raft himself, fast as he could, thrusting hand after hand into the furious water in front of his face, ignoring the pain in his ribs.

Kevin was the first one to the raft.

Then Paolo and Marcus.

Shy saw them right the raft and begin pulling themselves up by the handles, heaving their waterlogged bodies over the sides. Kevin reached out a hand, pulled in Christian, then he reached for Shy, and Shy fell into the raft on his back and lay there, staring up at the smoke-filled sky and sucking in breaths and listening to the voices all around him.

"Which way are the islands?"

"We have to move away from the ship! There's fuel all around us!"

"Look! That woman's alive!"

"Grab the oars!"

Shy told himself what was happening. They were lost at sea, and nobody was coming to their rescue. Carmen flashed through his thoughts, and he pulled himself up to a sitting position and scanned the water, but it was too dark to make out faces.

Kevin was in the raft with him. Paolo. Marcus and Christian. Several passengers he vaguely recognized. The bodies floating near the raft were mostly on their stomachs, facedown, but a few held up their heads and beat the water with flailing arms and shouted for help.

Two jagged fingers of lightning lit up the sky.

Marcus and Christian were on opposite sides of the raft, digging oars into the choppy sea, propelling the boat toward a screaming woman. Paolo grabbed her by the arm, pulled her into the raft. Shy watched her curl into a fetal position in the water sloshing around at their feet. She looked up at him in shock.

Shy turned back to the rolling ocean, looking for someone else to help, looking for Carmen, Rodney. He saw mostly lifeless bodies and ship debris. Three lifeboats in the distance. He saw pieces of the shattered lifeboat, the bottom half still floating near the ship, which was now mostly underwater, the front end lit up in flames.

A passenger suddenly stood in the middle of the raft and shouted: "Row faster, goddamn it!"

Shy spun around, saw another huge wave roaring toward them, at least as big as the one that slammed the lifeboat against the ship. And all they had to withstand it was a wide-open twelve-man raft.

He started hyperventilating again.

"The other way!" Paolo shouted. "Turn it around! We have to make it over!"

Kevin and Christian spun the raft around, started rowing directly toward the rising wave, fast as they could, Shy gripping the raft handle, unable to take his eyes off the towering wall as it rose higher and higher before them, Paolo now shouting it down: "Come on, you son of a bitch!"

Kevin and Christian rowed and rowed until the colossal wave was directly in front of them, carrying their tiny raft up its steep, roaring face, Shy leaning forward with everyone else, clutching the raft handle, clenching every muscle in his body.

At the last minute, Kevin and Christian pulled in their oars and leaned forward, too, everyone yelling and Shy losing control of his bladder as the raft went nearly vertical with the cresting wave, spray battering his face.

They were suspended like that for what seemed like forever, all gravity vanishing and sounds disappearing, Shy holding his breath and trembling—then the raft slipped over the thick lip and rocketed down the other side, dropping into what seemed like a hole in the ocean and at such speed Shy's whole body vibrated and he ducked his head down inside the raft to avoid being blown back into the growling giant.

When they made it to the bottom, they all turned and watched the wave explode into whitewash behind them, barreling over debris and life-jacketed bodies, colliding with the sinking ship, momentarily quieting the flames.

Shy's eyes darted around the raft as he sucked in desperate breaths. Everyone still there. Looking at each other. White-knuckled on all the raft handles.

But then several of them were screaming again, and Shy turned and saw a second rise in the distance, this one building farther out and already more massive, and he knew immediately they wouldn't make it over.

Kevin and Christian dug their oars back into the ocean and rowed as fast as they could, but it was pointless. Paolo yanked the oar from Christian's grip, tossed it into the ocean, did the same with Kevin's. He dug into the raft's emergency pouch and pulled out everything he could and shoved it into a dry pack, shouting: "Everyone off the raft! Diving under is our only chance!"

But for Shy this was impossible.

He stared at the cresting wave, a few hundred feet away, and then he stared at the water underneath them pulling back.

Paolo strapped the dry pack on his back and dove overboard and started swimming directly at the wave.

Kevin dove in, too.

Christian.

But everyone else continued gripping the raft handles like Shy, unable to let go, their faces all frozen in terror.

Then the wave was in front of them.

At the last second, and against every instinct he had, Shy pried his hand from the handle and rolled over the side of the raft, into the ocean, the current sucking him toward the roaring wave. He watched it stand on its toes, a dozen stories high, the thick lip curling over, slicing down toward him.

Shy pulled in one last painful breath and closed his eyes and dove underneath, far as he could.

The violent undercurrent snatched him up immediately, sucking his now powerless body deep below, into blackness, thrashing him and his life jacket every which way like a washing machine, until he had no idea what was up and his lungs burned and still the ocean kept twisting his body until he lost consciousness.

27
Truth of the World

Shy's eyes popped open.

He was bobbing on the surface of the black ocean in his life jacket, retching uncontrollably—warm salt water and bile flooding back over his tongue and teeth, fanning out in the water in front of his face, the awful taste of his own sick making him vomit again.

He heaved for several minutes, until there was nothing left to purge, and still his stomach convulsed and his eyes stung and the world was blurry.

He spit and looked all around the darkness, shivering.

He was alone.

No idea how long he'd been floating here or how long he'd been drowned. His life jacket must've brought him back up, saved his life.

He spun around looking for what was left of the wave that had pulled him under, but there was nothing. The ocean was calmer, in fact. The wind less severe. He spotted the cruise ship, surprisingly far off in the distance—only the front third still visible, pointing straight up into the sky and half covered in flames.

Nobody else around, dead or alive.

"Kevin!" he shouted.

"Marcus!"

Any name that came to mind, he shouted out, but nobody answered and he slapped at the water with both hands, feeling overwhelmed and hopeless and having no idea what swam below him.

He did nothing more than tread water in the dark for several minutes, battling his own thoughts. What if he was stranded for good? Nothing to eat or drink, no one there when he died? What if he never saw anything but water again? He felt like he'd been shown the truth of the world. The absolute power it held. People just meaningless specks that came and went as easily as flipping a switch.

He couldn't stop shivering in the cold wind and water as he looked around again, his eyes finally adjusting to the dark. A few ship pieces. Drowned bodies. An empty life jacket. An oar from a raft, maybe theirs. A rain slicker kept afloat by an air bubble trapped underneath.

He spotted a portion of a wrecked lifeboat, probably the one he'd seen slammed against the ship by a wave. Most of the bottom half just sitting there, maybe a hundred yards away.

He leaned forward without thinking and swam for it, picking up the oar and slicker along the way. His ribs throbbed as he splashed through the cold ocean, one arm in the slicker, tossing the oar in front of him and catching up, tossing and catching up, small waves sometimes washing over his head. Several times he swallowed mouthfuls of water and had to spit or vomit, but he didn't stop until he was able to reach out and touch what was left of the boat.

The top half was entirely ripped away, the sides jagged and sharp. Cracks and gashes running along the edges including one fist-sized hole that was half underwater. He floated around the boat twice looking for the least jagged side and then tossed in the slicker and the oar and pulled himself up to peer inside.

A handful of passengers. All lying in two feet of water at the bottom of the boat. None were Carmen or anyone he knew.

"Hello," he said.

Then louder: "Hello!"

No one lifted their heads to acknowledge him.

Shy floated there a few more seconds, looking back over his shoulder at the enormous black ocean, and then he pulled himself up and over the side and fell onto one of the bodies in the boat. He quickly rolled off and sat up and looked at the woman. Blood caked in her short gray hair.

Shy went on to his hands and knees and sloshed through the pinkish water to inspect the other bodies, too. He lifted faces, tried shaking them awake, checked for pulses. Nothing. All dead.

He picked up the oar and held it in his lap and looked outside the boat again. "Anyone out there?"

He turned his head to listen for a response, a voice calling back, or splashing, anything, but there was nothing.

Where were all the people on his raft?

Where were Kevin and Marcus and Paolo?

What if he was the only one left?

Shy set the oar back down and carefully got to his feet. He sloshed around the dead bodies and tried to turn on the motor. Nothing. He saw that the entire control panel had been bashed in. Blood splattered across the dash. He turned and looked in the supply compartment underneath the control panel. A large package of fishing line and hooks. Water dye. A length of rope. A flare gun and six flares. A fiberglass patching kit and a tarp.

No food or water, though.

He left everything where it was and considered the salt water at the bottom of the boat. It was about knee-high, which was a problem because one of the jagged sides was splintered so it was only a few inches higher. He reached a hand down near the bottom of the side to feel around the biggest gash—water rushing in.

He knew the boat surface had to be dry to use the fiberglass patch kit, so he pulled the soaking wet sweatshirt off the closest body, balled one of the arms and wedged it into the toothy hole. Then he started bailing water with his two hands cupped together.

He spent over an hour doing this, tossing the ocean water over the side of the boat, handful after handful, the inside water level falling at a painfully slow pace, and he tried to keep himself from thinking too far ahead.

Twice he stopped when he saw a bright light streaking across the dark sky. Looked like shooting stars, but they had to be flares. This gave him hope. Someone else had to be out there. He stopped bailing and fired a flare of his own in response and crouched there watching the sky.

He waited several minutes hoping he'd see something else, but he didn't, so he went back to work.

When he grew too tired to lift his arms he sat back to catch his breath and rest his aching ribs. But just sitting there was even worse. It allowed too much time to think about how dire his situation was. Stranded in the middle of an ocean without food or water or any sense of direction—in a boat full of dead people.

Panic rose in his throat and started to settle in his chest, making it hard to breathe. He pulled at his own hair for a few seconds, freaking out; then he closed his eyes and sucked in breath after breath until he calmed down and could resume bailing water.

It wasn't long before Shy grew exhausted.

He put on the slicker to protect himself from the wind and sank down into the water in the boat, which was slightly warmer than the air. He shivered and stared at the bodies. Two older men, one with glasses and a cast on his right arm. A youngish blond woman who might have been pretty before her head injuries. Two older ladies, the one closest to him with a hideous gash across the side of her face.

He thought about dumping them into the ocean so he didn't have to look at them, and because eventually they'd rot and start to smell, but he thought it might be bad luck. And a part of him still believed he might be rescued by morning. If the bodies were still on the boat they could be given a proper burial.

Outside the boat, the sky was slightly brighter. The sun would soon come up over the ocean. And before that it would come up over California.

How was this possible?

After everything he'd been through?

He tried to imagine his family back home, safe inside the strong hospital walls. But he couldn't picture their faces. Something was wrong with him. He'd swallowed too much salt water or lost oxygen to his brain. Because no matter how hard he concentrated, he couldn't picture the faces of his own mom and sister and nephew. He could only picture Carmen.

He looked back at the cruise ship, all but sunk now. Watched the last bit of the bow plunge beneath the ocean's surface until all that was left was the flicker of a few bright flames coming off the tip. And then only flames. And then nothing.

In its place, the first tiny sliver of morning sun.

Shy held himself as he watched the slow rise of the bright blurry mass, unable to wrap his mind around it. His teeth chattering and every breath killing his chest and his mind stuck on what might've happened to Carmen.

He reached a hand up to rub his tired eyes and found himself wiping away tears.

Day 3

28
The Other Survivors

Something jostled Shy out of his sleep.

He sucked in a deep breath and looked around, imagining the cold hands of a dead person gripping his throat, but the bodies were all facedown in the boat the way he'd left them.

It was light out.

The water level was dramatically higher, too. Up to Shy's chest when he sat up, which gave the impression of drowning. The boat was sinking.

The boat shook, like he'd run into something. A piece of the sunken ship or a person, maybe.

Shy crouched and scanned the glistening ocean, looking for signs of life now that it was daylight. He saw faraway ship pieces. A deflated raft. Empty life jackets.

He knew he'd been sleeping a long time because the sun was directly overhead now and beating down hot. The air warm and dry. The ocean lay mostly flat under the brightest blue sky he'd ever seen, like a postcard.

Then everything came rushing back.

The waves and the ship fires and California and his family. He should be on the Lido Deck now, passing out towels to passengers. Miniature golf clubs. Sneaking peeks at every woman in a bikini, including moms. Waiting for Carmen to cruise by with her coffee so they could talk. But the Lido Deck no longer existed because the entire cruise ship was at the bottom of the Pacific. And he was stranded at sea all alone. No other survivors anywhere.

The lifeboat shook again, more violently this time.

He leaned over the jagged edge, looked directly into the water, and his heart climbed up into his throat.

There were five or six sharks circling beneath his sinking boat. Jaws partly open and full of teeth. Eyes black. He watched, horrified, as one of them broke from the pack, rose up and banged its snout into the bottom of his boat, knocking him on his ass.

"What the hell!" he shouted, angrily pushing himself off one of the corpses and sloshing through the water to pick up the raft oar. Now he was pissed. On top of everything else he had to deal with this? He stood and started beating at the ocean and screaming down the sharks: "Get your asses away from here!"

They dispersed for a few seconds, then re-formed their pack and continued circling.

Shy pulled the oar into the boat and sat in the water trapped inside. He rocked himself back and forth trying to catch his breath and trying to think, his heart pounding against the inside of his chest as he looked around.

The sweatshirt had come out of the gash in the boat, which was why it had taken on so much water. If he didn't figure out a way to fix it, he'd sink, and if he sank . . . He remembered his grandma's warning in the library: *I have pictures of their teeth, though,* mijo. *They have rows and rows.*

Shy wadded up the arm of the sweatshirt a second time, shoved it back into the hole. Then he moved through the bodies and dug back through the supplies.

The boat shook again.

He pulled out the tarp, ripped open the packaging. But he couldn't figure out how to secure it over the hole, so he tossed it aside, grabbed the fiberglass patch kit. He had to bail out enough water so that the hole was no longer submerged and it had a chance to dry. Only then could he try patching it.

More scooping, two hands at a time, splashing the water overboard as quickly as he could. He did this for what seemed like hours, until his arms and shoulders burned and his back ached. All the while the sharks continued circling the boat. Sometimes knocking against the bottom or lifting their huge, menacing heads out of the water and flashing their teeth.

The sun traveled slowly across the sky and began falling toward the sea. By the time the sky was lit up with colors, the water level inside the boat was down near his ankles.

He kneeled, pulled the sweatshirt arm from the gash. It was no longer underwater, but it was still wet. And all the clothing on the boat was soaked, including his own, so he couldn't dry it. Finally he leaned his face down and blew on the gash, breath after breath, each deep inhale triggering that sharp pain in his ribs.

After several minutes, he felt around the gash with his fingers. It was dry. He opened the kit, positioned the patch over the hole, pasted on a thick coat of resin.

A shark slowly emerged from the water and showed its teeth,

gave a strange sideways glance. Shy leaped to his feet and grabbed the oar. He raised it over his head and came down with as much power as he could muster, cracking the shark in the teeth.

"That's right, shark bitch!" he shouted as it ducked back into the water. "Come back up here if you want some more!"

He stood with the oar poised above his head again, but the sharks all stayed underwater.

Eventually Shy sat against the tallest side of the boat and stared up at the swirling sunset sky, picturing Carmen's face when the ship alarm first started blaring. It killed him, that look.

His stomach was starting to cramp from hunger.

His mind felt cloudy.

The ocean continued whispering to him, the way it had since day one of his first cruise. But he knew he'd never understand.

As the sky grew dim, he moved across the boat and kneeled down to feel around the resin-covered patch. It was completely dry. Strong when he knocked against it with his knuckles. At least the boat wouldn't sink, he told himself. And the sharks had gone away.

Shy's thoughts soon turned to food and water. His stomach grumbled and his mouth was dry as a desert. It seemed unfair to be completely surrounded by water he couldn't drink.

He was staring out over the ocean and rocking himself against his favorite side of the boat when something in the distance caught his eye.

A faraway raft maybe.

With people.

Shy stood and waved his hands. "Over here! Hey!"

He dug into his supplies and fired another flare into the darkening sky, his second. Only four left.

He heard a man's voice in the distance and saw waving.

The oar was back in his hands, but how would he use it? He tried rowing from one side, but it only made the boat turn in a circle. He moved to the very front of the boat, dug the oar into the water on one side and pulled, then quickly switched to the other.

He wasn't able to get much leverage, but to his surprise the boat started inching forward, little by little, in almost a straight line.

A couple of the sharks were back now, swimming out ahead of him.

It took a long time for Shy to get close enough to make out actual people in the dark. He counted seven heads, most kneeling on either side of a raft, paddling toward him by hand, though it wasn't doing much good.

A man he didn't recognize shouted: "Hurry! We don't have much air left!"

"I'm trying!" Shy shouted back.

There were a few sharks circling the raft, too. And the half-deflated sides were dangerously close to the water.

Shy dug harder as he began recognizing some of the faces staring back.

The oilman. Toni from Destiny. Both wild-eyed, on their hands and knees, paddling.

Then Shy saw a second girl, just behind them.

The blonde he'd had to kick off the Honeymoon Deck during the storm. Addison.

29
Blood in the Water

Shy pulled his oar through the ocean, again and again, steering toward their weakening raft. There was less than a basketball court between them now.

He watched one of the sharks suddenly dart toward the raft. It bit into the side near the oilman, who quickly dove backward. Everyone screamed and moved away, holding each other. The shark shook the raft in its teeth, like a dog, then let go and sank slowly back into the water.

Shy couldn't believe how aggressive the sharks were acting. Like they sensed how close they were to getting these people into the water. The raft began sagging on the bitten side, and everyone pulled their hands out of the water and moved toward the middle of the raft.

A second shark broke from the pack, this one smaller and coming from the opposite side. It didn't bite into the side like Shy was expecting, it launched itself entirely out of the water, turning over in midair, and landed on the back end of the raft.

A few passengers were knocked off balance and fell overboard, splashing awkwardly into the ocean. They came up screaming and beating at the water around them, trying to get to Shy's boat. But the sharks quickly pulled them back under, their tails whipping around the churning water.

Shy was horrified.

To get away from the shark on the raft, two others dove into the ocean and swam for Shy's boat. One of them was Toni.

"Stop!" he shouted, watching the sharks pull them under one at a time, their screams piercing as they came up for air and struggled to get away.

Shy saw Addison still sitting near the front end of the failing raft, screaming. And he saw the oilman shoving things into a dry pack and then diving into the water, too.

"Stay on the raft!" Shy shouted.

Toni miraculously reached Shy's boat.

He extended his oar toward her, and she grabbed on. He pulled her in until she was close enough that he could grab her hand and her other arm and he heaved her up and out of the water. But just as he was getting her over the jagged lip of the boat, she screamed in Shy's ear, locked her terrified eyes onto his, then she was ripped from his grasp and pulled back into the water.

"Toni!" Shy shouted, leaning over the side of the boat. He watched her thrash against the shark, trying to fight it off. She broke away somehow and started swimming for the boat, but seconds later she was pulled under again, her screams turning to muffled gurgling and then nothing.

Shy's entire body was shaking uncontrollably.

He'd done nothing to help.

A few more sharks appeared, their fins and tails whipping the water into a boiling mass as they tore at Toni's body.

Shy dug his oar back into the water, moving toward the oilman and Addison, who were the only ones left. The oilman swam right up to the feeding frenzy, pointed a flare gun and fired. The dark water lit up bright orange and the sharks darted away. Toni's mauled body floating up to the surface, unrecognizable, her life jacket ripped to shreds.

The oilman dropped the gun and continued swimming the short distance to the boat. He reached out for Shy's oar and Shy pulled him in, then hoisted him over the side and turned his attention to Addison.

She was still on the mostly deflated raft, frozen in shock and staring down at the water in front of her. He inched the boat toward her, to the point that they were almost touching. A shark popped its head through the surface of the water. Its massive jaw yawning wide, water rushing over the endless teeth, one of its black eyes staring directly at Shy.

He swung his oar as hard as he could, cracked the shark in the side of the head. He raised the oar in the air, ready to strike again as the oilman snatched Addison by the arm and pulled her into the boat. She fell onto one of the dead bodies, quickly pushed herself away, and leaned up against the side, covering her face with her hands and sobbing.

Shy tossed down the oar and went to her. He didn't say anything, though. Nobody did. They only looked at each other and tried to catch their breath, listening to the splashing water and the feasting sharks. The sky entirely dark now, except a few scattered stars and the dull-looking half-moon that hovered in front of their boat.

Shy rubbed his eyes and gritted his teeth, but he couldn't shake it all from his head. Toni getting pulled under and the screaming and the blood.

The oilman reached into the dry pack beside him, pulled out a gallon of water. He unscrewed the cap and handed it to Addison, who was shaking so violently she could hardly lift it to her mouth. The oilman had to help her.

Then it was Shy's turn, and when the water hit his tongue his entire body came alive. He could've kept drinking for hours, but they had to conserve. Who knew how long the jug would have to last. He passed it back to the oilman, who took a sip of his own.

The oilman was holding a hand to his thigh, but even in the dark Shy could see the blood seeping through his fingers.

The man set down the bottle and looked up at Addison and Shy. He lifted his hand from his leg, and Shy cringed. The giant rip in his jeans exposed a grotesque wound. All the way to the bone. Blood pumped out rhythmically, soaking his pant leg, streaming into the water around his shoe.

The oilman put his hand back over the wound and told them: "I believe I've been bit."

30
Mr. Henry's Answer

Shy sat across the boat from Addison, listening to the oilman's whimpering and the hum of the nighttime ocean and the sound of tiny swells lapping against the side of the boat.

The man's leg was still bleeding, even though Shy had tied a tourniquet around his upper thigh—several inches above the wound, just like he'd been taught in training. But this wound was unlike anything he'd ever seen. It was jagged and uneven, the muscle chewed up and fully exposed. Shy didn't see how anyone could survive a wound like that.

Addison was in bad shape, too. She didn't appear to be hurt physically, but she wouldn't speak, even when Shy asked her direct questions about how they'd gotten on the raft and what had happened to their lifeboat. She just sat there against the side of the boat, shivering, eyelids drooping.

When she finally fell asleep, Shy covered her with the rain slicker. She'd been a bitch to him on the ship, maybe the hardest he'd had to deal with, but it no longer seemed to matter. He crossed back to the opposite side of the boat and stared out at the sea. He was freezing and hungry, thirstier than he'd ever been in his life. His ribs ached. He was with other people now—living, breathing people—but he still felt totally alone.

He sat there in the dark, his mind returning to the same simple questions. Why was all of this happening? Why'd he end up out here when he should be back home with his family, even if they all died together in the earthquakes? When he was a little kid his grandma had taught him to believe there was meaning in everything, even how his old man treated him. But now Shy understood there was nothing.

He cracked open his eyes a few hours later.

Still night.

Addison was passed out in the same position. The oilman was awake, though. He seemed to be over his shock. He cringed and held his leg in pain, but he appeared more aware of his surroundings. Shy went to him, picked up the jug of water and urged him to drink.

"Don't know why you'd waste it on me," the man said, waving the water away.

Shy took a baby sip himself and said: "It's not just you. We all need water."

"You know I won't survive," the man said, pointing to his mangled leg.

It was true, the guy looked worse than before. His eyes sagged and his shoulders slumped, his pant leg was caked with blood below the tourniquet.

"I don't wanna be here anyway," the man said. "Not without Angela."

"She's the one you were gonna give the ring to?" Shy asked.

The man nodded.

Shy figured he should keep the man talking or something, to take his mind off the pain. But he didn't know what to say. He tried pushing the water again instead, and this time the man took a small sip. When he handed back the bottle, Shy capped it and said: "I never got your name."

"William," the oilman said. "William Henry."

"I'm Shy." Shy reached out and shook the man's hand. He seemed so much different than he had on the ship. More humble. Maybe that's what a nasty shark bite did, Shy thought. It stripped away all the arrogant thoughts people had about themselves. "I wanted to tell you, Mr. Henry," he said. "Everything that happened with the ship was seriously messed up. Obviously. But, I don't know, it doesn't seem fair you never even got to ask her to marry you."

Mr. Henry forced a grin and shook his head. "I knew her answer, though."

Shy frowned. "Why do you say that?"

"Before dinner I told Angela to wear her pearls to the restaurant." The man winced and looked down at his leg, touched gently around the wound.

"I don't get it," Shy said.

"Most women get caught off guard when they're proposed to," Mr. Henry said. He coughed into a fist. "They look back after the fact and wish they were wearing a different dress. Or they wish they'd been wearing makeup. Silly things. We joked about this a few times. So when I told her to wear the pearls, she understood what it meant."

"She knew you had a ring and everything?"

The man shrugged. "But I saw the look in her eyes when I left her cabin that afternoon. She wasn't ever coming to dinner."

Shy had no idea how to respond to this, so he told the man: "You don't know that. She was probably just doing her makeup, like you said."

Mr. Henry shook his head. "I know."

Shy watched him lean his head back against the side and close his eyes, his fingers still touching around his wound. It didn't seem fair that a guy who got stood up would also get bitten by a shark. But then nothing about the last few days was fair.

Day 4

31

Lost at Sea

By morning Shy's stomach was cramping, and he felt weak. He was so cold he couldn't stop shivering, but he knew by the afternoon the sun would be beating down on them relentlessly. His lips were cracked and swollen from the day before, his face so sunburned it felt tight and stung in the salty air. Tiny sores had started popping up on his arms and legs and feet, and his skin was covered in a strange film.

For the first few hours of the day, the oilman slept and Addison shivered in her corner and remained silent. Shy tried to think of a plan. They couldn't just sit here and do nothing. The movement of the sun told him which direction was east, but what was he going to do, row them all the way back to California? It would probably take a damn year with his one stupid oar. He'd start them toward the islands everyone kept talking about, but he had no idea which direction they were.

When he grew overwhelmed by the hopelessness of their situation, he started watching Addison, remembering how weird she'd acted on the Honeymoon Deck during the storm.

A few hours later, Addison leaned over the side of the boat and said: "God, why won't they leave us alone?"

These were the first words she'd spoken on the lifeboat. Shy knew she was talking about the two sharks still hovering around the boat, but he took it as an opening to bring up what was on his mind. "Why'd your old man have a picture of me?"

Addison turned and looked at him.

" 'Cause that's what you said, right? When you were out there in the storm with your binoculars."

No answer.

Shy shook his head. "You wanted to know who I am—shit, who are *you*? And who's your dad?"

Addison's face crinkled up and she covered her face with her hands and started crying.

Seeing this made Shy lose his edge. He always caved when he saw a girl cry. "It's just a question," he told her, softening his tone. "Seems messed up to tell me your old man has a picture of me and then—"

"Are you fucking kidding me!" Addison shouted at him through her sobs. "I just watched my best friend die! Do you have any idea what that's like?"

Shy startled. He hadn't expected her to get all psychotic on him.

"And I don't know where my dad is!" Addison screamed. "He could be dead, too! And you want to talk to me about your stupid picture?"

"Jesus, calm down," Shy said, rubbing his sore ribs. "All I did was ask a simple question, damn."

Addison buried her face in her hands again and sobbed so loud Shy felt like an asshole. Maybe that's exactly what he was. Maybe he shouldn't have brought it up out here because nothing from the real world mattered anymore.

"Give it time," Mr. Henry said.

Shy turned to look at the oilman, who was staring back at Shy.

"I don't know what you all are talking about," he said, "but whatever it is, just give it some time."

Shy hung his head and inspected the sores on his bare foot, mumbling to himself: "Man, none of us *have* any time."

They all hid from the sun once it was directly overhead. Addison sat underneath Shy's slicker. Mr. Henry was covered by the tarp. Shy had taken off his life jacket and draped his shirt over his head and shoulders. He'd had enough of just sitting around and waiting, though. He needed to do something. Now.

He stood up and announced: "We need food and water. And we need to get to those islands."

Addison and Mr. Henry watched him pull the fishing kit out of the supply cabinet. He had no idea how they were going to get water—there wasn't a cloud in the sky, so rain definitely wasn't in the forecast—but he could at least try and catch a damn fish.

"That's real smart," Addison said sarcastically.

"What?" Shy said, turning to face her.

"Not wearing a life jacket." Addison looked away, shaking her head at him in disgust.

Shy stood there, staring. "What are you trying to say? You care if I drown?"

"No," Addison scoffed. "Do whatever you want. All I'm saying is it's stupid. Which isn't a big surprise, I guess."

Shy had no idea how to deal with a girl like this. In the normal world he'd probably flip her off and walk away. He'd never even *try* to interact with some spoiled-ass blond chick. He didn't want to get into another fight, though, so all he could think to do was shrug and turn his attention back to the fishing gear.

"What islands are you talking about?" Mr. Henry asked from under his tarp.

It was good to hear the oilman's voice. Anytime he went quiet for a long stretch, Shy was afraid he'd find the guy dead. "Ask her," Shy answered, motioning toward Addison. "It's her old man who supposedly works there."

"That's right, my *dad* does," she said. "Not me. I've never even been there."

"What's he do, anyways?" Shy said. "What kind of job is way out here in the middle of the ocean?"

"I'm his daughter, God," Addison said, "not his business consultant."

"Hold up," Shy said, unable to help himself, "you don't even know what your own dad does for work?"

"You probably don't even have a dad," Addison fired back. "Doesn't everyone like you grow up with a single mom?"

Shy just stared at her, amazed at what a bitch she was.

"What?" she said.

He shook his head, told her: "Nah, that shit's too ignorant to even comment on." He turned away from her all pissed off now, and broke open the pack of fishing lines and bait. He couldn't believe he was stranded out here with a damn racist.

It was quiet on the boat for a few minutes, then Addison cleared her throat and said: "I didn't mean it like that."

Shy ignored her.

Guys where she was from probably put up with her bitchy attitude because she looked good. But Shy wasn't playing that game. Anyway, she wasn't even that hot right now. She was as disheveled-looking as anyone would be who survived a sinking ship and got stuck on a broke-ass boat.

"Fine," Addison said. "Don't accept my apology. Like I give a shit."

Shy just shook his head as he put his life jacket back on. The girl had some serious emotional problems.

It didn't take him long to bait the line and cast it over the side of the boat. There was a school of colorful fish nearby. He tried to will them to his hook, but they didn't even seem to notice. So he sat there, waiting, thinking about Carmen and how much cooler she was than other girls. Especially *this* girl. And then he started thinking about back home.

Occasionally, he would reel in his line and recast it. Hoping it would do something. But it never did.

Shy stared into the water for what seemed like hours, watching fish swim right past his hook, trying to figure out what he was doing wrong. Maybe it was the fake bait he'd found in the supply cabinet. Or maybe he was fishing too shallow. Or maybe the sharks in the area had scared all the fish away or the ones who stayed were too nervous to eat.

At one point he overheard Addison saying something to the oil-man about a rescue boat finding them. Or a rescue plane. But Shy no longer held out hope for a rescue anything. Every emergency team that existed would be focused on the earthquake victims. Their tiny lifeboat, drifting in the middle of the Pacific, wasn't even on the radar.

An orange and white fish swam near his hook to investigate. It was thin and no bigger than the palm of his hand, but he begged it to bite. "Come on, you little bastard," he told it. "Swallow that hook for me. You know it looks delicious as shit."

But the fish turned and swam away.

Shy dropped his head in disappointment.

He could sense Addison behind him, judging his failure.

32
Eight Days

By late afternoon Shy felt amazingly weak. His muscles were cramping from hunger and dehydration. He stood at the front of the boat with the fishing line anyway, waiting for something to bite.

To take his mind off his discomfort, he started picturing random things from back home. The taquerias and liquor stores that lined his street. Neddie's Laundromat, where they took their dirty clothes on Sundays. The cracked pavement of his apartment complex parking lot, where he did all his ball-handling drills. His mom walking into the apartment from work, hanging her keys on the hook by the door and sorting through the mail.

He replayed the last time all four of them were together. Sitting at the kitchen table eating sweet bread from the corner bodega. Drinking orange juice. It was the morning before this second voyage, and they were mostly quiet because they still didn't know how to act after the death of his grandma.

Before Shy left, he turned to everyone, duffel bag slung over his right shoulder. "Guess I'll get back with you guys in eight days." He hugged his mom and sis, then held a fist out to Miguel, who gave it a little-kid bump. Then Shy was out the door, rumbling down the steps, climbing into the idling cab that would take him to the bus station.

Eight days.

Shy pulled his line back into the boat and stood there looking over the massive ocean and thinking about that. The sun burning his face. Empty stomach twisted in knots.

All these things from back home.

His life.

Gone.

It was the first time he'd actually thought about what he'd lost in a conscious way.

He glanced back at Addison and the oilman. Both watching him. Then he returned to the ocean, which stretched out beyond all comprehension. In every direction. The three of them in this tiny boat with no food and barely any water, crawling slowly toward their deaths.

A while later Shy heard Addison sloshing her way over to him. "They smell really bad," she said, pointing at the bloated bodies lying in the boat.

Shy nodded. At least they agreed on one thing. "Definitely getting a little ripe in here," he said.

"Well?" she said, her tone changing. "Can't you do something about it?"

Shy looked at Addison, and then he looked at the bodies. They'd always been a symbol of his hope of being rescued. If he kept them in the boat, the boat was more likely to be found. That's what was in the back of his head. And the rescue team would commend him for hanging on to the bodies so the families could take them back home and bury them. Shy realized something about himself right then. It was one thing to decide he'd given up hope. It was another to kill the symbol of it.

He went over to the first body and held his hand over it, cringing at the smell. He didn't want to even touch it. But he had to. He forced himself to lift the slimy, awful-smelling corpse into a sitting position and he looked at it. Bloated features stuck on a strangely crooked face.

He glanced back at Addison, who turned her head as if she couldn't watch. The oilman, too.

Shy looked back at the woman. "Sorry about this," he said under his breath. Then he turned his head to take a deep breath and held it as he strained to lift the heavy body up and over the side of the boat. He watched it splash into the ocean and slowly drift off in the life jacket as he stood wiping his hands on his pants.

He took the life jackets off the rest of the bodies before dumping them into the water, too.

When he was done he moved back over to Addison, saying: "Happy now?"

"At least we won't die of that smell," she said.

He picked up his fishing line and cast it back into the sea.

"Okay," she said, "now we have to get to those islands."

Shy turned to look at her, keeping his line in the water. "Too bad we have no clue which way to go."

She looked all around the ocean with a concentrated look on her face. "What if we just picked a direction? At least that way we'd be *trying*."

Her tone was super condescending, like she was blaming Shy for them being stranded. "Fine," he said. "Point which way, and I'll get us going."

"Why me?"

"Because it's your idea," he said.

She gave him an exaggerated frown. "Don't they train you people for this kind of thing?"

"What, sailing to some island nobody's ever heard of in a broke-ass boat?" Shy pointed near his feet. "With only one oar?"

"You don't have to be an asshole about it."

"Look, Addison," Shy said, not wanting to spend the last of his energy arguing. "I'm sorry about your friend, okay? And your dad. It sucks. But I lost people, too."

She looked down at her feet. It seemed like she was going to get upset again, so Shy said: "For real, though. Pick a direction and we'll give it a shot. Like you said, it's better than just sitting around doing nothing."

Addison turned to Mr. Henry and said: "Do you have an opinion about this?"

The man shook his head without looking up. Shy could tell he was coming to the end, and he wished he could do something. Give him painkillers, at least, to ease his suffering. But they had nothing.

"What about you?" Addison asked Shy.

He turned to the ocean. The tide seemed to be moving in one specific direction. Maybe it was being drawn toward one of the islands—though it could just as easily be the opposite. Shy shrugged and mentioned it anyway. "I guess we could go with the tide. We'll move faster that way."

"Okay," she said, looking up at him. "That makes sense."

Shy showed Addison how to bait the hook and cast the line, then he sloshed his way to the front of the boat with his oar and dug back into the water.

"It's Addie, by the way," she called to him from the side of the boat.

He turned to look at her, confused.

"My name," she said. "Only old people call me Addison."

Shy nodded. "Addie. Okay."

He went back to working his oar through the water, wondering if they were being nice to each other now.

33
Otay Mesa Cemetery

When the sun started setting, Addie came to Shy and suggested they trade for a while. He happily agreed and handed her the oar, then stood back to watch. It took her a while to get the hang of it, but once she did, she got them going pretty good. He was surprised a skinny, private-school racist had the strength to pull it off.

She turned around, half smiling, and said: "Is this right?"

"Damn, Addie," he told her, "you're not as useless as I thought."

She flipped him off, and he turned his attention back to fishing. But all he did was fail about a hundred different ways. He tried double-baiting the hook, tried tossing it as far from the boat as he could, tried dropping in two lines at once. Nothing worked. The closest he got was when a small, round fish nosed the bait, then darted away.

When it grew dark and a small shark started passing back and forth underneath his bait, Shy gave up and pulled his line back in and looked around. The night was brighter than usual under a mostly full moon. But there was still nothing to eat and no rain and no land in sight.

Shy sloshed his way over to Mr. Henry, who'd been silent for a while, no longer even whimpering in pain. His pant leg was torn wide open now. Shy pulled the man's hand from his leg to see how much worse it looked. Pus and blood oozed out of the gruesome wound. The skin around it had turned a purplish-red, and dark streaks ran up and down his leg. When the smell of it hit Shy, he turned away and went to get the jug of water. He held it out to Mr. Henry and said: "Drink some."

The man shook his head and closed his eyes.

"I'm serious," Shy said. "You need water."

No response.

Shy knew the oilman wouldn't last much longer, and they had less than a third of a gallon left. If he didn't force it, he and Addie would be able to stretch it that much further.

He turned and watched Addie working the oar. It had been over an hour, easy, and she still hadn't even taken a break. He was shocked. There was no way she'd ever done this kind of work before, yet she kept on rowing like it was her job.

He turned back to Mr. Henry and shook him by the shoulder. When the man opened his eyes, Shy told him: "You know I'm gonna keep bugging you till you drink some, right?"

The man reached out and took the jug, poured two small sips into his mouth and cringed as he swallowed. He wiped his chin on his shoulder and handed back the jug.

Shy patted the man on the back, wishing he could do more; then he sloshed his way over to Addie and made her drink some, too. "You're still not tired?" he asked.

"Of course I'm tired," she said, handing back the water jug. "I'm exhausted. This sucks."

Shy took a sip, re-capped the jug and then held it up to see how little was left. It was like sand in an hourglass, telling him: *Here's how much time you have left to live.*

"Look," Addie said, letting out a big breath, "I'll tell you what I know about the Hidden Islands, okay?"

"Yeah," Shy said, taken off guard. He was surprised she was offering information without even being asked.

"It isn't much, but whatever." She looked out over the ocean. "So, according to my dad, they used to be a cluster of four, but three are now underwater. Only Jones Island is still inhabitable, which is where he works." She shrugged. "Oh, and it's a private island, so you can't just go on vacation there. You have to be invited."

"You've never been there, though?" Shy asked.

"Are you kidding? My dad take me to his secretive, private work island?" She rolled her eyes.

"What's so secret about it?" Shy asked.

Addie grinned and shook her head. "I'm not sure how it looked back on the ship," she told him, "but I barely even know my dad. All he cares about is working and amassing his fortune."

"At least he took you on a cruise."

She rolled her eyes. "Oh yeah. The big father-daughter bonding trip. My dad's attempt at"—she did air quotes—"being more present in my life. I only agreed to go because he said I could bring Cassie."

Shy nodded. Even though the real world barely mattered right now, he wanted to know more about her dad, especially knowing he had a picture of Shy. "So, why'd he leave if you guys were supposed to be bonding?"

"You just have all the good questions, don't you?"

Shy shrugged.

"He told me he needed to check on some new research they were doing. But he was going to meet us in Hawaii." Addie's face grew serious, like she was thinking about what might have happened to him when the waves hit. She tapped the oar against the bottom of the boat a few times and added: "I guess his company has some arrangement with you guys. They let him get picked up by a private boat."

She looked like she was getting upset again, so Shy decided to ease up a little. "Anyways," he told her, "lemme take over for—"

"They make equipment for hospitals," Addie interrupted. She handed him the oar and stretched out her arms. "And some pharmaceutical stuff. See? I actually *do* know what my dad does for a living."

Shy didn't understand why a company that made hospital equipment needed to be on a remote island. Seemed kind of sketchy.

"For a while," Addie continued, "I honestly thought he wanted us to go on a vacation together. I mean, he usually takes a private jet to the island, straight from the Santa Monica Airport, which is close to our house. But that last night on the ship, Cassie and I overheard something we weren't supposed to."

"What?" Shy asked, more curious now. He sensed that she was moving toward something important.

"I guess like a week ago," she said, "someone from his company committed suicide on the ship."

Shy froze. The comb-over man worked for the same company as her dad?

"I'm pretty sure my dad's real motivation for being on the ship had nothing to do with me. I think he wanted to find out what happened for himself." Addie looked Shy right in the eyes. "So, were you working that trip? It was going to Mexico."

Shy pushed off the side of the boat, said: "Hell yeah, I was working. I'm the one who saw the guy jump."

"Wait, really?" Addie said, but she didn't look that surprised. He wondered how much she already knew.

"I grabbed him before he fell," Shy told her. "He died because I wasn't strong enough to hang on to him. Your old man tell you that, too?"

"He didn't tell me anything," Addie said. "I swear. We only found out about the suicide because we overheard one of my dad's security people questioning the maitre d'. And me and Cassie started talking after we saw you outside the gym. I mean, it seemed really random for him to just invite you to dinner like that."

"Yeah, what was *that* about?"

Addie shrugged. "It's one of the reasons we decided to do a little snooping."

Right then everything came together for Shy. "Do you know a guy named Bill?" he asked her out of the blue.

"I know a lot of guys named Bill."

"On the ship, I mean. Curly black hair. Always wears a black suit." Earlier Shy was unable to picture his own mom's face, but the suit guy was burned into his memory. "He had a mole on his nose."

"Oh yeah," Addie said. "That's one of my dad's security people. I didn't know his name was Bill, though. Why?"

"He asked me all kinds of questions about the suicide. Right after you and your friend left the Honeymoon Deck."

"I'm not surprised," she said.

"You're not?"

"They seemed really paranoid about what happened. The guy who jumped was named David Williamson—"

"Yeah, exactly," Shy interrupted. "He told me right before he jumped."

"He was one of the top guys in the company."

Shy thought back to his brief conversation with the comb-over man, or David Williamson. At the time he thought it was just some drunk rich guy rambling. Little did he know he'd be analyzing every word a week later while stranded at sea.

"Know what's strange?" Addie said. "He used to come over for dinner when I was little. He and my dad were friends." She shook her head. "I remember he seemed so normal. Don't you have to be a little unbalanced to jump off a ship?"

"He was definitely unbalanced when I talked to him on the Honeymoon Deck. He kept saying all this crazy shit about corruption and how he was hiding from people." It occurred to Shy that this was the most he'd ever shared about that conversation to anyone. Including his own family.

"I wonder what happened to him," Addie said.

"I wonder why your old man was so paranoid about it." Shy looked up at the moon, amazed at how everything now seemed to connect. The suit guy stalking him and his room being trashed and Addie's dad asking him to dinner—all of it went back to the suicide on his first voyage. And now him and this girl in the boat. "Hey, Addie," he said, wiping a hand down his face, "I still need to ask you about—"

"The picture my dad had," she said, finishing his sentence. "Right?"

"Uh, yeah, actually."

Addie reached into her jeans pocket, pulled out a folded photo and held it out to Shy. "You mean this one?"

Shy took it from her and unfolded it, stunned. The picture was wet and creased, but he could clearly see himself sitting alone beside his grandma's grave back in Otay Mesa.

"I took it from my dad's room," she said. "Never got a chance to put it back."

"How'd you get it?" Shy said, looking up at her.

"He left a key to his cabin with us," Addie said. "So we could have two showers. When they made us all leave the dining room early because of the storm, me and Cassie ditched my dad's security people and snuck into his cabin to look around." She pointed at the picture in his hand. "We found it just lying on top of his safe. You can understand why I was so weirded out when I saw you during the storm, right?"

Shy looked down at the picture again and the memory of that moment came flooding back. It was the night before this second voyage. He'd ridden his bike across town and through the cemetery gates to lean a sunflower against his grandma's small headstone. Her favorite flower. Then he'd just sat there, thinking about the last few hours of her battle with Romero Disease, and about his family's future. Not only had a great person been stolen from their lives, his grandma also paid half the bills. He had no idea how they were going to make it without her.

It made Shy sick knowing there was someone watching him that night, spying on his mourning.

He looked up at Addie, remembering what Supervisor Franco had said just before Shy went out into the storm to help clear the Lido Deck. "Does your dad by any chance work for a company called LasoTech?"

"Does my dad work for LasoTech?" she said, repeating the question. She scoffed a little. "More like my dad *owns* LasoTech."

34

Mr. Henry's Strange Request

They talked a while longer—about the company and what they were hoping to find out about Shy's conversation with the guy who jumped off the boat, David Williamson, and why everyone seemed so concerned about a guy who was already dead—and then Addie said if she didn't sit down she was going to pass out standing up.

"Go rest," he said. "We can talk more about it tomorrow."

She nodded. "Time to go freeze my ass off," she told him as she started over to her side of the boat. After she sat down she called to him: "Hey, Shy."

"Yeah?"

"I'm really sorry you got mixed up in all this."

She seemed like she genuinely meant it. "Same with you," he told her.

Shy moved over to Mr. Henry, who was sound asleep. He put his hand under his nose to make sure he was still breathing, then went to his own spot against the side of the boat. He sat down in the ankle-high water, leaned his head back and thought some more about everything he and Addie had just talked about.

Shy was so cold and hungry he had trouble falling asleep. He stared up into the star-filled night, letting his mind go wherever it wanted.

He pictured the man in the black suit cornering him in the Luxury Lounge. Pointing as Shy made his escape down the stairs. He pictured the look on Addie's dad's face when he stepped up to Shy's pool stand, offered to toss the foul-mouthed Muppet kid off the ship. Maybe that was some kind of vague reference to the comb-over man's suicide. Maybe he thought Shy was to blame. He pictured his grandma opening her scrapbook in the hall, pointing to the article about sharks. Then Shy found himself picturing something else, the sliver of Carmen undressing he'd seen through her bathroom door.

Shy closed his eyes so he could focus on that last image. He liked thinking about all Carmen-related things, including stuff that had nothing to do with her beautiful naked body. But right now, as he sat shivering against the side of the boat, all he wanted to do was think about her curves and her skin and the tattooed words below her belly button. It probably said something deep, he decided. A quote from some philosopher or a saying that he'd understand on the exact same level.

He missed how it felt to be around her. How his stomach would get butterflies when she even walked into a room. He wondered if she was on another boat right now, in some other part of the ocean, slowly dying by herself, the same as he was. And what if she had her eyes closed, too, and she was thinking about him? Could they be together in their thoughts even when their bodies were apart? He held himself for warmth and drifted off wondering about that.

Carmen showed up in Shy's dream, too.

She was walking up to his towel stand. Smiling. "Come with me," she said.

"Now?" he asked. "I can't just leave work."

"What are you talking about, Shy? It's your dream, isn't it? People can do anything they want inside their own dreams."

The sky suddenly shifted from morning to night. Supervisor Franco was there now, too. He was telling Shy his shift was over, to take a break, go get himself some dinner.

That was when Shy understood. He was somewhere between consciousness and sleep, where you can partly steer the story of your dreams.

He followed Carmen down the stairs, into the Southside Lounge. The butterflies in his stomach flapping like crazy. Because maybe she was bringing him here to confess her love. To explain how she was leaving her lawyer. The guy didn't understand her. Not the way Shy did. She'd finally realized how empty it was being with someone who never asked how she felt about things, who would never understand how bad it hurt to lose someone to Romero Disease.

But as they sat down at a table, he knew the look on Carmen's face wasn't the love-professing kind.

"I've been doing some thinking," she said. "About me and you, Shy."

"Me too," he said, though it was obvious their thinking wasn't the same.

"I believe the reason it's so complicated between us is 'cause I'm the only one in a relationship. If we were both committed to other people, we could be way closer as friends. Don't you think?"

The butterflies in his stomach stopped flapping.

They keeled over and died.

"Look," Carmen said, "you know I care about you, right?"

"I guess so."

"Well," she said, "over the past couple days I've gotten to know someone a little better. And I think she'd be perfect for you."

"A girl?"

"Yes, Shy. A girl." Carmen turned around and called out: "You can come join us now, Addie."

Shy looked up, shocked to see Addie approaching their table. She sat down, smiling, and gave him a little wave.

"You don't even like her," Shy said to Carmen.

"That's not true," she said. "Once you get past that bitchy front she puts up, and you ignore all her snobby tendencies, you'll discover that Addie's a pretty decent girl." Carmen then turned to Addie, said: "And I'm gonna be honest about Shy, too. He can be a little selfish and girl crazy. And he's into corny shit like handholding tests. But he means well."

"Corny can be cute," Addie said.

"Mmm, in Shy's case it's really not," Carmen said. "Trust me. But it's better than him being an asshole, right?"

Shy was starting to get frustrated. This was *his* dream. Why was he letting other people tell him what to do?

"Look at you two," Carmen said. "You're both shivering. You need each other right now."

Shy looked down at his own arms. Carmen was right. His teeth were even chattering. It was the same for Addie.

"So, what do you guys think?" Carmen said. "Are you brave enough to give it a try?"

Shy rubbed the hell out of his eyes, trying to wake himself up. When he dropped his hands, he found himself sitting across the table from Mr. Henry, who was turning on a power hacksaw. Carmen and Addie had vanished.

"Hold up, man!" Shy shouted over the roar of the saw. "What're you doing with that thing? And where'd the girls go?"

The oilman ignored his question and started lowering the blade toward his wounded leg, shouting: "I won't be needing this anymore!"

Blood sprayed everywhere. "Jesus, man!" Shy shouted, shielding his face with his hands, cringing at the awful sound.

After a few seconds the oilman turned off the saw and set it on the table, then he tore off the rest of his leg. "It was just getting in the way," he said, tossing it onto the floor of the Southside Lounge, where it made a surprising splashing sound.

Mr. Henry hopped around to Shy's side of the table and sat down, saying: "I came over here to thank you."

"To thank me?" Shy said. "For what?" His dream was so confusing now he just wanted it to be over. He clenched his eyes closed and rubbed them with his fists again, harder this time. Then he opened them as wide as he could, demanding himself to wake up.

It was still him and the oilman, but they were no longer in the Southside Lounge. They were inside the broken boat, leaning against the side next to each other. Addie across from them, asleep.

"For listening," the oilman said. "I needed to admit to someone that Angela didn't want me. It's like a weight has been lifted."

Shy's mind was foggy and slow, but he knew he was no longer dreaming. This was real. He could tell because the oilman's leg was back on his body, giving off a foul odor.

"You know, I've always had a certain belief about women," Mr. Henry continued, his face filled with pain. "They love to own expensive jewelry. But now I'm starting to believe there's a second part to that. Something I'd never thought about until I got out here on this boat. Women love expensive jewelry even more when it comes from the right person."

Shy watched Mr. Henry stare out at the dark ocean, wondering why he was talking about jewelry when he was in such bad shape. Sweat streamed down the guy's forehead. His teeth were clenched in pain. Shy would be focusing all his attention on staying alive.

"It hurts me to admit this," Mr. Henry said, turning back to Shy, "but even though I can afford any piece of jewelry, from any store, I've never been the right person to give it."

Shy opened his mouth to argue, but Mr. Henry raised a hand and said: "Now I have an odd sort of request."

Shy closed his mouth and listened.

"I'd like to hug you, Shy."

"Hug me?" This was the last thing Shy expected. "What are you even talking about?"

"I'm coming to the end of the line."

Shy was shaking his head now, saying: "Look, man, I'm sorry about everything that's happened. But I'm not trying to hug somebody out here—"

The oilman was already leaning over and wrapping his arms around Shy's shoulders. "I don't mean anything strange by this," he mumbled in Shy's ear. "It's just a hug. Nothing more."

"Get off me," Shy said, trying to push away. But he felt so weak. And Mr. Henry had a tight hold around his back. And it wasn't like the guy was trying to molest him. He was just doing a stupid hug, like Rodney might. And Shy felt so bad for the man.

The whole thing lasted maybe eight seconds. Then the oilman let go and pushed away from Shy. "Be the right person," he said. "Gifts are more meaningful when they come from the right person."

Mr. Henry scooted his way back across the busted-up boat and leaned against his part of the jagged side, massaging his mangled leg.

Shy rubbed his eyes again, trying to make sense of what had just happened. But he was too cold and hungry to think straight.

He sat there for a long while before he realized something

important. He was going to die, too. Sure, he'd last longer than Mr. Henry, but how *much* longer? Would he and Addie survive long enough to find the islands? To be rescued? Would they live long enough to see home again? And what if they no longer had a home to go to? What then?

He glanced across the boat at Addie. Her arms wrapped around her legs, eyes closed. Her whole body shivering in the cold. The oilman's eyes were closed now, too.

Shy was alone.

He stared up at the glowing moon again, and he listened to the whispering ocean. His thoughts were more staticky than before, but for the first time since the summer started, he felt like he understood the ocean's whispering. It all came down to this. The darkness. The loneliness. The mystery. The fact that everyone's days were numbered, and it didn't matter if you were in premier class or worked in housekeeping. Those were only costumes people wore. And once you stripped them away you saw the truth. This giant ocean and this dark pressing sky. We only have a few minutes, but the unexplainable world is constant and forever marching forward.

Shy felt nauseous from the realization, like he'd been shown something humans weren't equipped to see.

He pushed off the side and quietly moved across the boat to Addie and sat down next to her, slid his arm around her shoulders so they could share body heat.

She opened her eyes and looked at him.

Her chest moving in and out with each breath. But she didn't say anything. Neither did he. And eventually she leaned her head against his shoulder and closed her eyes and fell back to sleep.

Day 5

35

Unexpected
Good-Luck Charm

Shy woke up the next morning to the sound of his own chattering teeth, and he was surprised to find himself holding Addie. Her eyes were open, too, and he followed her gaze down the boat to where the oilman slept, except the oilman was no longer there, only his empty life jacket.

"What happened?" Shy said, struggling to his feet.

"I don't know," Addie said. "I woke up, and he was gone."

Shy sloshed through the ankle-high water to the life jacket, picked it up, looked over the side of the boat. No sign of Mr. Henry. He remembered the strange conversation from the night before.

The hug. He must've known all along that he was going to throw himself overboard.

Just like the comb-over man.

When Shy saw how upset Addie was, he dropped the life jacket and made his way back to her, saying: "At least he doesn't have to suffer anymore. You saw how bad it was getting."

"I know," she said, rubbing her temples. "It's not just him, though. It's everything. I want to go home."

"So do I," he said.

As Addie looked up at him, Shy noticed how much thinner she looked than when they'd first met on the Lido Deck. And her hair was a blond, tangled mess. Her face sunburned and peeling. For the first time since the ship went down, Shy wondered what *he* looked like, how much his own appearance had changed.

Tears started spilling out of Addie's eyes and running down her cheeks. She brushed a few off and said: "We're not gonna make it, are we, Shy?"

The look on her face killed him, and he leaned over and patted her shoulder, awkwardly. "Listen . . . ," he said, but then he trailed off. He wanted to say something important, something reassuring, but nothing like that came to him because it wasn't true.

"All I know is this," he finally said. "We're gonna spend the day paddling. Same direction as yesterday. And I'm gonna catch us a damn fish this time. You hear me, Addie? Even if I have to dive my ass in there and choke one out with my bare hands."

He thought she might smile at that last part, but she only nodded and looked to where Mr. Henry used to sit, wiping more tears from her face.

The sun climbed slowly into the cloudless sky, warming the air around them. Shy's hands were blistered, and his back and shoulders ached. He had so little strength now, he could only make the

200

boat creep forward a little at a time with the oar. But he kept working. And he kept thinking about Mr. Henry and Addie's dad, and he kept remembering the man in the black suit, Bill, asking all those questions in the Luxury Lounge and then hurrying away from Carmen's cabin after the ship alarm went off. There was something he wasn't understanding, something bigger than just a man jumping overboard. But his mind was too slow to put it all together.

After a few hours, they switched places. Addie took the oar without a word, and Shy moved to the back of the boat, and when he bent down to rebait the hook, he felt something scratch his upper thigh. He glanced down, expecting to find some kind of ocean bug biting him. Instead he found a small bulge in the pocket of his jeans and reached his fingers in for it. He was shocked at what he pulled out.

The oilman's seven-carat diamond ring.

He stared down at the massive diamond, then glanced at Addie, who was already busy working the oar.

The guy must've slipped the ring into Shy's pocket during that weird hug. It was probably the reason he hugged Shy in the first place. Shy dropped the fishing line and moved toward the edge of the boat. He held the ring over the side, thinking he should drop it in, let it float down after Mr. Henry. He didn't want someone else's ring. Didn't matter how big the diamond was. That kind of shit didn't matter out here. Plus, what if someone discovered them in the boat, long after he and Addie died. They'd probably think he was a thief.

But he couldn't drop it.

Couldn't let go.

"It's been two days," Addie called out, startling Shy so bad he almost dropped the ring by accident. "And we still haven't seen *anything*."

He slipped the ring back in his pocket and turned around, saying: "We will."

"No, we won't," she said, throwing the oar at the floor of the boat. "This is a waste of time. We're probably going the exact opposite way."

Shy scooped up the baited hook and sloshed his way to the front of the boat. "What do you wanna do, Addie? Give up?"

"I want to go home!" she shouted.

"So do I," Shy told her. "What do you think we're trying to do?"

Addie sat down in the boat and covered her face with her hands, but she didn't cry. She just stared at the water inside the boat.

Shy reached down for the jug of water, uncapped it, held it out to her. "Feeling sorry for yourself isn't gonna help you survive."

"You think I don't know that?" she said, snatching the jug out of his hands. "God, you're like the worst person to be stuck with." She took two baby sips of water and handed it to Shy, who did the same. After re-capping it, he held the jug up to see how much was left. About an inch high at the bottom.

Addie was looking at the same thing.

Their eyes met for a second, but she quickly cut away and reached down for the oar, then she stood up and turned away from him and dug back into the ocean.

Shy moved to the opposite end. He cast his line back into the ocean, wondering why he didn't want to tell Addie about the ring.

He'd only been standing there ten minutes, max, when he felt a sudden tug on the line. He grabbed it with both hands and stood up straight to look over the edge of the boat. There it was, deep below the surface, a thin yellow fish caught on his hook, jerking to get away. He got a rush of energy and started pulling in the line, fast as he could.

Shy heard Addie splashing down the boat, toward him. "What is it?" she said.

"Told you I'd catch a fish," he said.

Addie leaned over the side of the boat, said: "Oh my God."

When it was close to the surface, he reached down, pinched the line between his thumb and forefinger, only inches from the fighting fish, yanked it out of the water and flung it into the boat.

He and Addie watched the thing thrash around in the ankle-high water at their feet, still connected to his line.

"You actually did it!" Addie shouted.

"You doubted me, didn't you?" he said.

"Never again," she said, on the verge of laughter. "You're the fish master."

He wanted to tell her it was because of the oilman's ring. It was their new good-luck charm. But on the other hand, maybe it was only good luck if he kept it a secret.

"What do we do now?" she asked.

He looked down at the flopping fish, shaking his head. He hadn't thought it through this far. They couldn't eat the thing when it was still alive. He looked around, then went and got the oar, raised it up over his head, and brought it down on the fish.

It went still.

"Jesus," Shy said, staring at the gash he'd opened up on the thing.

"Here," Addie said, picking up the dry pack Mr. Henry had carried with him from the raft. "Put it on this."

Shy lifted the wet, scaly fish and tossed it on the pack. Wiped his hands on his jeans. They both stared at it.

The fish was a dull yellow and thin, but sort of long. Its eyes were seemingly fixed on Shy.

Addie surprised him when she reached down suddenly, removed the fish from the hook and then used the hook and her bare hands to split it down the middle, blood dripping through her fingers. She held out the bigger half to Shy, who looked at her like she was crazy. "What?" she said.

"I didn't know I was out here with a damn cannibal," he said, looking down at his mangled portion.

"I knew *you* weren't going to do it."

"I was getting around to it," he said.

"Yeah, right." She looked at the half a fish in her hand and said: "We just have to imagine we're eating sushi."

When Shy didn't answer right away, she looked up at him and said: "Oh, my bad. You've probably never had sushi in your life, have you?"

"I've had sushi," Shy lied.

They both cringed as they ate, sometimes pulling bones out of their mouths, chucking them into the ocean. It didn't taste like anything more than warm, fleshy iron, but the thought of it made Shy nauseous. He had to force himself not to throw it right back up. What felt good, though, was having something in his stomach, and soon he was skipping the chewing part and just swallowing his bites whole.

Half the fish worked out to be very little meat, but his stomach had shrunk up so small it was still satisfying.

Addie tossed the scaly skin overboard and rinsed her hands in the water by their feet. Then she looked up at him with a full-on smile—the first he'd seen from her since the ship went down.

He smiled back and picked up the oar. As he started toward the front of the boat to get them going again, he fingered the ring in his pocket, wanting to believe it was good luck for more than just catching fish. Maybe it could keep them alive, too.

36

Face of Corruption

As soon as the sun started dropping below the horizon, Shy and Addie staggered to Addie's section of the boat, completely exhausted, and sat beside each other against the side. It wasn't cold enough to need each other's body heat yet, so Shy didn't put his arm around her.

"Sorry about earlier," Addie said.

Shy frowned like he didn't know what she was talking about.

"My tantrum," she said. "I just—I don't want this to be it. And when I think about it too much I start freaking myself out."

"I'm the same way," Shy said. "I just keep it inside."

She shook her head and stared at the setting sun like she was thinking about something.

They were both quiet for a few minutes, and Addie leaned her head back against the side and closed her eyes. Shy thought they were done talking for the night, but then she bumped his knee with hers and opened her eyes again. "I've been thinking about you and LasoTech, by the way," she said. "It honestly doesn't make sense that they were so concerned about you, not if all you did was see David going overboard."

Now it was Shy's turn to lean the back of his head against the side. "They had to think I did something to him, right? But that Bill guy told me they knew it was a suicide."

"Yeah, that can't be it," Addie said. "I think they wanted to find out how David was acting before he jumped. Or maybe they thought he said something to you. Something that could get them in trouble."

Shy thought about that. He fingered the ring in his pocket, trying to remember the exact conversation he'd had with the comb-over man. Again. The vacation homes. The cofounding of his own business—with Addie's dad, he now knew. Tell me I'm fat.

"Can you think of anything important he might've said?" Addie asked.

"You think I haven't been trying?" Shy asked.

It was bad enough to think about all this stuff on the ship, when he believed he'd be home in eight days and he'd never have to think about it again. But then something occurred to him and he turned to Addie. "This was kind of weird," he said. "At one point he said I was looking at the face of corruption. You think he was talking about the whole company?"

Addie sat up. "Wait, he said that?"

"Yeah," Shy said. "At the time I just figured he was drunk—"

"*Of course* they were asking what he told you, then," she interrupted. "I bet the company's doing something illegal, and they thought David explained the whole thing to you. Like he was trying to clear his conscience before he jumped."

"I see what you're saying," Shy said. "Too bad he didn't explain *anything* to me."

Addie shook her head. "I wonder what they did. What my *dad* did?"

Shy watched the sun as it slowly dropped behind the water to the west of their boat, taking a good amount of light with it. "He also said he was my betrayer," Shy said, turning back to Addie. "Or something like that. Like he'd messed me over personally. Which obviously doesn't make sense because I'd never seen the guy in my life."

Addie stared at Shy for a few long seconds. "Maybe it has something to do with poor people, then."

Shy frowned at her.

"No offense," she told him.

"Yeah, right," he said.

"What if they charge poor people way more than they're supposed to?"

"But if they make hospital supplies," Shy said, "they wouldn't sell shit directly to people—"

"Or, wait," Addie said, "maybe it's some kind of insurance fraud. You can get in really big trouble for that."

Shy didn't know much about insurance fraud, but he was pretty sure Addie thought he was from some homeless family who picked through the trash for their dinner. Whatever. It didn't even matter anymore. "Or maybe your dad's company was just being paranoid," he said.

"God," Addie said, staring at the palms of her hands. "What if my entire life was stolen? My house, my car, my school. Imagine if all of it was paid for with fraud money?"

Shy realized how hard this conversation must be for Addie. She had no idea if her dad was dead or alive, and now they were talking about him possibly being a criminal. He was about to make a comment about that when Addie climbed to her knees suddenly and squinted, like she was looking at something in the distance.

"What is it?" Shy said, pushing up from the side, too.

She pointed directly in front of their boat. "I think I see something."

Shy's whole body started tingling as he scanned the darkening horizon, hoping to find land. What he saw was far away, but it definitely wasn't land. The longer he stared, the clearer it became, the dusky sky maintaining just enough light to see. "Is that a boat?" he said, turning to Addie. "That looks like a boat."

"I think it's a boat," she said, her face now lit up with excitement.

Shy stood and sloshed across the boat to the supply cabinet, where he flung open the door and grabbed the flare gun.

37

The Boat

There were four flares left. Shy loaded the gun and stood up. He knew from training to fire the first one straight into the air, then follow with another, five seconds later, so that any potential rescuers would see where the first flare had come from.

He aimed the gun at the sky and fired.

The flame shot up above them, and Shy turned his attention to the distant boat.

"Over here!" Addie shouted, waving her arms.

Come on, Shy thought as he hurried to load the gun with a second flare. In the distance, however, the boat just floated there.

He aimed the gun above his head and fired a second time. Watched the glowing ball of fire arc across the dim sky, then fall toward the water, where it landed in a soundless splash, maybe twenty yards from them. It fizzled into a tiny puff of smoke that lifted off the water and drifted apart.

Still nothing from the boat.

"Should we go to *them?*" Addie asked.

Shy stared ahead. There was no way they hadn't heard or seen the flares. What were they waiting for? Or was it someone who didn't want to help? He glanced down at the small amount of water they had left. There was no choice. They had to go.

"Hand me the oar," he told Addie.

She reached down next to her feet, held it out to Shy, and he hurried to the front of the boat.

The closer they got, the more it became clear. They were definitely approaching a boat. But it was just sitting there. He ignored the bad feeling in his stomach and kept digging through the water with his oar. Every now and then Addie would call out to the boat, to try and get some kind of response; otherwise they kept quiet as Shy moved them through the calm ocean.

Soon they were right in front of it.

It was a brown motorboat, about twice the size of their lifeboat. The engine turned off. A cabin underneath the surface with tinted windows and "Number 220" written on the side. There was no sign of anyone on board.

"Looks like it's abandoned," Addie said.

Shy called out toward the boat: "Hello? Anyone in there?"

Nothing.

Addie pushed her hair out of her face. "Why would an abandoned boat be way out here?"

"The tsunamis might've torn it away from its dock." Shy pulled the oar from the water and let their momentum carry them toward the motorboat. "Maybe we're closer to land than we realize."

"God," Addie said. "The tsunamis. What if the entire island's underwater?"

"We're not gonna think about that," Shy told her as he reached out for the front end of the motorboat to lessen the impact. Still, the lifeboat crashed into the bow of the thing. Shy grabbed the metal bar extending off the motorboat and called out "Hello?"

Still no answer.

"You coming with me?" Shy asked Addie.

She shook her head. "I'm waiting here."

Shy reached down for the length of rope he'd grabbed out of the supply cabinet and tied the two boats together. Then he stepped onto the jagged side of the lifeboat, balancing carefully, and pulled himself up onto the bigger boat. He walked around the perfectly dry deck, having no idea what to expect. He saw two empty life jackets. A folding chair on its side. He opened the tackle box near the stairs. Instead of fishing gear, a few shattered vials lay in the top tray, which seemed strange. It also smelled a little like smoke.

There was nothing else up there so he climbed down the three steep stairs, his heart pounding now, and peeked his head inside the open door of the cabin where the smoke smell was stronger. "Hello?" he said, but no one answered. It was so dark inside he could hardly see.

He stepped deeper into the cabin, using his hands against the wall to guide him, until the familiar smell of death hit him and he stopped cold. He saw a large shape on the ground and quickly backed out of the cabin.

Shy was ready to head right back up the stairs when he came across a flashlight in a holster on the wall. He grabbed it, powered it on and moved back into the cabin, shining the light on two men in lab coats. The one with red hair was lying on the ground, facedown. The bald one was slumped against the far wall.

Shy covered his nose and mouth with his left hand, seeing the pools of blood coming out from underneath the two men. He stood frozen for several seconds before forcing himself forward to nudge the body on the floor with his bare foot—he didn't know why, it was clear both men were dead.

He shined his light all around the bodies and spotted a gun half covered by an open duffel bag. He kicked it free and stared at it, feeling incredibly on edge. He'd grown accustomed to death on the ship, but this was different. This looked like murder.

He used his foot to turn over the first corpse and saw bullet wounds. The redheaded man had been shot in the chest and the leg and the right arm. There was blood crusted all over his white lab coat. The other man was thinner and older and he had a large gash on the side of his face, like he'd been struck by something. He also appeared to have been shot in the stomach. It was an awful sight of blood and gore, and Shy moved the light away, trying to figure out what the hell had happened.

He kneeled down, shined his light into the bag. A few packs of syringes, like the kind they use for flu shots, and none of them broken. Some kind of code written on each label. Dozens of pill bottles, too. They weren't anything like the illegal drugs he'd seen back home. These were from an actual hospital or a pharmacy—and he recalled Addie saying her dad's company was in the medical field. Which meant they had to be close to the island. Underneath the packs of syringes was a beat-up blank envelope with a few folded papers inside.

He shined the light on the bodies again. The men were dressed like doctors or scientists. But why had they been shot? And who did the shooting? Shy stood up and shined the flashlight around the rest of the cabin. Bullet holes in the walls. Some of the cabin looked charred, like someone had tried to set the boat on fire. But there was no water anywhere. The boat was somehow unaffected by the tsunamis.

Eventually the smell overwhelmed Shy, and he hurried above deck, back to where Addie was waiting for him.

"Anyone in there?" she asked him right away.

"Two guys," he told her. "They're both dead, though."

Her face filled with worry. "How?"

"I think they were shot."

Addie covered her mouth and started breathing more quickly. "Was one of them my dad?" she asked.

"No," Shy told her, shaking his head. "If I can get the motor going, we have to switch boats, okay? It's a little burned up, but it doesn't seem like this thing was affected by the tsunamis."

Addie nodded. "Are you sure my dad's not down there?"

"I promise." Shy glanced back at the motorboat, then told her: "I don't know what the hell happened, though. Who would shoot doctors?"

"They're doctors?"

"I think so," Shy said. "Or scientists. Look, lemme check everything else and I'll come back and transfer us over, okay?"

Once he saw her nod he started toward the bridge, pointing the flashlight out in front of him. He wasn't able to get the motor started, though, because the entire control panel had been shot up. The GPS, too. And there was no more fuel. Where were these guys going with no gas and a bagful of medicine? And who had climbed aboard and gunned them down? And where was that person now? Shy knew ship pirates were a possibility, but he didn't think anyone would be out stealing right after the tsunamis.

There wasn't any food or water in any of the supply cabinets. There wasn't even rope or extra flares.

Shy weighed the options. If they moved to the motorboat they would no longer have to sleep in cold ankle-high water. And the cabin would protect them from the sun during the day. But it was much heavier, and he'd never be able to reach the water from the front end, so using the oar was out of the question. They'd have to stick with their broken lifeboat if they wanted to keep moving.

Before he went to get Addie's opinion, he ducked back into the cabin to look around one last time. He shined his light on the bodies, the charred walls. Then he reached down and grabbed the gun, flipped open the barrel, saw that there were three bullets left. He dropped it in the brown and blue duffel, then slung the duffel over his shoulder and headed back up the stairs.

"Everything's all shot up," he told her. "And there's no gas or supplies. If we transfer to this boat we'll just be sitting here, waiting to be rescued. If we stay on the lifeboat we can keep moving. What do you think?"

They looked at each other for a while, then Addie said: "Shouldn't we keep moving?"

"I think so," Shy told her and he climbed down into their sad little lifeboat and undid the knot that had kept the two boats together.

They sat against the side in silence, Shy's arm around Addie's shoulders for warmth. Shy stared at the little bit of water they had left. And only two more flares and a flashlight. They had to reach land tomorrow or it would be over. He thought of the two dead men he'd found on the motorboat. Someone from the island must have shot them. But why? And what did that say about the island? Or what if they had shot themselves?

He looked up at the sky, thinking about the gun in the duffel bag. Would it get so bad that he and Addie would consider doing that? Using the bullets to stop their suffering? He fingered the ring in his pocket, thinking about that.

It was a starry black night that seemed to reach out forever, all the way back to the ruined coast of California. He tried to imagine all the lives that had been lost. All the families ripped apart, the property destroyed.

To believe that two kids on a boat had any special meaning was a fairy tale.

Shy listened to the change in Addie's breathing as she slowly fell asleep, and he watched the motorboat drift away from them, into the darkness, until it was only a shadow in the night, then nothing, and still he watched.

Day 6

38
The Subject of Love

By morning the water inside the lifeboat was several inches higher. Shy staggered to his feet and looked all around the boat, trying to figure out what had happened. He found a large, jagged crack in the hole he'd patched. It must've happened when the two boats collided.

He and Addie bailed as much water as possible, and he repatched the crack, praying it would take. Then he went back to working the oar through the ocean, concentrating on the sun as it slowly crept into the sky and warmed his stiff arms and legs.

Too soon it was directly overhead again, beating down on them. He put his shirt on his head to protect himself from it, though this time he resecured the life jacket over his bare chest. His lips were cracked and his stomach was cramping. Sores now blistered up and down his legs, under his jeans, and on the tops of his feet. He felt so weak he barely had the lifeboat moving at all, and his mind was beginning to slip. He stared out across the shimmering ocean with little hope of spotting land, aware of the two sharks that had returned. Like they sensed it was coming to an end.

Addie fished in silence at the back of the boat, the tarp over her head to protect her from the sun. One thought kept creeping into Shy's head: how strange that the two of them had ended up here together. They were from opposite worlds. In real life they wouldn't have been friends in a million years, but out here they were all each other had.

Addie eventually came to fish beside Shy.

She said when it was too quiet her mind got stuck on worst-case scenarios, and she'd have little panic attacks. "So, can you just talk to me?"

"About what?" Shy asked.

"Tell me about your high school. Or how you got the name Shy. It honestly doesn't matter."

He shrugged. Addie would never catch a fish on his end of the lifeboat, not with the baited hook so close to his moving oar. It would scare away any potential fish. He didn't say anything, though. He was better off when they were talking, too.

"My old man used to call me Shy when I was little," he told her. "And it just stuck."

"Why though? Were you quiet as a kid or something?"

"Not that I know of." As Shy pulled the oar feebly through the water, he thought about all the times he'd been asked about his name. He usually made shit up out of boredom. A different story for every new person. But out here, on this broken boat with Addie, it didn't seem right to make stuff up.

"According to my mom," Shy told her, "any time I fell or knocked something over my dad would be like, 'Damn, this kid doesn't know shit from Shinola.' It happened a lot, I guess, so he started calling me Shinola. By the time I started school he'd shortened it to plain old Shy. And everyone else just sort of went with it, I guess."

Addie looked horrified. "And what's Shinola?"

"Some old brand of shoe polish. The saying basically means 'You don't know anything.'"

Addie shook her head, staring at him. "That's like the saddest story I've ever heard."

"Nah, he's just like that. Always messing around." Shy wondered what she'd say if she heard the rest. About the abuse and why he eventually left. "Anyways, who knows why some nicknames stick and others don't."

They talked about a bunch of other things, too. Addie's friend back home who got hit by a drunk driver. Her private high school in Santa Monica, where celebrities showed up every afternoon to pick up their kids. The new Lexus she got at the start of summer for keeping a high GPA. Shy talked about his last basketball season and how tight his family was and how messed up everything got when his grandma passed from Romero Disease.

It was like they were getting to know each other while they still had the chance. And Shy realized there might be more to Addie than he first thought. Maybe it was like that with anyone you actually sat down and talked to.

Eventually they wandered on to the subject of love. Addie told him about the two high school relationships she'd had so far, but said neither of them were serious. "With both guys," she said, "we never actually broke up. We just sort of stopped texting and talking on the phone. Isn't that weird?"

Shy kept working the oar as he glanced back at Addie. "So, you never been in love, then?"

She shook her head. "I don't think so. But it's complicated.

Because how do you actually know if you have nothing to compare it to?"

"You probably just know," he said.

"So, what about you?" Addie stared at him for a few seconds. "Were you in love with that chick you work with?"

"Who, Carmen?" Shy was shocked Addie even knew who Carmen was.

"How would I know her name?" Addie said. "The girl I saw you talking to by the pool before you gave us stuff for Ping-Pong." Addie pushed her hair out of her face. "She's pretty."

"She's all right," Shy said. "But we were just friends. We grew up in the same kind of neighborhood."

"You sure?" Addie said. "I saw how you were looking at her. There was, like, drool on your chin, I'm pretty sure."

Shy frowned and shook his head. "We were actually in an argument when you saw us." An odd feeling came over him. Here he was starving and dehydrated, weaker than he'd ever felt in his life, and he was worried about being disloyal. Like it was wrong to even speak of Carmen to anyone else.

"So we've both never been in love, then," Addie said. "It's sad, isn't it? Like, what if we never get the chance?"

"You can't think that way," Shy told her, though he had just been thinking the same thing.

Addie shrugged and looked over the side of the boat at her fishing line. After a minute or so, she said: "There's only one thing sadder."

"Yeah? What's that?"

"How you got your stupid nickname," she said with a slight grin.

Shy turned to her in shock. "Really? 'Cause I don't know if 'Addie's' the sweetest name I ever heard either."

She gave him a dirty look and then they both started laughing. Hard. Like their little back and forth was ten times funnier than anything they'd ever heard. He pulled the oar out of the water and kneeled down and just let himself go. Because it felt good to laugh. He didn't care how much it hurt his ribs.

After a while, though, Addie's laughter changed.

Her face crinkled up and Shy saw that she was crying in silence. He dug the oar back into the ocean and kept his eyes fixed directly ahead so she wouldn't think he was watching.

39
Final Two Flares

The sun started to set, and Shy was now on the opposite end of the boat. But Addie still wanted to talk. "Tell me more about your grandma," she called out to him from the front of the boat.

"My grandma?" Shy asked.

Addie pulled the oar out of the water and faced him. "It's just, I heard Romero Disease was made up by the media to scare people."

Shy recast his line with the last of his hooks, trying not to get pissed off at her ignorance. "Didn't seem made up when her eyes filled with blood and she started clawing at her own skin. Or when she died within two days."

"I didn't mean—" Addie looked down at the oar in her hands. "God, that's what happened? I'm sorry."

"Who told you it was made up?"

Addie turned back to the ocean and resumed digging into the water with the oar. "My dad. I figured he'd know since he spent a bunch of time in Mexico the last couple years. That's where it started, right?"

Shy wished he could tell Addie the truth. That her dad was an idiot. But it didn't seem right with him missing, so instead he told her what he knew about Romero Disease. She was right, it had started in Mexico and then crossed into U.S. border towns like his. He listed all the symptoms his grandma had, explained how quickly her condition got worse and how freaked out his whole family was when she died so quickly of dehydration. He also told Addie, for the first time, how his nephew had it now, too.

"I'm so sorry," she mumbled.

It went quiet between them for a while, and then she cleared her throat and added: "I don't understand why he would lie to me. I'm not some naïve little girl he has to protect from reality."

A few minutes later Shy felt a powerful tug on his line. He peered over the jagged side of the boat and saw a pale fish, three times the size of the first one he'd caught, fighting to break free of his hook.

He wrapped the line around his shirt-covered hand several times, his heart speeding up in excitement, and lodged his foot against the base of the boat.

Addie was beside him now, peering over the side at the struggling fish. "Look how big it is!" she shouted.

Shy jerked the line toward him again, wrapping the slack around his wrist. He did this several times, as fast as he could, watching the fish get closer and closer to the surface. But then, out of the corner of his eye, he spotted movement—one of the sharks was darting toward the fish.

"Shy!" Addie shouted, ducking behind his line of vision.

It looked like the shark was preparing to launch itself right at the boat. But the fish was only a few feet away from the surface now, and Shy continued pulling. There was no way he was going to lose this fish.

At the last second, the shark opened its massive jaw, and Shy's gaze locked onto the rows of jagged teeth before turning his head, still pulling the fish but also bracing for impact.

The shark crashed right into the side of the boat, nearly tipping it over. Shy fell onto his back, staring at the severed line still wrapped around his shirt-covered hand and wrist. Not only had the shark made off with the fish, it had taken their last hook.

When he looked up again, he saw Addie leaning over the side of the boat, aiming the flare gun at the shark. Shy scrambled to his feet just as she fired, a ball of light shooting down into the water, where it quickly sputtered out and died.

"What are you doing!" he shouted.

But she was already loading the second flare and aiming the gun at the water. Shy got to her just as she was pulling the trigger and all he succeeded in doing was changing the direction of the flare. Instead of slicing though the water, at the shark, it launched overhead, and they both stood there watching it arc through the darkening sky and then fall uselessly onto the ocean's surface less than fifty yards away.

Addie fell to her knees, sobbing. "I can't take this anymore!" she shouted. "I just want it to be over!"

"It's okay," Shy said, kneeling down beside her. "We'll figure something out, Addie. I swear."

But they both knew there was nothing left to figure out. Not without the fish. Or hooks. Or flares. Or strength. With barely any water.

"It's okay," he repeated again and again.

Even when he saw that the water was dripping through a crack in his patch job again—because of the impact of the shark. Or when he realized the oar was no longer in the boat, but floating on the surface of the ocean somewhere.

Still.

He repeated these words to Addie.

"It's okay."

"It's okay."

40
Veins of the Earth

The dark quickly took over the sky and a nearly full moon rose above them. Shy and Addie were back against the side of the boat again, huddled together in silence. Shy was so weak now it took effort just to breathe. His thoughts were faraway and clouded. All he understood as he stared up at the moon was that they were going to die.

And once he accepted this fact, a weight lifted from his shoulders. Because this was how everything worked. The ocean's whispering and the earthquakes and the fires and the sinking ship and people diving overboard and dying and new people being born. Some are lucky enough to be given a part to play, but when that part ends the world doesn't end, too, it goes on spinning just like before.

Shy reached into his pocket to feel the oilman's ring, and it told him what he had to do.

He struggled to his feet, sloshed to the other end of the boat and grabbed the water jug. He held it up in front of the moonlight, saw the little bit that was left, then he went back to Addie and uncapped it.

He held it out to her, meaning that they were going to finish it and be done, and she seemed to understand.

Before putting the bottle to her lips, though, she reached out for his hand, linked her fingers in his—not a test but the real thing.

She took a sip and handed it back to Shy, who drank, too. They did this twice and then the water was gone.

He dropped the empty jug near their feet and continued holding her hand as they closed their eyes on the night, and Shy sat there wondering what he'd see next, if anything.

Time marched past him holding out a trayful of memories. Sprinkling food flakes into the bubbling fish tank in his and Miguel's dirty room. The alley behind his building where he'd sit alone on an overturned plastic bucket to think. Pulling books from his locker while Maria went off about some girl who had pissed her off. And he was finally able to remember the faces of his family again, even his dad.

Then he thought back to a basketball game from two years ago. One that had come down to the final seconds. They threw him the ball and he raced down the court, dribbled around a screen, and launched a long jumper over the outstretched hands of two defenders. Time slowed as the ball arced through the air—everyone's eyes stuck on its game-deciding path. The refs looking up, whistles hanging from their mouths. The players on both benches on their feet. The coaches holding them back.

When the ball found the bottom of the net the entire gym

erupted—everyone on his team jumping up and down and hugging him and shouting his name. It was the first and only time he'd ever nailed a game-winning shot. After a few seconds, he separated himself from the celebration to search the stands for his mom. Spotted her high in the bleachers, off by herself, waving her arms around and looking so proud of him.

Maybe this was the moment, Shy thought as his mind hovered high above the boat, in this other time and place. Maybe this was his reason for being here. Some people probably wanted to look back at the end and feel like they'd left some kind of legacy in the world. Like having kids. Or making a movie. Or inventing something that made lots of money. Or they wanted to feel like they'd done something heroic. But Shy decided he was happy knowing he'd made his mom feel proud.

Shy's eyes were still closed, his thoughts switching back to the sensation of the cold ocean water creeping up his legs, into his lap, when he felt Addie's breath against his ear. "Just so you know," she whispered, "I think I was going to love you, Shy." He tried to turn his head to look at her, but she stopped him with her hands. "Please don't say anything back."

He didn't, but his heart quietly swelled inside his chest. Because of her words. And the feel of her fingers linked in his. And because he now understood how lucky he was to have experienced a life in this world. He could never use a bullet on himself. Or Addie. The world would have to take them the old-fashioned way if that was what it wanted. And as his mind continued drifting away from his body, he had one final realization. The world itself was alive, too. It swirled around you and sped past your eyes and ears, so fast you could never see it, but slow at the same time, like a tree growing taller in a park. And all the sounds you heard—the wind whipping past your ears and the ocean's whispering and the trickle of whitecaps against your boat—that was the earth's blood pumping through imperceptible veins, and some of those veins were nothing more than people like Shy or Carmen or Addie.

And when the end came it smelled like morning dew and brine and everything around you morphed into a man, and that man shined a flashlight in your eyes and kneeled down beside you to pet your hair, and he said: *You're gonna be okay, young fella. Now come on.*

And he lifted you into his arms and carried you like a child into a hidden cave, where you would grow back into the earth's rich soil from which you came and where you would forever belong.

Day 7

41
Jones Island

Shy cracked open his eyes.

He found Shoeshine hovering over him, moving a syringe toward his right shoulder.

He flipped himself over and tried to push away, but Shoeshine was surprisingly strong. "Easy now," the man told Shy, pulling the needle away. "Just a few vitamins you're gonna need on the island. Trust me."

"What vitamins?" Shy's eyes darted around, taking everything in. It didn't make any sense. He'd come to the end. Yet here he was looking around a familiar-looking boat cabin. Alive. The oilman's ring still safe inside his pocket. Over Shoeshine's shoulder, Shy saw Addie standing against the wall, rubbing her arm.

"You gonna stop fighting?" Shoeshine asked.

"It's okay, Shy," Addie said. "He saved us."

Shy locked eyes with the man. Crazy gray hair and braided chin beard. Leathery face. No way Shy was gonna let some shoeshine guy stick him with a needle. But his mind was so clouded he couldn't think straight.

Shoeshine slowly lowered the syringe toward Shy's shoulder, the short needle piercing his skin, cool liquid pushing inside him. Instead of fighting, Shy looked around the cabin again. Identical to the one where he'd found the dead doctors. But there were no doctors on the floor now. And no bloodstain. The only thing he recognized was the duffel bag he'd found, which was wide open. One of the packs unwrapped and two of the syringes missing. The shot he was getting had come from the bag he'd found.

Soon as Shoeshine stepped away, Shy pushed off the thin mattress and hurried to a trash can to throw up. His eyeballs bulging from the pressure, lips cracking and bleeding. He was shocked by how much came out of him.

Addie put her hand on Shy's back. "He saw the flares," she told him, her eyes filling with tears. "And he found us. We've been rescued, Shy."

The look on her face told him it was true.

They'd survived.

When they got to the top of the stairs, Shy saw the island and it took his breath away.

And he saw a ship. Big enough to carry them home.

He was so overcome by emotion he dropped to his knees, fighting back tears of his own.

Addie kneeled down next to him and held out a banana. "Can you believe it?" she asked.

"I told you we'd be okay," he said weakly as he peeled his piece of fruit. "Didn't I tell you?"

"You told me," she said, wiping her wet cheeks with the back of her hand.

They both made quick work of their bananas, and Shy tossed his peel in the trash and looked around. This boat wasn't shot up. And "320" was written on the side instead of "220."

"Where'd you get this boat?" he asked Shoeshine, who was busy steering them toward the shore.

"Docked inside a cave on the other side of the island," Shoeshine answered. He kicked the cooler next to his feet. "There's more food in here. You all must be starving."

Shy pushed himself up to his feet again. "We found one exactly like this," he said. "Only burned up. It was just floating out there."

Shoeshine nodded.

"It's where I found the duffel bag." Shy looked for a reaction from Shoeshine, about the gun and the bodies, but there was nothing. "I also found two dead people."

Now Shoeshine turned to him. Shy could see in the man's eyes he wasn't surprised. And for a second he wondered if Shoeshine had something to do with the murders. But wouldn't he have taken the duffel, then?

"How'd you know what was in the bag?" Addie asked, rubbing her arm again.

"Because it was taken from the island," Shoeshine said, still looking at Shy. "There was a minor dispute about what to do with it."

"What's happening there?" Addie asked. "Is everything okay?"

Shoeshine turned to her. "Safer than being stranded at sea, I suppose."

"That's the truth."

"Who else is there?" Shy said, thinking of Carmen, Rodney and Kevin. And everyone else. But especially Carmen. "Other people made it, right?"

"There's about eighty of us," Shoeshine said. "They're staying at that hotel you see on the hill."

"Is my dad there?" Addie asked. "He's tall with gray hair."

"I hope so," Shoeshine said. "More than a few who fit that description."

Shy looked toward shore again. The island had beautiful green cliffs. The large building at the top, overlooking the ocean, was obviously the hotel. "How'd you even find us?" he asked, turning back to Shoeshine.

"Like the young woman said. Saw a flare go up near sunset. I've been out looking for folks the past three days. But you're the only two I've come back with."

"Why don't I remember?" Shy said.

"You were half dead." Shoeshine let up on the gas and allowed the boat to coast. "But I had a feeling about you, young fella. Somehow I knew we hadn't seen the last of you."

Shy got a weird feeling looking at Shoeshine. Like the guy was genuinely looking out for him. Even back on the ship he'd felt that way. But why?

He turned back to the hotel on the cliff. It was blue and white and lined by densely packed palm trees—easily the biggest building visible on the small island. The whole island itself seemed no bigger than a few football stadiums wide. Lush cliffs wrapped all the way around, the ocean running right up into them except for a long grassy section, which was where they were headed. Shy spotted four Paradise lifeboats lined up on the shore. To the side of them was a large sailboat on its side in the rocks with a torn sail flapping in the wind. He saw that the ship was carrying a helicopter.

"Whose ship is that?" he asked.

"Showed up here two days ago," Shoeshine said. "Introduced themselves as a team of researchers. There were about a dozen of them or so."

Addie went right up to the railing. "But they're going to take us home, right?"

Shy watched Shoeshine stare at the ship for a long time before he answered. "That's what they've promised."

"What about the phones in the hotel?" Shy asked. "Can we call home?"

"No electricity. And all the satellite phones we've found are dead. We've been looking for backup generators."

"What about radios?" Shy said. "Does anyone even know we're out here?"

"The researchers say they've alerted the authorities about us."

Shy glanced down at the duffel bag near Shoeshine. "So, who were those doctors I found on the boat?" he asked. "And why'd you give us vitamins from the bag? Why would we need a shot?"

Shoeshine put a hand up, interrupting Shy. "Plenty of time for questions, young fella. But what do you say we get you two back on land right now." He powered down the motor and lowered the anchor.

They were directly in front of the long manicured patch of grass that looked like part of a golf course.

"Gotta keep the boat offshore a ways because the pier's underwater," Shoeshine said. "Same as the runway they used for small planes."

Addie tapped Shy on the arm and pointed at the island. "He thinks that's only a quarter of what it was before the tsunamis."

"As the water goes down," Shoeshine said, "we find out more and more about this place. Now, you all feel strong enough to swim a ways?"

Shy and Addie both nodded.

Shoeshine ducked back down the stairs, into the cabin. He came out with his notebook wrapped in plastic and shoved it into the duffel bag with the medicine and slung it over his shoulder. "Okay if I carry this for now?" Shoeshine asked Shy.

"You can have it," Shy said, meaning the gun, too.

Shoeshine nodded. As the three of them moved to the side of the motorboat, he said: "Before you all set foot on that island, there's one more thing you need to know."

Shy peered down into the water. It was so clear he could see all the way down to the bottom. No sharks. But instead of sand or reef, he saw what looked like a thin paved road. A shed. Part of the island really *was* underwater.

"Some of the folks who made it back . . ." Shoeshine paused. "Well, there's something wrong with them."

"What do you mean?" Addie asked.

Shy could tell by Shoeshine's face it was something bad.

Shoeshine shook his head. "Nobody's exactly sure yet. They've been separated from everyone else for now. The doctor can tell you more."

Shy could also tell Shoeshine was holding something back. About the syringes in the duffel bag maybe. Or the gun. Or the people who had something wrong with them.

The man turned and looked Shy dead in the eyes, like he sensed all his questions. "Main thing is this. I didn't give you no vitamins out here, you understand?"

"Why not?" Shy said.

"And you all never saw this bag I'm holding." He patted the duffel hanging from his shoulder. "It's important this part stays between us three, you hear?"

Shy and Addie looked at each other. Before Shy could say anything else, though, Shoeshine told them: "I know all this seems confusing right now. But trust me, the less you know, the better. Now come on." He turned back toward the water and jumped in.

42
Dry Land

Addie jumped in feetfirst with her life jacket on, her blond hair fanning out in clumps on the water's surface. Shy took off his life jacket and flung it back into the boat. He was weak, but he didn't care. The shore was close. And he felt free as he leaped off the boat, a cool rush of ocean water quickly enveloping his body, bringing him back to life. For a few surreal seconds his head was underwater, feet dangling a few feet above the grassy bottom, then he dog-paddled his way up and his face broke through the surface.

He and Addie looked at each other, smiling, and Shy recalled the last thing she'd said to him on the lifeboat, about how she was going to love him. He wondered if it was something she had said because she thought she was going to die, or if she really felt it. And what did *he* think about that?

Shy reached down into the water and squeezed Addie's knee through her jeans. It was the closest he could come to acknowledging what she'd said. Addie grinned and turned onto her stomach, started swimming for shore.

Before Shy swam after her, he glanced back at the motorboat that had just saved their lives. And then he looked beyond the boat, at the massive sparkling ocean. Hours before they'd been lost in it. Left for dead. But here they were now, less than twenty yards from land.

He could feel his entire body coming back to life as he turned and set off after Addie.

Shy stepped onto shore last.

He walked up the closely cut grass on shaky legs and allowed himself to collapse near Addie, where they both looked around in silence.

They were on what was once a golf course—most of it was now underwater. The research ship with the helicopter was a couple hundred feet offshore, and Shy spotted a couple people moving around on the top deck. He turned around and looked at the island. Old-looking stone stairs zigzagged up the face of the cliff. A thick cable came up out of the water, ran all the way up to the hotel where a fancy aerial tram sat. The cliffs themselves were intensely green with densely packed trees and bushes. A group of squawking seagulls chased after each other low in the sky.

It was like they'd landed in paradise. Shy put both his palms on the ground beside him, amazed that he was actually back on solid ground. He studied the broken-down sailboat on his left. He saw now that there were gashes in the side and the bar that held the torn sail was badly bent. No way this thing would ever sail again. It was a major reminder of what damage the waves had caused.

"That was the easy part," Shoeshine called to them. "Still got four hundred sixty-five steps to go. I've counted."

"It's so strange," Addie said to Shy. "In a few minutes I'll know if he's still alive."

He nodded.

"Even if he's done bad things," she said, "he's still my dad, you know?"

"I get it," Shy said as he struggled to his feet. But he didn't want to think about Addie's dad right now. Or the shady things he may have been doing. Like the picture of Shy Addie had found in his room. His legs were incredibly wobbly. He could barely walk. All Shy wanted to think about right now was the fact that he was alive. And he was on dry land.

Addie looked up at Shy, said: "I don't even know if I can make it up these stairs. I'm so weak."

"I bet there's food and water up there," Shy told her. "And a bed." He helped Addie up, thinking about how close he now felt to her. They'd survived together. No one could ever take that away. But he also knew the butterflies flooding his stomach were about something else. Something that made him feel like a bad guy.

As Shy and Addie followed Shoeshine up the stairs, side by side, he remembered Carmen's dark brown hair and brown eyes. He tried to stop himself, but he couldn't. He remembered how she'd stepped into the hall outside her cabin with wine when he couldn't sleep. All the early-morning talks they'd had on the Lido Deck, when she stopped by with her coffee.

Come on, Carm, he thought as he closed his eyes and touched the ring in his pocket.

You gotta be up there.

Please be up there.

Shoeshine stopped as they neared the top of the stairs. He glanced up at the hotel, then looked out at the men on the research ship. He pulled his notebook from the duffel bag, hid the bag with the gun and syringes inside the thick bushes growing right up against the stairs and continued on.

"What was that all about?" Shy asked, glancing at the beat-up leather notebook in Shoeshine's hand.

"We know the world has changed," Shoeshine answered, "we just don't know which way."

Shy and Addie looked at each other, confused. "I don't get it," Shy said.

Shoeshine shook his head and pointed toward the hotel. "Plenty of empty rooms. Doors are all open, keys on the desks inside. Once you claim your room you can lock it. Food and water in the restaurant out back. Extra clothes in the lobby."

"Aren't you coming?" Shy said.

"I need to check something on the other side," Shoeshine said. "Ask for Christian, the doctor I told you about. He'll tell you whatever else you need to know."

After they watched Shoeshine disappear around the hotel, Addie turned to Shy. "So you know him?"

"Shoeshine? Sort of." Shy turned toward the hotel. "I know Christian a little, too. We started out on the same life raft." Shy remembered being right next to Christian as the giant wave roared toward them. He shook the memory out of his head and wondered if he'd find Kevin and Marcus inside. And Paolo.

"I don't understand why everything's so secretive," Addie said. She squatted down and put her hand on the ground.

"Same here." Shy looked up at the hotel, which was about a dozen stories high, with big windows and balconies. He turned to Addie, who was now rubbing her temples. "You all right?"

She nodded. "Just a little dizzy. Getting up here took all my strength. I think I need to lie down or something."

"Can you make it inside? I'm sure we'll find you a better spot."

Addie nodded, and Shy helped her to her feet.

They cut across the puddled lawn together, pushed through the hotel doors and stepped into the lobby.

"Damn, look at this place," Shy said. It reminded him of the ship's atrium, only ten times the size. High domed ceilings and massive chandeliers. Giant framed paintings on every wall. Thick carved pillars. Antique-looking couches. Marble floors and a marble staircase that wrapped in a circle up to the second level. Shy wondered if those stairs would lead him to a room where he'd find Carmen.

"I knew they had a hotel here," Addie said, "but I never pictured it like this."

"So, this is where people from your old man's company stay?" Shy asked.

"And the doctors they fly out for vacation. My mom said it's one of the ways they get people to invest in their products."

They both turned when they heard people walking across the marble floor. It was Christian and two men Shy didn't recognize.

Christian stopped suddenly. "Shy? Is that you?"

Shy nodded, surprised at how emotional he felt seeing someone who'd been with him on the raft.

"Jesus, man! I'm so happy to see you!" Christian hurried across the lobby toward them, gave Shy a quick hug, then hugged Addie, too. "How'd you guys get here? We didn't think anyone else survived."

"Shoe found us," Shy told him. "In the middle of the night. We thought it was over."

"Shoeshine. Of course. Man, thank God you guys are okay."

"They're more than okay," one of the men said, stepping forward. He had a long, dark beard and a receding hairline. "How would you feel if I told you you're going home? Tonight?"

"Tonight?" Shy said. "Are you serious?"

"That's right," the shorter man said. He was wearing a Hawaiian shirt, khaki shorts and flip-flops. "We're departing just after the sun sets."

The man with the beard smiled and held out his hand to Shy. "I'm Greg Walker, and I'm in charge of the research expedition. This is my head assistant, Connor Simms."

Shy gave his name and shook hands with both men. Addie did the same.

"You two showed up just in time," Greg continued. "We were sent here to study the tsunamis' effects on the sea life just off the coast of the island. But that went out the window when we found all the survivors here. Our mission now is to get you back home to your families."

Shy squeezed Addie's arm. He was so excited he could hardly contain himself.

She smiled back at him and nodded, but she seemed to be swaying a little, too. Shy gripped her elbow, trying to steady her.

"What about California, though?" he asked the two men. "Isn't it messed up really bad?"

"There's a lot of damage," the shorter man, Connor, said. "It's terrible. But the entire country has come to the aid of all the western states affected. You'd be amazed how much people are coming together."

"They said the death count wasn't quite as high as the media originally reported," Christian added. "All we can do is pray that our families and friends are okay."

Greg slapped Shy on the shoulder Shoeshine had just stuck the syringe into. "We'll be explaining everything in a few hours over lunch. One-thirty, if you're near someone with a watch. Go get some rest. We'll make sure everyone knows when it's time to gather in the restaurant. I'll be going over all the logistics of our departure."

"You're safe now," Connor said.

Greg nodded. "And we're thrilled to be bringing two more home with us."

Shy felt Addie suddenly start slipping through his grip. He caught her at the last second and lowered her to the ground. "Jesus, Addie," he said, kneeling down to pick up her head. Her eyes were closed. "Addie? Can you hear me?"

Christian reached into his bag and pulled out a bottle of water. He took Shy's spot, uncapped the water and put it to her lips, saying: "Addie? Can you hear me? I need you to take a small sip of water if you can."

Her eyes fluttered open, and she looked up at Christian. She took a small sip and turned to Shy. "What happened?"

"You fainted," Christian said. "We need to get food and water in both of you."

Shy put his hand on her forehead. "You okay?"

"She needs rest," Connor said. "Let's get her into one of the bedrooms."

Shy looked over his shoulder when he heard other people hurrying across the lobby toward them. "There are still plenty of open rooms on the first floor," someone said.

In a few seconds, a small crowd of people had converged around Shy, Addie and Christian—everyone shouting advice and asking how they'd made it out of the ocean alive. Shy looked up at all of them, recognizing a few of the faces from the cruise ship.

And then, near the back of the group, he saw the face he'd been imagining since the moment the ship went down and he'd found himself alone in the dark ocean.

Carmen.

43
Under the Gazebo

Shy, Christian and a few others, including both researchers, helped get Addie into the closest unclaimed room, 117, and laid her on the perfectly made up king-sized bed.

"She needs air," someone said.

"And something to eat," another person said. "Look at her."

Shy watched them all swarming around Addie's bed, but he kept checking the door, too. His heart pounding. Carmen hadn't come into the room yet. She had to be waiting for him in the lobby.

"She'll be able to rest all the way back to California," one of the researchers said.

An older woman told someone to go get Addie a change of clothes.

"Is my dad here?" Addie mumbled.

"Who's your dad?" the older woman asked.

"Jim Miller. He's tall with gray hair. He worked on the island."

"You rest for now, honey," the woman said. "I'll go ask around, see what I can find out."

The two researchers backed away from the bed and left the room after the woman.

Shy and Christian remained with one other woman as everyone else began filing out. Christian looked into Addie's eyes and ears with a tiny doctor flashlight, then he listened to her heart with a stethoscope. Shy watched, torn between making sure Addie was okay and going in search of Carmen.

"Shy?" Addie said, looking up from the bed.

"I'm here," he answered.

She let her head fall back onto the pillow. "God, I don't even know what happened to me."

"You've been on the ocean for five days," Christian said. "Both of you." He turned to the woman next to him. "Mary, would you go to the restaurant and get some bottles of water and fruit."

"Right away," she said, and she hurried out of the room.

"You need to rest, too," Christian said to Shy. "Go to one eighteen, across the hall. I'll come see you next."

"Okay," Shy told him, but there was no way he was doing anything until he saw Carmen. "You feeling a little better?" he asked Addie, squeezing her foot.

"I think so," she said.

Shy nodded as Christian began asking her questions.

When two women came in carrying a change of clothes for Addie, Shy slipped out of the room.

The second he walked into the lobby he spotted Carmen, who motioned for him to follow her.

As he moved across the marble floor, though, toward the doors, a few other survivors from the cruise ship approached him. Word had gotten out that he and Addie had been rescued, and they marveled at how long Shy had survived at sea.

Shy smiled and nodded at them all, but he hardly heard a word they were saying. He was too anxious to talk to Carmen, who was now standing in front of the hotel doors, waiting for him.

"Make sure you're in the restaurant at one-thirty," a man said. "They're going to tell us when we can expect to be home."

"I'll be there," Shy said, waving as he moved past the group.

His legs were wobbly as he followed Carmen outside the hotel and along the cobblestone path. For some reason she continued walking a few paces in front of him, like she didn't want to start talking until they were completely alone.

They moved around the entire exterior of the hotel. Puddles everywhere, especially out back. Seaweed strung through some of the manicured bushes like tinsel. A woman wearing an oversized Raiders jersey called to him from across the lawn: "We heard about you! Thank God you were able to survive!"

"Thank you!" Shy shouted back.

They walked past others who greeted Shy the same way. Finally Carmen led him under a large gazebo where they were alone. She spun around and faced him, her head tilted a little to the side. "Shy," she said, her face breaking into a big smile.

Just hearing her say his name sort of choked him up. "Carm," he managed to say back.

She was wearing a plain white T-shirt he'd never seen her wear, baggy jeans and tennis shoes. She covered her mouth and her eyes got a little glassy, but there were no tears. Carmen was too tough for that. "Come here," she said.

He moved toward her and she wrapped him in a tight hug, saying in a quiet voice: "I thought I lost you."

Shy was so overcome with emotion he wanted to melt into her. He cupped the back of her head and held her against his chest, breathing in her hair. He was exhausted to the point that his knees were shaking, but he didn't care. He was willing to stand like this forever.

She looked up at him. "I thought of you every single minute. I even tried praying."

"I thought about you, too," Shy told her.

Carmen reached up and grabbed Shy's face in her hands, stared right into his eyes. "How'd you get rescued? It's been *five* days. I almost lost hope."

"Shoeshine," Shy told her. "He found us out there in a sinking lifeboat."

Carmen hugged him again.

Shy closed his eyes this time and concentrated on the feeling of her body against his. Being with Carmen again made it sink in that he'd made it to the other side. That he had a second chance.

When she pulled away from him this time, she said: "God, look how skinny you are, Shy. It's like breaking my heart."

"I only caught one fish the whole time," he said.

She laughed a little and shook her head. "I never saw you as the life-skills type. Why do you think I was praying?"

"It was the sharks," he told her. "For real. They scared away all my fish."

"You smell, too," Carmen said, grabbing him by the elbow. "Let's get you cleaned up."

Carmen led Shy back into the hotel and behind the reservation desk, where he picked out a change of clothes, and then she took him out back to the freshwater pool where she said everyone had been bathing.

"Go on," Carmen said, turning away from him. "I'll keep a look out so nobody tries to sneak a peek at your stuff."

Shy slowly peeled off the damp clothes he'd been wearing for the past five days and grabbed one of the small hotel-style bars of soap lying beside the pool. Being rescued was a trip: one minute he'd be stressing about getting back home and finding his family, and the next minute he'd get a lump in his throat just looking at a bar of soap.

He dunked himself in the cool water and began lathering his hair and body, which felt incredible, as Carmen caught him up about her own lifeboat's journey to the island and the island itself.

She was on the first boat to make it to the island, along with about thirty others, including Christian, who they'd pulled out of the ocean. A disheveled redheaded man in a lab coat, Dr. Sullivan, greeted them on the golf course and led them up the stairs to the hotel. Soon as they walked into the lobby, though, he had them all sit down so he could explain what was happening on the island. He'd been working in the lab on the other side, with a team of other scientists, when the first tsunami hit. In seconds, the entire lab was underwater. Only a few of them made it out alive. But that wasn't all. The next morning, most of the people who worked on the island—in the hotel and the restaurant and on the grounds— started getting sick. Really sick. He'd been putting them all upstairs, in the penthouse, where he was giving them medication.

"Then the doc ducked behind the registration desk," Carmen said over her shoulder, "and came back with a duffel bag. He explained that the virus going around was very contagious and that each of us would need to have a shot for protection."

Shy had stopped lathering and was staring at the back of Carmen's head. He knew she was talking about one of the dead people he'd found on the motorboat. And the shots they all got were the same ones Shoeshine had just given to him and Addie.

"So you let him give you the shot?" Shy asked.

"Of course I did," Carmen said. "Only two people from my lifeboat refused it, and they're both sick now. They're up in the penthouse."

Shy started rinsing himself off, debating whether or not to tell

Carmen about the dead scientists. Or about him getting the shot, too. If everyone already knew about it, why did Shoeshine want him to keep it secret?

"So where's the bag of medicine now?" he asked.

"Gone," Carmen said, turning all the way around to face him. "That's why I'm worried about you."

Shy thought about ducking back into the water to hide himself. But he didn't. He just stood there.

She glanced down at him for a quick sec, but her face stayed serious. "Shy, your chest. What happened?"

He reached up to feel it. He had a pretty big scab that was slowly healing. And he was pretty sure he'd broken a rib or two. "No idea," he said. "Happened on the ship."

Carmen cringed. "Anyway, Dr. Sullivan disappeared, too. The day after we got here. We don't know where he went or what he did with the medicine."

"Was there another doctor?" Shy asked.

"There were four of them," Carmen said. "But Dr. Sullivan was the only one who came around the hotel. The rest of them mostly stayed on the other side of the island, except when they went to the restaurant to eat. They claimed their entire life's work was buried underwater."

Shy started drying himself off with one of the towels stacked near the pool, trying to decide how to tell Carmen what he knew. He didn't want to betray Shoeshine, but at the same time, he couldn't keep this from Carmen.

She turned away from him, as if she'd just remembered he was naked. "Everyone on the second boat is fine, too, but by the time the third and fourth lifeboats showed up, Dr. Sullivan was already gone. Same with the medicine. So none of them got the shot."

"And they got sick?" Shy asked, putting on a fresh pair of pants. He transferred the oilman's ring from his old ones.

"Almost all of them," Carmen said over her shoulder. "Only Shoeshine is still fine. And a few others. It's crazy contagious, like Dr. Sullivan said. That's why Christian and those research people aren't letting anyone go up to the penthouse."

"By any chance," Shy said, "was that duffel bag of medicine brown and blue?"

Carmen spun back to Shy. "How'd you know that?"

Shy slipped his second arm into his T-shirt and pulled it over his head. "Look," he said, "Shoe told me to keep this quiet, okay?"

"Just tell me what you know."

"Okay." Shy was so tired he had to squat down. "Me and Addie stumbled into that Dr. Sullivan guy's boat while we were paddling around out there. You said he had red hair, right?"

Carmen nodded.

"So, yeah, someone shot him," Shy said. "Shot his boat up, too. And tried to burn it."

The color went out of Carmen's face. "Who shot him? Why?"

"No idea," Shy said. "I found him that way. Some other doctor had also been shot."

"But that doesn't make sense," Carmen said. "Why would anyone shoot a scientist? He was helping us."

Shy looked over Carmen's shoulder to make sure they were still alone. "You don't think Shoe had anything to do with it, do you?"

Carmen composed herself and shook her head. "The reason he didn't get sick, I think, is because he never stays in the hotel."

"Where's he sleep?"

She shrugged. "Outside, I guess. He spends all day exploring the other side and fishing and writing in his notebook. He's also obsessed with that wrecked sailboat. Maybe he sleeps on *that*." Carmen shook her head again. "Nah, Shoe's been good to us. He rescued *you*, didn't he?"

Shy looked up at the top floor of the hotel, where the penthouse was. "I grabbed the duffel with the medicine off their boat. I don't even know why. Anyway, when I woke up on Shoe's boat this morning, he was sticking me with one of those syringes."

"Shy," Carmen said, grabbing his forearm, "that's really good. Everyone who got the shot is still healthy."

"He told me they were vitamins," Shy said. "But obviously that was a bunch of bs. What kind of sickness is it, anyway?"

Carmen shook her head. "Some tropical thing, I guess. Brought on by the flooding. And we were all calling the shots vitamins." She let go of his arm. "All I know is the illness must be bad 'cause nobody's recovered enough to come down from the penthouse yet."

They were both quiet for a few seconds. Shy stood and scooped up his dirty clothes.

Carmen cleared her throat, said: "There's something else, Shy. I wanted to make sure you heard this from me first."

Shy looked at her, preparing himself for more bad news.

"Rodney's up there. He's one of the sick people."

It was like a shot to the midsection. Shy looked up toward the top floor again. His legs felt even weaker all of a sudden, like any second he might collapse like Addie had. But he wouldn't let himself. "He'll get better, though, right?"

"That's what Christian says. And the research people promised to take everyone back to California, no matter how sick they are."

"We can't go see him?" Shy asked.

She shook her head. "At least, we're not supposed to."

As they walked back into the hotel, they were both quiet. Shy could tell Carmen was thinking about the same thing he was. Rodney. It killed him that the guy had made it all the way to the island only to get sick. He vowed to make sure he took care of his roommate on the voyage back home.

Carmen led Shy right past Addie's room and the room Christian told him to take, toward the stairs. "I think I'm supposed to be in room one eighteen," he said.

"Says who?" Carmen said.

"Christian."

She shook her head. "You can take any room you want. Come on."

She led him to an open room on the third floor, across the hall from hers, and stood by the door as he went inside. He sat on the end of the king-sized bed. It was a super nice hotel room. Art on all the walls, a big window overlooking the ocean. Clean-looking bedding and pillows. But Shy didn't care about all that. He was still thinking about what he'd just learned.

When he'd seen the island from Shoeshine's motorboat, he had assumed the worst was over. And maybe it was. But things were still pretty messed up. California had been rocked by an earthquake. And he had no idea about his family. And now he'd found out a bunch of people, including his boy Rodney, were sick.

"Get some rest," Carmen said. "I'll come get you before we meet for lunch."

Shy looked at her hovering near the door. "Thanks for telling me about Rod," he said. "Guess I shouldn't even ask about Kevin and Marcus."

"Marcus is here," she said. "The people on the second boat fished him out of the ocean."

"So he's not sick?"

Carmen shook her head. "He's been holed up in his room the past couple days trying to fix some portable radio. He found it at the bottom of a huge puddle, though, so I have my doubts."

"And Kevin?"

Carmen shook her head, looking at Shy. "He wasn't on any of the boats."

Shy nodded.

Not only did he feel exhausted, he felt empty. Just a few days ago they were all hanging out together on the ship for Rodney's birthday. Now Rodney was sick. And Kevin, the strongest and smartest of all of them, was missing. Drowned, probably. Or mauled by a shark. It proved to Shy that the most important part of surviving was dumb luck.

Carmen stared blankly at the floor a while. "Look," she finally said. "A lot of bad things went down. We both saw the footage of what the earthquakes did." She shook her head. "I can't even sleep really 'cause all I do is think about my family. And Brett. And whether or not they're still alive."

Shy nodded.

"But me and you are still alive," Carmen said. "And we're going home. That's what we need to focus on, you know?"

"You're right," Shy told her.

"Now get some rest. I'll come wake you up in a few hours." She picked up one of his room keys and slipped it into her pocket.

"Thanks, Carm."

She smiled. "You're family, too, Shy. Remember that." She turned to leave but then stopped herself and looked back from the door. "Before I go, you know the rules. Give me one thing I don't already know."

Shy looked out at the ocean, thinking. Carmen had just told him the truth about Rodney and Kevin. He wanted to tell something truthful, too. "You know that girl Addie?" he said, sitting down on the bed. "The one I was out there with?"

Carmen nodded.

"She's actually not that bad. I probably never would've made it back without her."

Carmen stared at him for a few long seconds, like she was trying to figure out what he meant. Then an understanding came over her face and she said: "I'm happy you had someone." She smiled at Shy and stepped out of his room, slowly pulling the door closed behind her.

Shy lay back on his pillow and stared up at the ceiling. He thought about everything he and Carmen had just talked about, and he thought about Kevin and Rodney. He was definitely grateful to be where he was. Alive. Back on land. About to return to California on the research ship. But at the same time he felt guilty, too.

Why should he live and Kevin die?

What made him any more worthy?

Nothing.

He closed his eyes, remembering Kevin following him to the Lido Deck on the first night of the voyage. Warning Shy about the guy who'd been asking about him. Saying with his eyes that he had Shy's back.

Kevin was a good guy. He was probably a better guy than just about anyone else Shy had ever known, including himself.

44
Giving Thanks

Shy felt like he'd just fallen asleep when he opened his eyes and found Carmen shaking him awake. "Sorry I can't let you rest longer," she said. "But we need to find out about this departure."

Shy sat up. "How long was I out?"

"It's one already. So almost three hours."

"For real?" Shy wiped the sleep from his eyes and got to his feet. He followed Carmen out of his room, saying: "I probably could've slept for three *days*."

Carmen stopped in the middle of the hall. "So which room is hers?"

"Who?"

"Blondie," Carmen said. "Ol' girl you were stranded with."

Shy gave her a confused look. "What are you talking about?"

"Just gimme the room number, Shy. I decided me and her are gonna be friends."

Shy was still too asleep to know what he thought about this. He reluctantly gave her the room number and followed her down some stairs and through a hall. Before he fully comprehended what was happening, they were standing together outside Addie's room.

"Go 'head," Carmen told him. "Knock."

Shy did.

As they waited for Addie to answer he got a strange nervous feeling in the pit of his stomach. Carmen and Addie, together? It was too weird, like worlds colliding.

The door opened slowly, and there she was. Blond hair tangled in her face. But she looked alert, like she'd been up for a while. She smiled at Shy, then turned to Carmen and said: "Oh. Hi."

"Addie, meet Carmen," Shy said, trying to act like it was no big deal. "Carmen, Addie."

He watched them smile at each other and shake hands like two businesspeople. Then it got all quiet and awkward.

"You feel better?" Shy asked Addie.

She shrugged. Something was seriously bothering her.

Shy thought he understood what it was. "I know you wanna look for your old man," he said, "but everybody's supposed to be coming to this meeting, right? So I guess . . ."

"He'll either be there or he won't," Addie said, finishing Shy's thought. She glanced down at the ground, all sad-looking.

It went quiet again, so Shy told Carmen: "Addie's dad was on the ship."

"Yeah, I kind of figured that out," Carmen said.

"No, but then he got on a boat and headed here," Shy added. "She's not sure if he made it or not."

"Oh," Carmen said. "Sorry to hear that."

It went quiet again, until Carmen said to Addie: "No offense, girl, but you look like you might need to spend some time with a bar of soap."

"Come on, Carm," Shy said. "She was in here resting."

"I know that, Shy. I'm saying, I can show her where the fresh-water pool is. We still got time before people start showing up at the restaurant."

"Wait, what?" Shy tried to imagine them hanging out, just the two of them. "Or how about we could all go together," he said.

Carmen rolled her eyes and looked at Addie. "You see how this *vato* is, right? Next he's gonna wanna soap up your back."

Addie smiled uncomfortably and looked to Shy for help. But before he could say anything, Carmen was walking into the room and grabbing Addie's stack of fresh clothes off the foot of the bed. She linked her elbow in Addie's and started them out the door, telling Shy: "Meet you in the restaurant in fifteen, Sancho."

Addie looked over her shoulder at Shy, but he was helpless. Carmen did what she wanted. Nothing he said was gonna change that.

Shy sat down at an empty table inside the buzzing restaurant. There was food on a buffet-style counter near the miniature stage: chips, cookies, pretzels, oranges, bags of beef jerky and hundreds of personal-sized bottles of water. Nothing that needed refrigeration, because, as Shoeshine had told him, the island didn't have electricity.

Shy started wolfing down everything he could get his hands on, and he looked around at all the survivors. A couple of them had worked with him on the cruise ship. Everyone else had been a passenger. They were all wearing clothes left behind by previous hotel guests or the people who worked on the island.

Shoeshine wasn't there.

Neither was Marcus.

But he recognized many of the other faces. One of the women the oilman had shown the ring to by the pool. An older gray-haired man from Shy's muster station. A mustached guy he always saw at the blackjack table in the casino. When Shy noticed that someone was staring back at him, his stomach dropped.

It was the man in the black suit. Bill.

He was all the way across the restaurant and no longer in his suit—their eyes stayed locked for a few long seconds until Shy looked away. He flashed back to when he helped the guy get out from under the chandelier in the Destiny Dining Room. He remembered the heat from the fire as he'd leaped through the flames. How he and Kevin got the man onto one of the lifeboats. How was it that this Bill guy was still alive and Kevin was dead?

Carmen and Addie walked into the restaurant just then and headed straight toward Shy's table. Carmen pointed at him and said something he couldn't make out and both girls laughed a little. When they sat down he frowned and said: "What's so funny?"

"That's between me and her," Carmen said.

Shy turned to Addie, who was grinning. It didn't seem as fake this time. She was dressed in baggy jeans and an oversized blue T-shirt, hair all wet and clean-looking. She looked a hundred times better than she had on the lifeboat. "Addie, you gonna help me out here?"

Carmen cut in again. "This is an A and B, bro. So why don't you C your ass out of it."

Addie shrugged.

"That's like something you tell people in third grade," Shy said to Carmen.

"Sometimes you gotta speak to children in a language they understand." She winked at Addie, all proud of herself.

Before Shy could think of anything to say back, three people from the research crew walked to the front of the restaurant and stood near the tiny stage. The one with the beard, Greg, tapped a fork against a drinking glass until everyone quieted down and faced them.

"Ladies and gentlemen," he said. "As many of you already know, we were sent here to study the effects of the tsunamis on this tiny island. Some of the most unique sea life in the world lives in the reefs off the northern coast. However, as soon as we discovered you guys, our agenda changed. We've radioed back to our base and received clearance to cancel our original mission effective immediately. I'm happy to report that we will be setting off for California tonight."

Everyone cheered.

Shy felt a surge of emotion as he looked around at all the happy faces. He thought of his mom and his sister and his nephew. He couldn't wait to get back to Otay Mesa to try and track them down.

"The coast guard has agreed to meet us halfway and guide us back to Long Beach Harbor."

A man with his hair pulled back into a ponytail stepped forward. "Many of you have asked about the state of the West Coast after the earthquakes. We've been hesitant to say too much until we gathered more facts. But I can now say this: there is major damage and a pretty significant loss of life near all the fault lines. But rescue crews from all over the country, and even other parts of the world, are there in full force. They are confident that the affected states will be built back up much sooner than anyone expected."

"The moral of the story," the bearded man said, "never underestimate the resilience of the American people."

Shy watched the crowd of survivors smile and turn to each other. Everyone was as excited as he was. But at the same time, he wanted to hear more details about the earthquake. He wanted to know specifics.

The ponytailed man raised his hand, waiting for the reaction to die down. "The fact is, you people may have caught the worst of it.

Scientists are saying that the tsunamis you experienced were the most powerful in recorded history. As you can see, they've all but decimated this island. They also caused major damage in Hawaii, Japan, Taiwan and the Philippines."

Shy was now wondering if these guys were trying to sugarcoat shit. Just tell us the truth, he wanted to say.

The man in the beard looked at his watch. "I'm sure you all have more questions," he said, "but there will be plenty of time on our voyage home. That must be a great word to hear right about now, huh? 'Home.'" He motioned a fourth man up from the front table. "Larry here is going to run you through the launch procedures. We're leaving tonight at seven-thirty, just as the sun sets. It's imperative that everyone follow his directions exactly. We want to get you all home as safely and efficiently as possible. And this includes our friends currently recovering in the penthouse."

Shy and Carmen nodded to each other, thinking of Rodney. Shy wanted to raise his hand and ask about San Diego, but the first three researchers were already walking away.

The guy who'd just been called up to the stage, Larry, began describing how they needed everyone to line up single file along the shore by six o'clock. Motorized rafts would take them out to the ship, a dozen at a time. The sick would be loaded last. They had a team of fifteen, he said, and if they did things as efficiently as they hoped, the ship would be on its way by seven-thirty. Their estimated arrival back in Long Beach was roughly two days.

Shy couldn't help smiling at the thought of leaving on the ship. Neither could Carmen. But Addie looked super stressed as she kept scanning the restaurant. She seemed to spot Bill.

"He might know something about your old man," Shy told her. "You should go ask him."

Addie shook her head.

Carmen reached across the table, put her hand on top of Addie's.

A few minutes after all the researchers had left to go prepare the ship, one of the former Paradise passengers suggested people go around saying what they were thankful for.

The crowd caught on pretty quickly.

A woman with long brown hair said she was thankful for her husband, who had shielded her with his own body during the second tsunami. She started tearing up and said: "We'd only been married two years. After we got home from this trip we were going to start thinking about children." The tears quickly turned into full-on sobbing, and the people sitting around her patted her back and rubbed her shoulders.

Christian stood up next. "I'm thankful to everyone who helped pull me out of the ocean. You had enough to worry about. And there wasn't any extra room. But you *made* room. I'll never forget you for that."

People clapped as Christian sat back down.

Addie told Shy and Carmen that she was going back to her room to try and rest a little more.

"I'll walk you out," Shy said, getting up from the table.

Addie nodded.

Carmen winked at Shy as he led Addie toward the door. Addie avoided eye contact with Bill.

Outside, Shy told her: "Sorry your dad's not here. But it doesn't mean he's not on the island. Shoeshine didn't show up to the meeting either. I bet a bunch of people didn't."

Addie looked Shy right in the eyes, but she didn't say anything for a few seconds. Then she took his hands in hers and sighed. "You were really nice to me when we were stranded, Shy."

"Wish I could say the same about you," Shy said. He expected to get at least a grin out of her, but she kept a straight face.

"I want you to know I meant what I said." She squeezed his hands. "That last night."

Shy didn't know how to respond to that, so he just sort of nodded and smiled and squeezed her hands a little, too. "Go rest," he said. "We'll come get you when it's time to go down to the beach."

"I just want to make sure you understand that," Addie said.

"I do," Shy told her. "And I'm glad you said it. But there's no need to get all sentimental, right? I'll see you in a few hours."

Addie sighed. She leaned forward on her toes and kissed his cheek. She stood there looking at him for a few seconds with a pained expression on her face, like she still hadn't fully recovered from fainting. Then she turned and started down the hall.

When Shy returned to his table in the restaurant, Carmen was shaking her head. "I know what it's like losing your old man," she said.

Shy wanted to tell Carmen about Addie's dad's shady business on the island. They had to be in some deep shit for people to have guns and bags of needles, for doctors to end up dead on a boat. There was no way it was just insurance fraud. But it didn't seem like the right time or place to get into all that now, so he just nodded and turned back to the people saying what they were thankful for.

"I'm thankful to the men who are taking us home," an older woman said. "It's because of them that, God willing, I might get to see my grandchildren again."

More applause. Some people raised bottles of water and gave cheers.

Bill stood up next and pointed a finger at Shy. "You see that young man sitting over there?"

Everyone turned to Shy. He instinctively sank down in his chair a little, afraid of what the guy was going to say. Carmen was staring at him, too.

"His name is Shy," Bill said. "And he saved my life on the ship."

People clapped for Shy, but Bill wasn't done. "My leg was trapped under a chandelier in one of the dining rooms. He and another young man lifted it off, helped me through the burning room and got me onto a lifeboat. If it wasn't for Shy's bravery, I wouldn't be here right now."

More cheering. This time it went on for several seconds. Carmen pointed at Shy over the table and mouthed, *You're my hero.*

Shy shrugged uncomfortably and looked at Bill. He felt uneasy with all the attention. Truth was, he'd trade Bill's life for Kevin's in a second. It's not like Shy could just forget everything else that happened on the ship—how the guy had followed him all over and messed up his and Rodney's room and threatened him in the Luxury Lounge.

Others stood and announced who and what they were thankful for, but Shy was no longer listening. He was staring into space, thinking about the conversations he and Addie had had on the lifeboat about her old man and his company. Back then it didn't seem to matter as much. His sole focus was on surviving. But now he was sneaking looks at Bill, wondering what the guy's deal was. And what about LasoTech? And then a different thought crossed his mind: Bill must've had something to do with the dead doctors Shy found. And if that was true, it meant Addie's dad had had something to do with the murders, too. Even if it was indirect.

45
The Penthouse

Shy and Carmen labored up the stairs, toward the penthouse on the twelfth floor. He'd spent the last two hours at the restaurant with everyone, doing nothing more than eating and resting and thinking, but it hadn't seemed to give him a whole lot more strength. He was already out of breath and there were still seven flights to go. He made himself a promise: the second he got on the research ship he'd find himself a bed, or a cot, or even just a spot on the floor, and he'd let himself sleep for twelve straight hours.

"So someone's actually guarding the doors?" he asked Carmen.

She nodded. "A few of the guys take shifts. But don't get all nervous, they're only passengers. And a few people who worked at the hotel."

Shy didn't see what the big deal was. Especially if he and Addie were supposedly protected by their shot of vitamins. And someone had to make sure the sick people knew the plan, right? They were leaving in two hours. And how were they going to get down to the water? He wasn't so sure he trusted anyone right now.

Mostly, though, Shy just wanted an excuse to visit Rodney.

As they passed the eighth floor, Carmen said: "So, what are the chances we'll find our neighborhoods still standing?"

"No idea," Shy said. "I don't wanna jinx it."

"Hearing them talk about it at lunch," Carmen said, "I don't know. It made me feel better and everything, but I got the feeling they were holding something back. I mean, you saw the footage in the theater. It was *bad*."

"I was thinking the exact same thing." Shy started assisting his tired legs by using the handrail. "Wanna hear something else?" he asked. "That guy at lunch who said I saved him, he was the dude who was following me all over the ship."

"Stop it," Carmen said. "Really?"

"I promise. Me and Kev were doing our sweep, and I heard someone calling for help. I didn't even think about it at the time."

"He seemed really appreciative about you helping him out."

Shy shrugged. "He still creeps me out. I don't trust the guy."

As they passed the tenth floor, Shy switched subjects. "So, what'd you and Addie talk about?"

"I just gave her a little nutritional advice," Carmen said.

"I'm being serious," Shy said.

"Me too. That girl's too skinny. She needs protein."

Shy shook his head. "So, you were checking her out?"

Carmen grinned. "I peeped her out a little. So what?" She climbed a few more steps and said: "Don't start having some big deserted-island fantasy, okay? We just talked. She told me how you blasted a shark with an oar. And how some injured guy threw himself overboard when you two were sleeping."

Shy felt the ring in his pocket as they climbed the final flight of stairs. He decided he needed to tell Carmen about Addie's dad. The picture Addie had found in his room. How he was partners with the guy Shy saw jump off the ship on his first voyage and how there was something seriously sketchy happening on the island.

But just then they reached the top of the stairs and peeked around the corner. Two men were sitting on metal folding chairs outside the double doors of the penthouse. "What now?" he whispered to Carmen.

"Best way to deal with shit like this," she said, "is to act like you know what you're doing." She popped out from behind the wall and started walking directly toward the men.

Shy followed.

Both men stood up at the same time. The heavier, balding one moved in front of the door. The other guy, who was rocking a military flattop, held his hands up and said: "Sorry, guys, nobody's allowed in there right now. Doctor's orders."

"Christian's the one who sent us," Shy said.

Carmen slowed and put her hand on the guy's elbow. "We're supposed to go in there and run them through the launch details."

"Sorry," the flattop guy said. "*Nobody's* allowed inside. Not even us."

"It's for our own protection," the heavier guy by the doors added. "Plus Larry was just up here talking to them. Christian must have made a mistake."

Shy and Carmen glanced at each other. There was no way Shy was gonna climb all those stairs without seeing Rodney. "Okay," he said, turning back to the two men. "I guess it was a misunderstanding, then. We'll just go back downstairs and tell Christian—"

Shy suddenly shoved his way past both men and pushed through the doors.

"Hey!" they shouted from behind him.

Shy spun around, saw that one of the men had fallen to the floor. Carmen was hurrying past them, too, and they both ran through the hall, into the main living area, where an awful smell hit Shy.

And then he saw.

Fifteen or twenty people were lying on their backs on temporary cots. Their arms and legs tied down. Some of them looked up when they heard Shy and Carmen come into the room. Others didn't move.

Carmen covered her mouth with her hand.

The two men who had been guarding the door hurried into the room after them, shouting: "You can't be in here! We'll all get sick!"

But then they went quiet, too, and stared at the strapped-down bodies.

Shy pulled Carmen by the wrist and they moved from one body to the next, looking for Rodney. The patients were in various conditions. Some seemed alert and shouted at Shy and Carmen. Others had vomit all over their shirts and they moaned and twisted in pain. Others clawed frantically at their own thighs.

A few weren't moving at all.

"No," Shy started mumbling as he and Carmen continued through the rows of patients. "No, please."

The men were after them again, shouting: "We have to get out of here before they come back!"

"There!" Carmen shouted. She was pointing to a cot in the far corner, where Rodney was lying, and they both rushed toward him.

Rodney's face was turned toward the wall.

His eyes seemed open, but when Shy shook him he didn't respond. Carmen turned Rodney's head toward them, and Shy's entire body went cold. The whites of his eyes were entirely red and fixed on nothing.

Carmen continued shaking Rodney and calling out his name, until Shy grabbed her by the wrists and said: "Let's go."

As the men dragged Carmen and Shy back through the room, Shy stared at each body they passed. Everyone in the penthouse was infected with Romero Disease. And some, like Rodney, were already dead.

And they'd been left there to rot.

46
Two Paths Along the Cliffs

After the two men led Shy and Carmen out of the penthouse, they hurried down the stairs together in shock. "How'd it get way out here?" Carmen said. "And why has nobody told us?"

"I need to get the duffel bag," Shy said. "And find Christian. The shot we got has to have something to do with the disease. Like a vaccine."

"There *is* no vaccine."

"Then why haven't you gotten sick?" Shy said. She glanced at him as they continued down the stairs, but she didn't say anything. Nothing made sense. A few minutes ago they were excited to be going home. Now there were people on the island with Romero Disease. And Rodney was gone. And they'd just left him there.

"The bag had pills, too," Shy said. "Maybe it's the kind of medicine they gave my nephew."

"What's happening!" Carmen shouted. "Did you feel how cold Rodney's arm was? Did you see his eyes?"

Shy stopped her as they got to the bottom of the stairs. "I know where Shoeshine hid the duffel. We have to get the meds on the ship or the rest of the patients will die before we get home. I'll get Shoe. He has to know more than what he told me."

"I'll find Christian," Carmen said. "He's about to explain why everyone's been lying to us. I'll get Marcus, too."

Shy looked out across the lobby, where a few passengers were lounging on the couches, talking, laughing. They had no idea that people just a few floors above them were dying. "I'll meet you back here before six, okay? So we can line up for the ship together."

Carmen nodded. "It doesn't make any sense, Shy. Why would they lie to us?"

All he could do was shake his head.

Before leaving the hotel, Shy hurried to Addie's room and knocked on the door. Her dad's company had to know about the disease. How else would there be a bagful of the vaccine and medicine? And Shy was sure that was what he'd found on the motorboat. He remembered Addie saying LasoTech made hospital equipment. But if they had scientists who worked in a lab, it only made sense that they'd make drugs, too. Maybe they'd been working on a way to protect people from Romero Disease.

He knocked again and called out: "Addie, open the door! It's Shy!"

When there was still no answer he hurried back through the lobby, pushed open the doors and went outside. He made his way back to the top of the stairs, where he saw the helicopter slowly lifting off the ship. He watched it lean to the side and start moving away from the island; he wondered who was in there and why they'd be leaving ahead of the ship.

Shy skipped down a few stairs and sifted through the bushes where Shoeshine had hidden the duffel bag, but it wasn't there. Someone had taken it. Maybe Shoeshine.

He stood up again and watched the flight of the helicopter, trying to figure out what was happening. He kept picturing Rodney's lifeless face. His blood-red eyes. And everyone else who was strapped down to cots in the penthouse. The minute he'd found those dead scientists in the ocean he'd known something bad was happening here. But he never would've guessed it involved Romero Disease.

Shy took the trail beyond the gazebo, which led him higher up the cliff, through dense trees and bushes, around large boulders and exposed roots. He had no idea where he was going, he just knew he needed to find Shoeshine. And the last time he'd seen the guy he'd been headed in this direction.

He came upon a few of the researchers, who were spraying the bushes and trees with some kind of squirt bottle. They didn't even look up, so Shy scooted right past them. When the path broke off into a Y, he chose the route that led farther up the hill. His lungs burned as he climbed. His legs felt like Jell-O. But he had to make sure the duffel bag got on the ship. And he had to talk to Shoeshine.

Shy glanced up as he ran. The sun was already dropping from the sky. He only had about an hour and a half before he had to get back to the hotel. He tried to pick up his speed.

The land leveled out and the path began to narrow. Shy kept running, ducking under tree limbs, leaping over puddles. The faster he ran, though, the more his mind flooded with questions. How had the disease gotten all the way out to the island? Was someone on the cruise ship sick? One of the hotel workers? And where were the two scientists going on that motorboat with the duffel bag? And who shot them?

Shy didn't notice that the path came to an abrupt end until the last second. He tried to stop, but his momentum made him slide through the dirt. At the very edge of the cliff he grabbed a thick tree branch to keep himself from falling.

He looked down, his heart climbing into his throat as he watched the rocks he'd just kicked tumble fifty, sixty feet, into the ocean. He'd survived giant waves, a sinking cruise ship, circling sharks, only to almost fall off a cliff. He squatted down to catch his breath.

There was a large clearing to the right. A cement platform that looked like a helicopter launchpad. To the left he saw what had to be the flooded lab sticking up out of the ocean. A tall security fence wrapped all the way around it.

No sign of Shoeshine.

Shy doubled back to the Y in the path and was starting down the other route when he heard someone calling his name. He stopped and turned around. It was Bill, limping up out of the brush, using a stick as a cane. "Shy! I've been looking all over for you!"

"Me?" Shy answered. "Why?" He looked around to see if anyone else was there. Even after the nice things the guy had said about him during lunch, Shy still didn't trust him.

"I wanted to thank you personally," Bill said. He was wearing a generic baseball cap now and a green backpack. He looked kind of scratched-up from walking through the brush. "I meant what I said back at the restaurant. I wouldn't be here if you and your friend hadn't pulled me out from under that chandelier."

"Anyone would've done it," Shy said cautiously. He needed to shake this guy and continue looking for Shoeshine.

"But it wasn't anyone. It was you." Bill pulled off his cap, ran his fingers through his hair and put it back on. "What's the matter, Shy?

You seem upset. Everyone else back at the hotel is so excited to be going home."

"That's 'cause they haven't been up to the penthouse," Shy fired back. He was sick of all the secrecy. It was time for people to start being straight with each other. "There are people dying up there, man. And nobody's telling us shit."

"You're right," Bill said, balancing on his stick. He adjusted his cap again. "I don't think they want to alarm anyone. We've been through enough already, haven't we?"

"And what about LasoTech?" Shy continued. The questions were just flowing out of him now. "You work for them, right? What do you guys do?"

"We produce pharmaceuticals," the man answered. "Well, I don't personally. I'm only a member of the security team."

Shy knew it. There had never been any hospital equipment. He wondered if Addie had straight-up lied to him, or if she really didn't know. "And what do you know about a brown and blue duffel bag with vaccinations?" Shy found himself shouting now. He could feel the heat rising in his face as he pointed out toward the ocean. "And how about two scientists who got shot on a motorboat out there?"

Bill nodded at him for a few seconds; then he glanced at his watch. "Listen, there's still a little over an hour before we need to be on the beach. Let me show you something, Shy. It won't take long, I promise."

Shy scoffed at the guy. "I'm not going anywhere with you," he said. "All I'm saying is I know your company is shady as shit. And sooner or later, everyone's gonna find out." He turned and started back down the path, pissed off but scared now, too. Because maybe he'd said too much.

"It involves the loss of your grandmother!" Bill called after him.

Shy stopped in his tracks and spun around. "What are you talking about?"

"Your grandmother," Bill said. "Or more specifically, the disease that killed her."

Shy stared at the guy, breathing hard, trying to make himself think straight.

"I'm only telling you this because of what you did for me on the ship." Bill waved with his stick for Shy to follow him. "Trust me, you'll want to hear what I have to say."

The man turned and started limping up the path.

47

The Roles We Play

Shy followed Bill up the hill, to a lookout point just off the path where he pointed to an even better angle of the submerged lab. "You see that building down there?"

Shy nodded. "I already know, it's your company's lab."

"It *was* the lab," Bill said. "Before the ocean surge destroyed it. Do you know what took place inside those walls?"

Shy shrugged. He'd come to hear about his grandma, not to listen to some long, drawn-out story.

"The most important drug research and development in the country," Bill continued. "But it turns out that's not all LasoTech developed. The man you saw jump off the ship—"

"David Williamson," Shy said.

"Yes, Mr. Williamson. He left a letter in a cave that's a few hundred feet away from the lab. We used the cave as a second dock for our boats. The scientists also used it as a storage facility. The day my lifeboat landed here, I learned that a scientist had discovered this letter. I then read the letter with my own eyes. It was long—seven typed pages—and it revealed some very disturbing information."

Shy vaguely remembered the comb-over man mentioning a letter before he jumped. "So what does all this have to do with my grandma?"

"Everything," Bill answered. "This letter explained exactly how Romero Disease originated. I believe Mr. Williamson had what people call a crisis of conscience. Kind of ironic that the information I was seeking this whole time was printed on lined pages, isn't it?" The man limped a few steps toward a small boulder on his left. "God, this leg is killing me."

Shy watched him sit down and take off his backpack, set it between his feet.

Bill looked up, said: "Mr. Williamson had been part of the company from the beginning. He developed many original medications that helped a lot of people and made the company a lot of money. But according to his letter, he wasn't satisfied. He wanted to do something no scientist had ever done before. That's when he and Mr. Miller came up with a novel idea. Instead of always reacting to the environment, they wanted to *create* the environment. So they worked backward."

"I don't get it," Shy said.

"Instead of developing a drug to treat a disease, they set out to develop a disease that would need a drug. And that's exactly what they did."

When it hit Shy what the guy was saying, his whole body went numb. "They created Romero Disease in a fucking lab?"

"According to the letter we read," the man said, nodding. "Trust me, we were all as blindsided by this information as you are."

Shy could feel his anger rising as he stared at the man. "So how'd people get infected?"

"That's where Mr. Miller came in—your friend's father. According to the letter, Mr. Miller opened a free clinic in Mexico—under a different name, of course. For two years they treated poor border communities for everything from the common cold to breast cancer. But they also secretly infected the first few patients with their deadly disease."

Shy stared at the man, horrified.

"They knew it would eventually make its way across the border, into America. And they knew the fear it caused would drive up demand for treatment. When reports first started surfacing, they sat on it for a while, knowing it wouldn't look right if they had a treatment too soon. A few weeks ago their medicine that treats the disease was approved by the FDA. Their plan was to submit their vaccine by the end of the year. But the earthquakes changed all that, of course. We've received word that the disease is ravaging the entire West Coast now. It was determined that the best course of action was for the company to distance themselves from the situation completely."

Shy couldn't believe what he was hearing. They hadn't committed insurance fraud, they'd made up a disease that killed people. His grandma. Carmen's dad. Rodney. Shy felt so light-headed he had to squat down and put his hand on the ground for balance.

"It's beyond comprehension," Bill said. "I know. According to the letter, Mr. Williamson claimed he never really thought about what might happen once the disease was introduced to the public. He'd been focused on the science of the thing. Only Mr. Miller understood how much of a profit it would bring them."

Shy was so pissed his whole body started shaking. Addie's dad was responsible for everything. How could Addie not know herself? Shy lost his shit and stood back up. He marched right up to Bill and shoved him off the boulder, shouting: "You killed people, man!" He stood over the guy, breathing hard and trying to think. "You killed my family!"

Bill got back up slowly and brushed himself off. "I didn't do anything, Shy," he said calmly. "I didn't even know about this until a few days ago."

"You were part of it," Shy said. "Why else would you be following me all over the ship? Why'd you ask me what that guy said before he jumped?"

Bill sat back on the boulder. "Those were Mr. Miller's instructions. He wanted to know what Mr. Williamson said to everyone he spoke to that night. He was worried his partner had leaked top-secret information. But I had no idea what he was looking for, I swear to you."

Shy was so confused. He thought about being stranded on the broken lifeboat with Addie. Back then he'd had no clue he was stuck with the daughter of the guy who killed his grandma. It made him sick. *She* made him sick.

"I agree, Shy, it's horrible." Bill unzipped his backpack, still looking at Shy. "But judgment isn't my profession. Protection is."

Shy watched as Bill pulled a gun out of the bag and pointed it at him.

Shy froze in disbelief. "What are you doing?"

"And Mr. Miller pays me a lot of money for protection," Bill continued. "As long as he's alive, I will always protect his interests. The company may be ruined, but he's assured me my services are more valuable to him now than ever before. No one on the mainland knows about his vaccine, and I intend to keep it that way."

"He's dead, though," Shy said.

"Oh no," Bill said, standing up. "Jim Miller is very much alive. He's on his way back home as we speak."

The helicopter, Shy thought.

"Oh, and as far as the two men you found on the ocean," the man went on, "one of them was a doctor who intended to get the vaccine to California. To protect those who are still healthy and to expose us. The other man was one of mine. His instructions were to make sure this man never arrived. I'm sorry to hear I lost a good man, but at least his mission was a success."

The man motioned with the gun for Shy to sit on the ground. He did, staring directly into the barrel. His whole body shaking uncontrollably now. Out of a blinding fear. What if this guy didn't let him go? What if he wasn't able to get on the ship with Carmen and Marcus? And he never made it back home to look for his family?

"I'm going to teach you something," Bill said. "And I'm only doing this because you helped me on the ship. Otherwise you'd already be in the ground."

"I got you on a lifeboat," Shy said weakly.

The man took a deep breath and stared at Shy. "We all have roles to play in this life," he continued. "It's simple really. Mr. Williamson had a gift for science. Ego led him to create the perfect disease. Mr. Miller had the business sense to make money off that creation. My role is to protect Mr. Miller. And do you know what your role is, Shy?"

Shy stared as the man continued pointing the gun at him. "It's not right, though," he barely managed to say.

Bill shook his head. "I learned a long time ago to never get caught up in right or wrong. The problem here, Shy, is that you know too much. Maybe you've known too much since the night Mr. Williamson decided to end his life. Or maybe you only know too much because of what I just told you. Either way, your role comes to an end today."

Bill cocked the gun and moved forward a little, so that the barrel was only a few inches away from Shy's forehead.

Shy looked down at the ground in front of him and then closed his eyes, waiting to hear the explosion that would end it all. His mind furiously flashed through hundreds of images: boarding the ship and his grandma lying in her hospital bed and Rodney's red eyes and his nephew sleeping and his mom climbing the steps to their apartment and Addie tearing the fish in half and meeting Carmen for the first time on the ship.

And then he heard it.

The shot.

And he let his head fall toward the ground, assuming he was dead.

But he was still sitting there. Smelling the dirt. Breathing. Thinking.

He slowly opened his eyes and looked up.

Bill was lying facedown two feet in front of him, blood already pooling in the dirt around his body.

At first Shy thought he'd shot himself, but then he sensed someone to his right and turned.

Shoeshine was standing there.

The gun in his right hand still pointed at the man.

The brown and blue duffel bag slung over his shoulder.

48
Kicking Down the Door

Shy stumbled to his feet, watching Shoeshine check Bill for a pulse. "Is he dead?" he asked.

"He's dead." Shoeshine peeled the gun out of Bill's right hand and shoved it into the back of his waistband. He picked up the green backpack and then looked out over the ocean.

Shy knew he was in shock, because he couldn't process what had just happened. But seeing Bill with a bullet wound in his back made him kneel down like he was about to be sick. He'd almost gotten shot in the head. After hearing that Addie's dad's company planted the disease to sell their drugs. He spit and looked up at Shoeshine, told him: "You saved my life. Twice now. Who are you?"

The guy shook his head, still looking over the water. "Just a guy who shines shoes, young fella."

"No way, you have to be something else, too." Shy wanted to do something for the guy, to show how grateful he was. He reached into his pocket and pulled out the ring, thrust it forward in his palm. "Here, you should have this," he said.

Shoeshine looked down at the ring and shook his head. "No thanks. Never been big into jewelry."

"But you could sell it or something. When we get back to California."

"Not interested," Shoeshine said, unzipping Bill's green backpack and sifting through it.

Shy shoved the ring back into his pocket, watching. He thought of all the things Bill had just told him about the disease and Addie's dad and everyone's role. It disgusted him that anyone could make people sick on purpose. How would he explain it to Carmen? And what about Addie?

He turned toward the flooded lab, where it had all started. "How'd you even know we were here?" he asked Shoeshine.

"Been watching that man watch you since back on the ship," Shoeshine said. "I could sense something wasn't right." He turned to face Shy for the first time. "Felt the same way about this whole island, soon as we landed here. It ain't done with yet, young fella."

Shy nodded. He wasn't sure what Shoeshine was talking about, but he knew he agreed. The man hadn't been wrong yet. Shy stood up and moved closer to Bill's limp body, studied the bloody bullet wound in his back.

Shoeshine pulled a clear spray bottle out of the green backpack and held it up to the sun, which was much lower in the sky. The bottle was filled with a yellow liquid. Shoeshine sprayed a little onto the back of his hand and smelled it. Then he tasted it and spit.

"What is it?" Shy asked.

Shoeshine shook his head and looked back toward the island.

"What is it, Shoe?"

Shoeshine turned suddenly and tossed Shy the duffel bag. "Make sure everything in there stays safe," he said. "It's very important, you hear? There's something else I gotta see about." He started hurrying down the hill.

"Where you going?" Shy called after him.

Shoeshine didn't answer.

"Everyone in the penthouse is sick!" Shy shouted. "They have the disease, too!"

"Stay off that ship!" the man shouted over his shoulder. "Long as you can! You hear me?" Then he ducked around a corner, out of sight.

Shy started down the hill a few minutes later, obsessively running through everything he'd just learned from Bill and replaying the sound of the shot he thought had ended his life. When he heard two people talking in the distance he stopped cold and ducked out of sight. It was two of the researchers coming down from the other path, toward the Y.

Once they passed, he looked around, trying to figure out what to do with the duffel bag. He didn't want to take any chances, since it was the one job Shoeshine had trusted him with. To be safe, he climbed partway up a tree and stashed the bag in the elbow of a high branch that was covered by a dense layer of leaves. He'd come back for it, he decided, just before he lined up to get on the ship.

Shy hurried down the rest of the path, past the gazebo and into the hotel lobby. A few passengers were leaving just as he got there. "Where you going?" Shy asked.

"A bunch of us are heading down early," one of the women said. "We're just so excited."

"Come down when you can," the guy next to her said. He held up a deck of cards. "Might play a little poker to pass the time."

"I'll be down there soon," Shy told them, trying to maintain his smile. He didn't understand why Shoeshine wanted him to stall getting on the ship. Everyone else was going early. And it wasn't like Shy was gonna let the thing leave without Shoeshine. He owed the guy his life.

Shy watched the group leave, then started down the hall toward Addie's room. He needed to ask her some serious questions about her dad, who was still alive.

He knocked and waited.

No answer.

"Addie!" he shouted. "Open the door, I need to talk to you!"

When there was no response again, he looked up and down the halls to make sure no one was around. Then he kicked at the door, hard as he could. It barely budged. He backed up and kicked again, right next to the doorknob. On the third try the door swung open and he went inside.

The room was empty.

The bed was made up perfectly, like nobody had ever been in it. Where was she? Down on the beach already? Shy sat on the couch in the corner to try and think. He was mad as hell. And he was scared. Addie's family had killed his own. It made him hate her. But he'd looked into her eyes on the lifeboat. She wasn't like her dad. Or maybe he'd read her wrong the whole time.

And then he remembered the helicopter leaving the island. He punched the wall. What if Addie had been on it with her dad? But that didn't make sense either. She didn't even know he was still alive.

Shy left Addie's room and hurried down the hall. Another group of passengers was cutting through the lobby toward the exit. "We figured we might as well go line up now," the woman in the Raiders jersey said.

One of the men looked at his watch. "Only about twenty-five minutes before we're supposed to be down there. We'll see you soon, I hope."

Shy promised he'd hurry.

49
Spotty Reception

Carmen wasn't in her room either, so Shy started looking for Marcus's room. Since he didn't know the room number, or even the floor, he wandered through every level, calling out their names.

"Carmen!"

"Marcus!"

Shy was almost at the end of the fourth floor when he heard a door open behind him. He turned around and saw Carmen standing there. She didn't say anything, just waved him over.

He followed her inside the room, where he saw Marcus sitting at the end of the bed, working on the radio. Occasionally, there would be a burst of static, but nothing more.

Marcus looked up. "Shy," he said, setting down the radio and hopping to his feet. They slapped each other's hands and gave a quick dude hug. "I'm so happy you made it."

"You too."

"Tell Shy what you heard," Carmen said, looking upset.

Marcus sat back down with his radio. "I got it coming in pretty clear for a couple minutes," he said. "Just before Carm showed up." Marcus glanced at Carmen and turned back to Shy. "I'm not positive, man, but it sounded like some British dude talking about America being in a state of emergency."

Shy looked down at the radio. "What's that even mean?"

Marcus shrugged. "I'm not sure."

"Tell him the rest," Carmen said.

"According to the man, they got people crowded in stadiums all over the West Coast. And because they were all so close to-gether . . ." He paused and looked at Carmen again. "That disease spread through everyone."

"Romero," Carmen said, gripping Shy's arm. "They all got it now, Shy. Everyone in there. And they're not letting 'em leave the stadiums."

"Jesus," Shy said. It lined up exactly with what Bill had told him. What were they going back to?

Carmen reached out and banged the side of the radio. "Why won't it come in clearer?"

"Don't hit the thing," Marcus said, holding the radio away from her. "You're making it worse."

She sat down on the edge of the bed, seething.

"At the meeting they tried to say things were okay," Shy said. "I knew it didn't sound right."

"We were just talking about that," Carmen said. "I guess they didn't want us to worry about back home until after we got rescued."

Marcus started playing with the tuner again. "Like I said, I'm not completely positive. It was sort of hard to make out."

291

"You find the bag of medicine?" Carmen asked Shy. "I told Marcus all about the penthouse."

"Sorry to hear about Rodney, man," Marcus said, shaking his head. "He was a really good dude."

Shy nodded. "Shoeshine gave me the duffel bag," he said, looking back and forth between them. "But something else happened while I was out there."

"What?" Carmen said.

"Come with me to get the bag," Shy said. "I'll tell you on the way."

Carmen stood up. "But then we gotta hurry and get down to the beach. We can talk about all this shit deeper once we're on that damn ship going home."

Carmen covered her mouth after Shy finished telling her and Marcus everything Bill said about Romero Disease. "Do you believe this asshole?" she asked.

Shy shrugged. "Why would he make it up?"

"How can they even do that?" Marcus said. "Just invent a disease?"

"I guess if they're scientists," Shy said, switching the duffel from one shoulder to the other. He'd pulled it out of the tree on their way to see the body they were now standing over. He kept looking down at the man, Bill, remembering him pointing the barrel right in his face. It made Shy feel like a ghost. Like he shouldn't actually be standing here, breathing.

"He had the gun right against my head," Shy said, trying to make sense of what had happened. "I thought it was over."

"And that's when Shoeshine blasted him?" Carmen said.

"He saved my life," Shy told her. "Twice in one day."

"This is really freaking me out," Carmen said. "We have no idea what we're going back to."

All three of them stood there, looking at each other and at the body. "So no one knows a vaccine even exists?" Marcus asked.

"I don't think so," Shy said. "He made it sound like they wanted to back away from the whole thing."

"You know what they basically did, right?" Carmen kicked the dead body right in the ribs. "They sacrificed poor people to scare money out of rich people. They sacrificed my fucking dad."

"Beyond shady," Marcus said. "That's, like, some kind of genocide or something."

"Soon as we get back," Carmen said, "we're telling everyone. Cops, FBI, CIA, whoever we can find."

Shy just kept staring at the man's head. He was so angry he was shaking and his teeth were chattering. And then a thought occurred to him. The envelope in the duffel. He unzipped the bag and reached past the pack of syringes and opened the beat-up envelope enough to see inside. His jaw dropped. It was the letter written by the comb-over man. David Williamson. They had their proof right here.

"We better get down there," Marcus said.

"Shoe's still out there somewhere," Shy said. "He wants us to stall a little."

"How 'bout we stall on the damn ship," Marcus answered, picking up the radio.

Shy shrugged and zipped up the duffel and led the three of them back down the narrow trail that would eventually take them to the stairs. When they passed the hotel, though, he started thinking about Addie again. And the helicopter. He wondered if he should go try her hotel room one more time, just in case. And then something else occurred to him.

"Wait," he said as they neared the top of the stairs.

Carmen and Marcus turned to look at him.

Shy glanced out at the ship, which was facing the island. He saw where the helicopter once was. If Addie's dad was really still alive, he had to have been on that helicopter. And the helicopter had been on the researchers' ship. Why would they let some random guy take their helicopter unless . . .

"Come on, Shy," Carmen said.

Shy looked down at the beach. They had a perfect view from the top of the stairs. The passengers were all lined up and the research people were walking around them wearing backpacks. Green ones. Just like the one Bill had been wearing. The wrecked sailboat was gone. He thought about Shoeshine telling him to stay off the ship. Maybe he was saying for them to *never* get on the ship. Maybe it was a warning.

"Everyone's lined up already," Carmen said. "We gotta get down there."

"Let's go, man," Marcus said, trying to pull Shy by the wrist.

"Hold up," Shy said, yanking his arm free. "I gotta think." He was remembering something else now: Shoeshine pulling the spray bottle out of Bill's backpack, smelling the substance on the back of his hand. And the researchers he'd seen on the path, spraying the bushes and trees with this same kind of spray bottle.

"Shy!" Carmen shouted.

"We can't go down there," he said, looking up at her. "Not yet. We got time, right? They still gotta get the sick people on."

They all turned to the water when two motorized rafts started buzzing toward shore from the ship. The drivers steered the rafts right up onto the golf-course grass and gave the researchers on land a thumbs-up.

"Look," Marcus said. "You can hang around up here if you want, but I'm getting my ass on one of those rafts. *Now.*" He turned to Carmen. "You coming with me?"

Carmen looked back at Shy with sad eyes. "I just wanna go home," she told him.

"Me too," Shy said, wiping a hand down his face. "But something's not right."

Shy moved closer to the edge of the cliff near the stairs when he heard one of the researchers start shouting orders. He watched over a dense wall of bushes. Instead of loading the first group of survivors onto the first raft, the team of researchers all reached into their green backpacks at the same time and pulled out machine guns. They aimed them at the line of survivors and started firing.

Screams filled the air.

The quick rattle of gunfire.

A few of the passengers tried to run, but no one made it more than a few steps before getting shot.

Shy ducked behind the edge of the cliff, pulling in quick breaths. Carmen and Marcus hurried back up the stairs and dove in behind him.

He watched horrified as body after body fell limp onto the putting green and the screams became fewer until there was nothing left but the sound of gunfire and nobody remained standing other than the researchers, who were not researchers at all but LasoTech security, just like Shy feared.

"Oh my God. Oh my God," Carmen kept chanting in Shy's ear.

Marcus only stared, his eyes bugged, mouth hanging open in shock.

Shy's heart pounded in his chest. He couldn't move. The men were now piling dead bodies onto the rafts, and several men on the ship were positioning two rocket launchers so they were aimed back at the island. Another man was lighting all the lifeboats on fire so there would be no way to escape the island. When he was done, he pointed up at the stairs and shouted something back at his guys, and soon two other men were raising their guns toward Shy, Marcus and Carmen and firing.

Shy ducked behind the tram and pulled Carmen and Marcus

down with him, and the three of them held each other, trembling, as shots ricocheted all around them. Some continued on toward the hotel, causing mini-explosions in the walls and sparking fires. The trees and bushes were catching fire, too, and Shy immediately connected it with the substance in the spray bottles.

The gunfire lasted nearly a full minute, and when it let up for a few seconds, Shy lifted his head over the lip of the wall and saw that two of the gunmen were bounding up the stairs toward them.

"They're coming!" Shy shouted, grabbing Carmen and Marcus by the backs of their shirts and yanking them to their feet. In seconds they were in a full sprint past the hotel and the gazebo, back up the trail, and all Shy could hear was bullets ripping through the bushes and trees around them and the muted sounds of their footfalls as they climbed higher up the cliffs.

Seconds later the gunfire stopped and Marcus shouted: "They're leaving!"

Shy and Carmen stopped running, too, and spun around to watch the gunmen hurrying back down the trail, away from them. Shy pulled in desperate breaths next to Carmen and Marcus, who were both leaning over, hands on knees.

"Where are they going?" Marcus said between breaths.

Shy shook his head. He couldn't comprehend any of it. Not the slaying of the survivors or the chase up the hill or why they'd just stopped and turned around. But he knew it wasn't over.

Many of the trees and bushes down the hill were in flames, which lit up the darkening sky.

The three of them waited in silence.

"I'll go look," Shy said.

"You're staying right here!" Carmen said, latching herself on to his arm. "What if they're waiting for us?"

"We have to help the sick people," Shy said.

Marcus was shaking his head. "Let's get off the trail. Maybe we'll be able to see the ship from the edge of the cliff."

They stepped off the trail together, Shy leading the way, until they were at the edge of the cliff, where they looked out over the ocean. Their angle was poor, but Shy saw one of the rafts at the side of the ship, and the researchers pulling the dead bodies up into the ship. They didn't want to leave any evidence of what they'd done.

"Where's Shoeshine?" Shy asked.

No one answered.

As soon as the last of the bodies was loaded onto the ship, the gunmen climbed aboard, too, and then a group of them pulled the rafts up.

"They're all on," Shy said. "We have to go get the sick people out of the hotel and down to the beach. Part of the hotel is already on fire."

Just after he said these words a ball of fire shot across the water from the ship and crashed into the side of the hotel, and the wall exploded in flames.

More thunderous shots came from the ship, the sound exploding all around the island, the hotel taking blow after blow until the whole thing was in flames, including the penthouse where some of the patients had still been alive. Shy had never seen anything like it. The men were firing rocket launchers at the island, trying to burn everything down. He was choking on fear now.

They started running again, back down the trail, Shy leading with no idea where he was going. But then a ball of fire landed in the brush right in front of them and without saying a word all three of them spun back around and took off, back up the hill.

Every other tree and bush they passed was on fire, the flames leaping from branch to branch, reaching into the sky, lighting up everything. Smoke blanketed the path, and soon they were all coughing and covering their mouths with their shirts. There was nowhere to go, no safe place. They were going to be burned alive with everything else.

Suddenly, another man came ripping through a patch of burning bushes and fell to the ground, rolling to put out the flames on his clothes. Then he sprang to his feet.

Shoeshine.

"It's napalm!" he shouted. "They're torching the entire island! Follow me!"

Shy sprinted after Shoeshine, Carmen and Marcus right behind him. They took the trail up the hill, fire spreading all around them.

Shy couldn't think, but he could run. And he was hyperaware of his surroundings. The flames and the smoke and each twist and turn Shoeshine made and Carmen and Marcus running behind him.

But the farther up the trail they went, the more it became clear to him that they would be trapped. The only way down from the towering cliff was the stairs, where they'd be in clear sight of the men on the ship. But the rest of the island would soon be engulfed in flames. There was no way out.

Shoeshine led them off the path, toward the edge of the cliff, and Shy recognized the helicopter launchpad. It was where he'd slipped and almost fallen. The four of them stood at the very edge and stared down at the water some sixty feet below, the fire already pushing up against their backs.

"What now?" Shy shouted.

Shoeshine grabbed the radio out of Marcus's hands and the duffel bag off Shy's shoulder.

"What are you doing?" Marcus shouted.

"I've got it!" Shoeshine shouted back, shoving the radio inside the duffel and zipping up. He then leaned into Shy's ear and told him: "You make sure they follow."

He turned and leaped over the edge, throwing the duffel out in front of him.

Carmen screamed as the three of them scrambled to the edge to watch Shoeshine falling feetfirst, arms and legs flailing, until his body exploded into the water.

"No way," Marcus said, shaking his head. "No fucking way."

Shy glanced at the flames surrounding them.

There was no choice.

He moved toward Marcus, holding up his hands and saying: "We don't have to jump. We can just go back down the trail—" Then he shoved Marcus, as hard as he could, off the cliff, watched him fall screaming toward the water.

Shy took Carmen's hand and looked at her.

Her face was contorted with fear but she nodded to him, and they both took two hurried steps toward the edge and leaped together.

In the air, Shy reached out for nothing with his arms and kicked, the air whipping past his ears and the lost feeling of weightlessness and freedom, and he saw the comb-over man falling from the ship and he saw Carmen's bugged eyes beside him and then he smacked into the water and sank down into it, deeper and deeper, even when he fought to stop himself, and then he let his body go limp and the water wrapped its arms around him and lifted him back up toward the surface, slowly and steadily, and he fought his burning lungs, waiting until he burst back through the surface to suck in a huge breath, and then he spun around in the water, desperately, until he found Carmen staring back at him.

50
Five Knots

"Over here," Shoeshine said, waving for them to follow him. He was in the water with the duffel bag, against the cliff.

Shy's entire right side was numb where he'd slammed into the ocean. And his mind was numb, too. He saw Carmen and Marcus swimming up ahead of him. And he saw the sailboat with the torn sail floating off to the right. The one Carmen claimed Shoeshine had been obsessed with. It seemed impossible that he'd gotten it to the point that it could float again. But here it was.

Shoeshine was slowly climbing up the rocky cliff now, which didn't seem like a good idea since the entire island was still engulfed in flames.

By the time Shy got to the cliff, he saw that Shoeshine was crawling toward a cave in the side of the cliff, about fifteen feet above the water. Shoeshine reached down for Carmen and helped her into the cave. Then he helped Marcus. Shy climbed up after them and Shoeshine pulled him up and in as well. Inside, the cave opened up much wider. Shoeshine walked over to a pile of life jackets, tossed one to each of them, saying: "You're gonna need these." They all strapped the jackets on. Then Shoeshine lifted a large folded blanket.

"What are we doing?" Carmen said.

"Getting on that sailboat out there," Shoeshine said.

Shy was shivering as he turned to the water again.

"We can't!" Marcus shouted. "The ship's moving toward it!"

They all rushed to the cave opening and looked out, saw a ball of fire screaming through the air, toward the boat. It landed only fifteen feet away and quickly died in the water.

"They're trying to burn it down!" Carmen shouted.

Shoeshine leaned out of the cave and shouted at the research ship: "Come on, you bastard! Just get up to five knots!"

Another fireball fell short of the boat.

Then a third.

Shy watched the ship start gaining momentum toward the boat and he watched the balls of fire continue arcing through the air toward it. One landed right next to the boat, nearly turning it on its side. The fire jumped up and set the tattered sail ablaze.

"Come on!" Shoeshine shouted. "Speed up for me!"

Above them, Shy heard the earth-shaking sound of fire sweeping over the island. He was so confused. "Why do you want it to speed up?" he said.

"I spent all afternoon rigging the damn thing. Just in case."

Carmen slid up next to Shy to watch the ship bearing down on the helpless sailboat.

Another fireball missed, and then the research ship itself exploded in a burst of flames that shot into the sky. A second explosion followed on the back half of the ship and pieces of it blew out in every direction, some of them landing as far as the mouth of their cave.

The three of them looked at Shoeshine all bug-eyed as Shoeshine nodded calmly.

"What the hell happened?" Carmen asked.

"I rigged their own explosives to the ship's propeller," Shoeshine said. "Soon as it got to five knots she was gonna blow."

"So you knew they were gonna kill everyone here?" Marcus said.

Shoeshine shook his head. "Just knew it wasn't a research ship." He looked out over the water, at what was left of the ship. "Didn't set the trigger, though, until I realized they were aiming to torch the island."

"What if we had all gotten on the ship?" Carmen asked.

"I would have disarmed it."

They all stared at Shoeshine in awe.

"Jesus, dude," Marcus said. "Who are you?"

"A guy who shines shoes," Shy interjected, recalling all the times he'd asked the exact same question.

Shoeshine grinned at him and added: "May have spent some time in the military, too. Special ops."

Shy turned with everyone else to watch the flames continue to engulf the decimated ship, lighting up the sky. And they watched the shadow of the flames on the island, flickering against the water in front of their cave.

Shoeshine pointed to the sad-looking sailboat sitting a hundred yards to the right of the burning ship. "You all ready for another swim?" he asked, tossing the duffel back to Shy.

They all nodded and Shoeshine picked up the folded blanket and let himself drop from the cave back into the water.

Shy slung the bag over his shoulder and followed right behind him.

Day 8

51
The Living

Shy awoke early the next morning on the ragged sailboat, trembling and in a mental haze. So much had happened the day before he could hardly formulate a coherent thought. And he couldn't speak. Nobody could. He reached into the duffel and pulled out the comb-over man's letter and read every word of it, over and over. It was so crushing, though, he had to eventually put it away and stop thinking about it. He looked around instead, taking in his surroundings.

They hadn't gone very far over the course of the night. Only a few hundred yards away from the island. Shoeshine had stripped the tattered sail from the boat and was just starting to replace it with a different one. What Shy had thought was a blanket the night before was actually a sail the man must have been piecing together out of random scraps since landing on the island. He hadn't finished until right before Shy awoke, like maybe he'd been up the entire night.

Marcus was at the front of the boat with the radio. He had it coming in a little more clearly now, and Shy was able to make out many of the words. The reporter was talking about a makeshift border that had been erected in America. The earthquakes had caused the disease to spread so rapidly among the western states, people were no longer allowed to travel east, in hopes of keeping the disease contained. The coasts of California and Oregon and Washington were essentially giant quarantine areas for now, until scientists could develop a vaccine and replenish the medication used to treat the disease, which they'd already exhausted. A number of pharmaceutical companies were working day and night, trying to develop a vaccine, but so far none of them had had any luck.

Shy clutched the duffel bag in his lap. He understood they'd have to get it to the right people as soon as possible. Thousands of lives probably depended on it.

He remembered the last time he was on the sea in a boat, gripping the duffel bag. He'd been with Addie. He thought about how they'd spent nights close to each other for warmth, and how they sometimes talked. He could still see her splitting that fish in half with her bare hands. Could still hear her whispering in his ear that last night.

Where was she now?

Did he even care?

He was convinced that when he last saw her, she already knew she was going to leave the island in the helicopter with her old man. It was the look in her eyes when they talked after the lunch meeting. And the things she had said. And that kiss on the cheek. She was telling him goodbye.

But the more Shy thought about it, the more he decided Addie hadn't known anything when they were stranded together on the lifeboat. Back then she was just as confused as he was. He trusted what he'd seen in her eyes. Which meant her dad must have gotten to her on the island at some point.

Anyway, it didn't matter anymore. He was with Carmen now. She was sitting against the side of the boat right beside him, staring out at the wreckage from the ship, which floated all along the surface of the ocean. And they were holding hands—though he still wasn't sure who'd initiated that part.

Shy closed his eyes and breathed, feeling her hand in his. He understood it was a miracle they were even alive, but he wanted their families back home to be alive, too. He wanted everything to go back to the way it was.

In a few minutes Shoeshine muttered from atop the forward hatch: "Believe I finally got it." And he slowly began raising his homemade sail until it was all the way up and secured. The wind immediately caught it and started the boat moving through the ocean at a decent speed, farther away from the island. Shoeshine hopped down from the hatch and hurried around to the tiller, where he began steering, occasionally looking down at a homemade-looking compass.

They all watched him and asked what they could do to help, but Shoeshine insisted that they just rest for now.

The tattered boat moved swiftly through the ocean as the sun crept into the perfect blue sky. Shy listened to more bits and pieces of the reporter on Marcus's radio, and he felt Carmen's heartbeat in her hand, and he stared at the devastated island, which was completely scorched and still smoldering in places. He wondered what they'd find when they returned home, and who would be there to greet them. And then he decided to stop thinking about things he couldn't control. For now he should focus on how fortunate he was to be on this sailboat, with Shoeshine and Marcus and Carmen. He fingered the good-luck ring in his pocket and looked at each of their faces, feeling incredibly close to them. Marcus tinkering with the antennae. Shoeshine opening up his leather journal. Carmen staring at the sea and breathing steadily, clutching his hand. He had no idea how long it would take for a boat this size to sail all the way back to California, but he was convinced they'd make it there eventually. They had to.

Shy turned back to the massive ocean, which spoke to him more clearly now, trying to process everything that had happened over the past eight days. But it was impossible. All he could do was watch the island get smaller and smaller on the horizon, until it was just a tiny dot on the water, and then it was gone.

The fight
for survival
continues in

THE **HUNTED**

Available Fall 2014
from Delacorte Press

Acknowledgments

I'd like to thank the following folks for helping make this novel possible. Krista Marino: Your guidance through this story was truly remarkable. Thanks so much for all your hard work. Shy and I owe you a fancy dinner at the New York restaurant of your choice. Steve Malk: Thanks for always taking the long view and for coaching me through far more than just career decisions. Working with you is one of the best moves I've ever made. Matt Van Buren: Thanks for reading all fifty-eight thousand drafts of this novel. Your notes and conversations (often in a Park Slope bar) were vital to my figuring things out. Thanks also to all the great folks at Random House who work so hard to get good books into the hands of readers, especially Beverly Horowitz, Dominique Cimina, Lauren Donovan, Lisa Nadel, Adrienne Waintraub, Tracy Bloom Lerner and Lisa McClatchy. Thanks to my medical expert peeps (and friends): Quan Luong and Tanya DiFrancesco. Thanks to my supportive family: Caroline, Al, Roni, Amy, Emily, Spence, the Suns and Annie the cat.

Last but not least, I'd like to thank all the supportive friends who agreed to accompany me on the cruise I took to research this book. Oh, wait, none of you would go with me. Even when I begged and offered to pay. Even after I posted several desperate pleas on Facebook: "Come on, someone come with me on this cruise. I can't board a ship for a full week by myself." No responses. Zero. Oh, and the cruise I randomly picked turned out to be a "family" voyage, too. So all the moms and dads kept shooting me dirty looks and shielding their kids from me. I could read their minds: *Who's this random guy creeping around the Lido Deck by himself sipping piña coladas?* So, yeah, thanks for the company, guys. Way to come through for your boy.

About the Author

The Living is Matt de la Peña's fifth novel. He attended the University of the Pacific on a basketball scholarship and went on to earn a Master of Fine Arts in creative writing at San Diego State University. He lives in Brooklyn, New York, where he teaches creative writing. Look for Matt de la Peña's other books, *Ball Don't Lie*, *Mexican WhiteBoy*, *We Were Here*, and *I Will Save You*, all available from Delacorte Press.